HAUNTED EVER AFTER

JULIET MADISON

CHAPTER I

'Hello, is anybody there?' My voice quivered as I pulled open the bedroom door and stepped into the dark embrace of the hallway. God, I sounded like one of those stupid people in horror movies who never turn on the lights and walk directly into the path of a three-eyed monster or serial killer.

I crept along the hallway, wincing as I stepped on the dreaded creaky floorboard then shook my head at the silliness of it. I'd called out to the possible intruder and I was worried about a creaking floorboard? I reached the entry to the kitchen and felt around the corner of the wall for the light switch, then hesitated. What if someone was waiting for me, ready to pounce when I switched on the light? No, the sound was coming from beyond the kitchen, possibly the laundry. A dull thumping, whirring, and an occasional shrill like a bird on helium. I'd put the dishwasher on the heavy-duty clean cycle before bed, but it couldn't be that. It sounded like my clothes dryer was on.

I don't remember turning it on.

Who put it on?

Did Greg's flight arrive early and he decided to do laundry the moment he got home?

I scrunched my face in confusion. Greg *never* did laundry and flights were more likely to be late than early.

I drew in a deep breath and flicked the switch. The granite benchtops glistened and the white floor tiles glowed under the light. I squeezed my eyes shut at the sudden intrusion on my retinas then snapped them open and scanned my surroundings. No serial killer visible in the kitchen, and the dining and living areas were as I'd left them — perfectly clean and tidy.

Maybe it wasn't the dryer making that noise. It *was* windy, it could be that tree outside the laundry flapping against the wall. That would explain the thumping. And the whirring... well, wind whirred, didn't it? And the shrilling could be a bird, not on helium, obviously, but simply upset by all the wind.

I tiptoed through the kitchen, angling my ear towards the sound. Whirr, thump, shrill, whirr, thump, shrill. Definitely my dryer. Although I hadn't heard the high-pitched squealing before, maybe there was a problem with the spinning mechanism or something.

My mind tried to rationalise but my body knew the truth. Heart pounding at twice its normal speed, nerves shaking like my electric toothbrush, and despite being winter, sweat glued my pyjamas to my back.

Something was wrong. *Very* wrong. And not just the idea that an intruder might be inclined to do a spot of laundry whilst awaiting his prey.

Damn, where's a convenient baseball bat when you need one? The victims in horror movies always had one at the ready. My eyes darted around for the nearest object with weapon potential and I silently cursed the fact that all my sharp knives were in the dishwasher. Always the way. Could have done with the bonus set of steak knives from that Kitchen Whiz infomercial I saw last night.

I plucked a wooden spoon from the utensil holder, then cringed. What was I supposed to do with this — stir the intruder to death? Smack his bottom like a naughty child? I grabbed an egg whisk for good measure and crept towards the laundry. Maybe I could poke him in the eye. Light from the kitchen shone through, enough to see if anyone was in the room. I clutched a utensil in each hand, as though about to play drums with a set of pots and pans, and arched my body to the side, peering into the laundry.

Something was spinning inside the dryer, as suspected. I crouched slightly and crept towards it. As I squinted, the sight before me came into focus, and I flinched, realising what was inside.

My pounding heart practically cannonballed out of my chest and I jumped backwards, the ironing board falling from its wall hook onto me, followed by the broom and mop. 'Argh!' I screamed, fumbling around on my butt and trying to stand among all the household equipment toppling around me. 'Argh!'

I grabbed the fallen broom and jabbed it at the power point to turn off the dryer. The machine continued working. 'How on earth?' My eyes wide open, I gripped the broomstick with shaky hands as heat pounded through my bloodstream. Tentatively I reached towards the circular door, and was about to yank it open when it burst open by itself. I gasped and fell back against the equipment.

My breath froze high in my throat as my mind tried to comprehend the sight in front of me.

A woman.

A pale, semi-translucent woman in purple polka dot pyjamas flew out of the dryer and sat herself on the edge of the machine. 'That was the most fun I've ever had in my entire life! Oops, I mean *death*!' She tidied her messy mop of curly hair and tucked red strands behind her ears. Her eyes looked straight into mine and I shook. 'I was wondering when you'd come and say hello.'

'Who... what...' Words snap-froze on leaving my voice box and icicles of fear took their place.

She jumped off the machine and stood in front of me. I scrambled to my feet, mumbling, 'No, no, no... this isn't happening!' I waved the spoon and whisk frantically like I was trapped in a spider web. 'Go away, go away! It's only a dream. Wake up, Sally, wake up!' I lurched through the doorway and dashed around the corner to the kitchen, running through to the living room, squealing like a little girl and waving the utensils. I shoved the egg whisk into my pyjama pants pocket, then the wooden spoon but it fell out, and dug the key in the lock of the front door.

'Hey! Don't leave me here all alone!' the woman shouted. Then laughed. 'Well, if you really want to, go right ahead.'

I flipped my head sideways. She sat on the dining table with her arms crossed. I turned the key and pulled at the door handle, but it wouldn't budge. I tried locking and unlocking it again. 'Open, damn it!'

'You might as well give up. It's not going to open,' she said.

Panting, I turned around and my eyes homed in on another possible route of escape — the sliding door to the patio. Except I'd have to get past Psycho Ghost Woman to get to it. The door that opened to the outside from the laundry was the only other option, but I didn't know if I could *ever* go into that room again. I pulled at the door one last time. It remained shut.

'I told you, it won't open. Didn't you believe me?' She pouted as though I'd hurt her feelings.

My mind visualised the route back to the dreaded laundry. I

should be able to make it around the corner without being caught.

Just.

I sucked in a few sharp breaths and ran, through the living room and around the corner into the kitchen, the egg whisk falling from my pocket on the way.

'Argh!' I skidded and stumbled backwards. The woman was at the open doorway that led to the laundry, hands on hips, obstructing my escape route.

'You can't get out this way either.' She shook her head.

I turned and ran towards the patio door, but as I reached for the handle she appeared there too.

There was no running from this crazy bitch. I was trapped.

A glimmer of hope overshadowed the fear as I eyed the phone on the kitchen counter and lunged for it. It flew from the charger and onto the floor. I dove to pick it up but it shot from my grasp and into the living room, like one of those plastic frogs that you press and they spring up and land a metre away.

My iPhone! In my room. Why didn't I grab that as soon as the bloody thumping/whirring/shrilling woke me up? I knew the woman might just teleport or disapparate or whatever again, but what could I do? I had to try. I dashed into the hallway and into my bedroom, slamming the door behind me. Ha! I'd beat her. I tugged the charging cord from the iPhone and pressed Greg's number.

'Hi, you've reached Greg Simons. I'm either in a meeting, on a plane, or playing a very important game of golf, which I'm most likely winning. Leave a message and I'll call you back as soon as possible.'

Damn it, Greg! I ended the call and tried again, then checked the time — 12:17am. As long as his flight had been on time, he'd be due back pretty soon.

'Hi, you've reached—'

Double damn! He should be in a cab by now, why wouldn't he pick up?

'You've got to be kidding. Don't you have *anything* decent in here?' a voice said.

I spun around. The woman rifled through the clothes in my wardrobe, her face scrunched up in disgust. 'Not *one* dress, I can't believe it! Seriously, what do you wear when you go out? *Do* you ever go out?'

How dare she! Breaking and entering, and now, ridiculing my practical dress sense!

Anger boiled over my fear and my nostrils flared. 'Leave me alone!' I picked up a terracotta vase and threw it at the woman. It went straight through her and hit the wardrobe door, falling onto the carpet without breaking. Damn. Could have been a good way to get rid of the revolting gift Greg's mother had given us for our engagement.

She laughed. 'Nothing can hurt me, you know. Not even a kitchen utensil or ugly vase — although the sight of it has upset my sensory harmony somewhat.' She laughed again, her high-pitched, piercing tone stinging my eardrums.

I covered my ears and stormed out, retreating to my favourite spot in the corner of the living room couch. I huddled under a blanket and hugged a cushion tightly to my chest, hoping to muffle the sensation of my heart pounding.

'Wheee!' The woman burst forth from the hallway and cartwheeled across the living room floor.

She cartwheeled again, and as confusion and disbelief overtook my mind, I shook. Who was she? *What* was she? Was I going mad?

'I can't believe how different I feel; the pain, the suffering — it's all gone. I feel so light and free.' She looked at me and smiled. 'You and I are going to have so much fun!' My body shook even more and the woman's smile turned into a curious stare. 'Why are you so scared? I'm not going to hurt you.'

Her words seemed genuine but still I trembled, unable to comprehend what was happening.

She perched herself on the dining table and crossed her legs.

'Who...' my voice joined in the shaking, 'who are you?'

She flicked her hand as if the answer was nothing important. 'Oh, I'm just a boring housewife.' She chuckled.

'And... you're a... *ghost* or something?'

But I don't believe in ghosts.

The woman scanned her body like she was looking for a stain. 'Ha! I didn't even notice how see-through I am.' She looked up and nodded. 'I guess so, I never really thought of myself as a...' she curved her fingers like quotation marks, '... g*host*. Until now, I just thought of myself the way I've always been — only lighter in body and clearer in mind.'

Oh boy. As long as I wasn't hallucinating, this was real.

A real live ghost was in my house!

I mean... not *live*... but, you know. 'So, um... you were like, a real person, and then you, um...'

'Died, yes,' she said, with such acceptance.

'Why are you here? Why me? I don't recognise you at all. Shouldn't you be haunting people you knew in real life?'

'I tried, but couldn't. And it's too...'

'Too what?'

Her eyes glazed over for a moment and she flicked her pale hand. 'Nothing. Anyway, I ended up here.'

'So it's random? You stuck your hand in a hat with names of potential scaredy-cats to haunt and plucked me out?'

She uncrossed her legs and crossed them again. 'Not exactly. We *are* connected. The thing is, I used to date someone you know.'

Whoa. 'Who?'

Her slender hand rose and a long finger pointed in the direction of the bookcase behind me that displayed an array of happy snaps. Unless she was gay (and one of my friends had kept their preference for women hidden from me), there were only three possible options:

1. My brother, Rick.

2. My friend and colleague, Dale.

Or...

The front door opened. 'Sally, honey, what are you doing up?'

3. Or Greg. The man I'd be marrying in two weeks.

CHAPTER 2

My eyes darted towards the dining table, then back to Greg. The woman had disappeared. 'Oh, thank God you're here!' I flung myself at him.

'What's wrong?' He pulled away and studied me, concerned creases lining his forehead, his hands grasping my shoulders. 'You're shaking.'

I opened my mouth to explain the trauma that had unfolded but no words came out. Nothing would sound remotely sane.

There was a woman spinning in our clothes dryer.

A ghost did cartwheels across our living room floor.

I see dead housewives.

See? Crazy.

'Sally?'

'The wind. It was quite strong and I was worried the tree outside the bedroom might fall on the house.' Well, it was kind of true. I had worried about that for all of two minutes before I heard the noises coming from the clothes dryer.

Greg pulled me close in an embrace. 'Oh, honey, is that all?

9

That tree is solid and sturdy and the wind isn't as strong as it's been in the past. It won't fall.'

'I guess I overreacted a little, with you not here. I'm not used to having you away overnight so often after your promotion at work.' I gulped. I'd never lied to him before. It felt weird and wrong and, okay, a little thrilling, but I was only doing it because I had to. I couldn't tell him our house was haunted, he wouldn't believe me. Heck, I didn't know if *I* believed me.

'Don't worry, honey, I'm here now. Let's get to bed, hey?' He kept one arm around me and we walked towards the bedroom, his other hand rolling his suitcase across the floor. 'Oh, would you mind popping this in the dryer for me? It was pouring rain when I got into the taxi.' He lifted his jacket that had been draped over the top of his suitcase and handed it to me.

I froze. 'The *dryer*?'

'Yeah, it's still soaked as you can see.'

And as he *couldn't* see, there'd been a ghost in our dryer only moments ago and no way in hell was I going near that appliance again. I never thought a clothes dryer could give me Post Traumatic Stress Disorder but I was sure I'd collapse in a fit of panic if I had to open that circular door.

'Um, I'll just...' I walked to the dining table, which also had PTSD potential thanks to the memory of Ghost Woman perched on it. '... hang it on this chair overnight. No need to waste electricity when good old air can do the trick.' I forced a smile as I positioned the jacket on the back of the chair, and from behind it looked like the ghost of a headless man sitting at the table waiting for his dinner. Not that he'd be able to eat it on account of the missing head, but still. Freaky.

'As long as it doesn't get that rain smell. Maybe it should be washed instead, whack it in the washing machine overnight?'

'No. Let it dry first. It'll be fine.' I ushered him to the

bedroom before he decided to unpack his suitcase and instigate a washing and drying spree.

Greg kicked off his shoes and yawned. 'I need a quick shower, back in a sec.'

I huddled under the covers as still as a rock until he returned, thankful that a certain woman didn't return. Maybe Greg had scared her off. Maybe she'd had her fun and was making her way down the street, visiting every house to see what other terror she could evoke. But the woman had said she'd dated someone I knew, so it mustn't have been a random visit. Did she mean Greg? Greg had never mentioned anyone he knew dying. Maybe it was Rick. My brother was never that talkative about his love-life, or apparent lack of one. Or it could be Dale. But why would she haunt me, why not Dale's sister or someone else closer to him?

Greg's warm, fresh-smelling body sidled up close to me and I sighed with relief. It was all okay now. I was safe. I strung my arm across his chest and nestled in.

'Mmm,' he whispered. 'I've missed you.'

'I've missed you too.' I smiled and kissed his forehead, then his nose, then his mouth, and he moaned in that way that told me he wasn't quite ready to fall asleep. He rolled on top of me and caressed my face, sprinkling me with warm, soft kisses, his lips still wet from the shower. I wrapped my arms around him and savoured his affection. It had been two weeks since we'd had any. As his kisses trailed down my neck I ran my fingers through his damp hair, watching the shadows from the windswept tree dance across the ceiling.

'Sure, go right ahead. Forget I'm even here!' Ghost Woman appeared above us, her arms crossed and face creased in annoyance.

'Argh!' I pushed Greg off and scrambled to my feet, yanking the blanket off the bed and wrapping it around me. My heart pounded and my nerves sharpened at the ready like soldiers awaiting attack.

Ghost Woman laughed her ear-splitting laugh.

'Sal, what on earth is wrong?' Greg's dumbfounded expression replaced his desire-filled one from before, as he lay semi-reclined on his back, propped up by his elbows.

There's a ghost watching us make out.

I drew a deep breath and clenched the blanket to my chest. 'Um... it was just...' I glanced at the ghost who was circling her hand as though waiting for me to spill the beans. 'There was a spider. On the roof.' I pointed.

'Where?' Greg stood and turned on the bedside lamp, peering at the roof. 'I don't see it.'

'You don't see *anything*?' The woman was still there, floating near the ceiling.

'Only the peeling paint in the corners. We really must get this place repainted.'

Oh great. I was dealing with an annoying, perverted ghost and all he could think about was home renovations?

'Are you sure it wasn't just a shadow?' he asked, glancing around the room, lifting pillows and peering behind furniture.

'Oh. Maybe it was. It looked like a spider, but I'm probably still on edge from before.'

'Well, I can't see anything. Let's forget about it and continue where we left off, yeah?' He flashed a grin and the room darkened as he flicked the switch.

My body was tense and the moment was gone. I couldn't exactly get in the mood with some otherworldly being floating above us, could I? 'Actually, I think I'll go get a drink. I need to calm my mind.' Even though I knew the woman might follow me out there, I had to get out of the bedroom. Sure, I was scared, but I wanted to tell her off. How dare she interrupt our... our... our romantic endeavours. What a cow.

I hesitated near the door and turned back to my fiancé. 'Ah, Greg? I was just thinking... we've never really talked much about our past relationships. Who were you with before me again?' I leaned against the doorframe like it was the most casual thing to chat about at this moment in time.

'Huh? Why are you asking this now?'

'Curious, that's all.'

'Becky. Remember? She was the one before you. Ran off overseas with that Italian guy?'

'Oh yeah. And before her?'

'Sal, do we really have to get into this now? C'mon!'

'Did you ever date anyone who, I dunno, later... died, or anything?'

'What? Why would you ask that? Sal, I think you should have some of that chamomile tea or whatever it is and chill out.'

'I'm just interested. Did you?'

'No. I mean, I don't know. I haven't exactly kept in touch with all my exes, so how would I know? But I'm sure they're all alive and well.'

'What about a redhead? Did you ever date a woman with red hair?'

He shuffled awkwardly on the bed and sat with his hands clasped around his bent knees. 'Um, I might have, a couple of them had red hair, I think.'

'You think? Have there been that many women that you can't remember?' Whatever 'mood' I'd had before was long gone now.

'Oh, Sal, give me a break. It's late and I'm tired. I can't think straight. And women are always changing their hair colour, it's hard to keep up.'

'Fine.' I sighed, and exited the bedroom. I wanted this night to be over. As soon as I could say my piece to this woman, I'd go straight to sleep and leave this crazy night in the past where it belonged.

I switched on the kitchen light. A sudden noise sounded to my left and I flipped my head to the side. A photo in a frame lay face down on the floor. Had she knocked it off, or was it a draught? Where was she? I inched closer to the fallen photo, cautiously, as though it might spring up and hit me in the face if I got too close. I picked up the frame. The photo was of Greg in his golf attire, proudly standing with one foot crossed over the other, his hand resting on his expensive golf club set like it was his most prized possession. Well, it probably was. Apart from me, of course. Not that I was a possession, but I'm sure if there was a fire he'd grab me first and not his golf clubs.

Hang on. If she did knock it over. That probably meant...

'Uh-huh.' Ghost Woman manifested right in front of me, nodding. 'Me and Greggy-boy were once an item.'

I glared at her. 'So you think you can just come in here and get in our way, huh?' I whispered in the harshest whisper I could muster. 'Well you can go jump. Greg's mine, so leave us alone!'

She stepped backwards and seemed to shrink, then sat on the floor and hugged her knees, her head bowed.

Oh geez. Talk about giving me the guilts. Maybe I shouldn't be so hard on her. She wasn't exactly in the most enviable position right now, being dead and all.

'Hey, what's your name?' I asked. 'Do you want me to, ah, let Greg know what happened to you? Is that it?' She shook her head. 'Then what do you want?'

She stood and glanced around as if she was considering her options, then her gaze focused beyond the kitchen window and her eyes widened. 'I want to swing on that!' A swirl of colours replaced her form, then nothing. I dashed to the window and peered outside into the small yard, the moonlight casting an eerie glow on the roof of our shed. Colours swirled again and she appeared outside, her hands gripping the clothesline as she swung around in circles, a childlike grin of delight on her face.

I shook my head in disbelief, and as I turned around my gaze fell on the invitation stuck to the fridge with a Basic First Aid instruction magnet. *Bridal Bonding Weekend*. My shoulders relaxed. Only one week to go and I'd be enjoying a couple of rewarding days away with my best friends. No ghosts invited.

CHAPTER 3

**YOU ARE INVITED TO
SALLY'S BRIDAL BONDING WEEKEND!**

*Join us for a long weekend of fun, frivolity and food as we celebrate
Sally's upcoming transition into wifehood.*

When?
*Friday 21st June (Winter Solstice) to Monday 24th June (one week
before the wedding!)*

Where?
Barron Springs Country Guest House, Barron Springs

Who's invited?
*Sally, of course (last one to get hitched!)
Mel (leave the kids at home please)
Georgie (our appointed bridal bodyguard — and chef)
Moi — aka, Lorena (maid of honour and organiser extraordinaire!)*

What's on the agenda?
Several exciting 'Bridal Bonding Activities' — you'll have to wait and see!

RSVP ASAP (or else)!

&.

It must have been a fluke. A one-off. I hadn't seen Ghost Woman all week, and thank God for that, because I'd told myself if I saw her again I'd book in for an MRI and neurology assessment at the hospital. A bonus of working in one meant I had connections and could get the odd favour granted if needed. I'd decided I'd say I was suffering with constant headaches, or dizziness, or something so they'd have to do immediate testing to rule out anything sinister. But luckily it hadn't come to that. Maybe I imagined the whole thing, somehow. Pre-wedding jitters? Pre-wedding psychosis? Women could get pre-menstrual psychosis, although rare, so why not pre-wedding? All the planning, decisions, flowers, dresses, hair, make-up, guest lists, music, calligraphy place cards, menus... it was enough to send anyone bonkers. Even an organised person like me.

Anyway, all was good with the world again. Things were back to normal. As normal as they could be when my wedding was only a week away. Lorena's well-planned bridal bonding weekend would be a welcome escape from flitting about at home or work, obsessing over last minute wedding details. My friends were the best. And I trusted Lorena's promise that this would be an enjoyable weekend to remember, just for the girls.

I smiled as I turned the shopping trolley into aisle eight of Barron Springs Supermarket, where we were stocking up on supplies for the weekend. But despite the promise of fun and frivolity (not that I was frivolous, that was Lorena's domain), I couldn't quite shake the memory of last weekend...

I'd never believed in ghosts. Not once did I consider that a person's soul, or spirit, or whatever you wanted to call it, lived on after death. Even after seeing countless patients die on the hospital ward, and hearing distraught family members talk about their loved one now 'being at peace'. I'd nod in sympathy of course, but I knew, or *thought* I knew, that death was the end. You die, and that's it. That's what I was taught, that's what I believed. Until now. Now things weren't so black and white.

I distracted myself with the shopping list Lorena had given me. All four of us were spread throughout the supermarket like a search party, each with a designated list of supplies to get. *Toilet paper, toilet paper...* yes, you never could rely on self-contained accommodation to have enough. Good thinking, Lorena. I took my attention off the shopping list and peered down the aisle, when a rude woman grabbed hold of my trolley and pulled it so it went faster.

'Um, excuse me!' I attempted to be assertive.

She turned around, her red curls swinging and bouncing around her pale face.

Oh no. No way. 'You again,' I sneered.

'Well, good afternoon to you too, Miss Friendly!' She huffed, then sat on the edge of the trolley with perfect balance. She wasn't as translucent as before, and could almost pass for a normal, living human.

'Go away!' I whispered between gritted teeth as I pushed the shopping trolley. 'Leave me alone!' My vision obscured, I leaned to the side of the ghost and spotted the toilet paper up ahead. Maybe if I went about my planned task and ignored her she'd leave. Stopping next to the array of white rolls, I plucked a couple of six-packs that were on a two-for-one special.

'Why don't you get the deluxe four-ply rolls? I thought this was supposed to be a luxurious weekend away,' Ghost Woman said. If she kept bothering me I'd need to buy a six-pack of another kind to get through the weekend.

'I'm not listening to you.' I covered my ears for a moment, then pushed the trolley further down the aisle, grabbing two bottles of anti-bacterial hand sanitiser from the shelf, two boxes of tissues, and two bottles of bug spray.

The ghost crossed her arms and pouted, then disappeared and reappeared directly in front of me, making me drop the packets of paper towel I'd just picked up.

'Geez!' My hand flew to my chest to ease my thudding heart.

'I'll make you listen to me.' She sang an out-of-tune rendition of Beyoncé's 'All the Single Ladies', complete with a pathetic attempt at dancing.

'Shhh!'

'Only you can hear me, you know,' she said between 'Oh-oh-oh's'.

'Exactly, so be quiet so I don't look like a complete nutcase!'

She sang louder, her mouth only an inch from my ear as she floated alongside me. I came to an abrupt halt and covered my ears. I grabbed one of the cans of bug spray and took off the lid, spraying the chemicals towards her.

She laughed riotously. 'Like that's going to get rid of me!'

I glared at the purple polka dot pyjama-wearing nuisance, when Lorena turned into the aisle carrying a basket of meat, eggs, cheese, and crackers. 'Why are you spraying that stuff around?' she asked, waving her long fingernailed hand about.

I popped the lid back into place and tossed the can into the trolley. 'Um... there was a fly. A big nasty fly that wouldn't leave me alone.' I slid a menacing glance toward the ghost as I spoke.

'That's weird, flies in the middle of winter?' Lorena looked around, coughing at the mist of insect neurotoxins in the air.

'Well, you must have got rid of the sucker, I can't see it.' She glanced at my shopping trolley and furrowed her brow. 'Sally, why have you got two of everything? We're only staying a couple of nights at a guest house, not Noah's Ark.'

'I want to be prepared.' My voice became high-pitched in defensiveness. 'We don't want to run out of supplies in the middle of the night or anything.'

'Somehow I don't think we'll need two cans of bug spray, probably won't even need one, hun.'

'You never know, it's an old house. There could be spiders. We can put one can upstairs, one downstairs.'

'But hand sanitiser? They said soap would be provided for us at the house.'

'Lorena, soap is not the same as sanitiser. It doesn't kill *all* germs. With all the viruses roaming around these days, you should carry a bottle of hand sanitiser in your handbag at all times.'

'Fair enough.' Lorena shrugged, adjusting the strap of her Gucci handbag on her shoulder, a cheeky smile arching into her warm, brown cheeks. 'We should have put you in charge of buying the treats instead of the household supplies. We certainly *could* make use of two boxes of chocolates, two tubs of ice cream, and two bottles of wine. Although not that I can drink any.' She winked, rubbing the mound of her belly. 'I'll go and tell Mel to double up so we don't run out.'

With Lorena out of sight, I turned my trolley around and pushed it back to the hand sanitisers, grabbing an extra bottle. One for each bathroom, and one for the kitchen. I nodded sharply in satisfaction.

'You really should see a professional about your issue,' Ghost Woman said, jumping into the trolley like a child.

'What issue? I don't have an issue.'

'Your germ phobia.'

'It's not a phobia, I'm simply being cautious.'

The ghost nodded, as if saying, 'Oh, yes, of course, dear.'

'Don't patronise me!' I blurted a little too loud, then quickly covered my mouth and faked a cough.

'I didn't say anything.' The ghost held her palms up and shrugged, feigning innocence.

'You didn't have to. The look on your face said it all.' I pushed the trolley back down the aisle.

'Look, if we're going to be spending time together, we really should learn to get along with each other.' She held out her hand.

'Are you kidding? I don't want to spend time with you, and I certainly don't want to shake your ghostly hand!' I gripped the trolley and pushed it faster down the aisle, hoping the speed would somehow make her fall off.

It didn't, but still I pushed, swerving around the corner as the cart bumped over something and skidded to a halt.

'Christ!' A man bent down to rub his foot. 'What do you think you're doing, going that fast around the corner?' He winced as he removed his shoe and a red bruise manifested across his bare foot. 'You might have broken my toes!'

The ghost shook her finger at me like a naughty child and heat rushed up my face. 'Oh my God. I'm so sorry! I didn't see you there.' I bent down and reached towards his foot. 'Let me take a look, I'm a nurse.'

He pushed my hand away. 'Don't touch it! You've done enough damage for one day.' He glared at me and put his shoe back on, hobbling away.

I stared helplessly at the man, and couldn't help but notice his sculpted arms bulging beneath his long-sleeved shirt, and the tight roundness of his —

I shook my head. *What was I thinking, drooling over the*

incredibly attractive man I'd injured? I'm a happily engaged woman!

'Sally, what happened?' Mel approached, mostly obscured by a trolley full of wine, chocolates, chips, cookies, and colourful packets of sweet indulgences, followed by Georgie who'd been in charge of the fruit and vegetables. 'Did that guy have a go at you for some reason?'

I nodded.

'The bastard, I'll give him a piece of my mind,' Georgie said, taking a long-legged step forward.

I grasped her arm. 'No, don't. He had every right to be angry with me. I ran over his foot with the shopping trolley.'

Mel burst out laughing, and Georgie's blue eyes widened. 'How did you manage that?'

'I was pushing it a little too fast and didn't see him when I rounded the corner.'

'Why the rush, Sal? We're here in Barron Springs to relax,' Georgie said, moving her trolley aside with one hand for a customer to pass, as if it was as light as a feather.

I was trying to dislodge the ghost riding on my trolley.

'I guess I'm still in wedding panic mode. Besides, I can't wait to get to the guest house and enjoy ourselves.' I flashed a smile, and glancing around I noticed that the ghost had indeed disappeared.

'Me neither,' Mel said. 'I need to make every kid-free moment count. Let's go, girls!' She heaved her bulky load towards the check-out.

We paid for our purchases and packed the groceries into Lorena's glossy, black four-wheel drive. As she expertly manoeuvred across the bumpy country roads, Lorena sang along to a song on the radio, and then in a singsong voice announced, 'We're heeeere!'

She pulled into the long driveway of Barron Springs

Country Guest House, a grand old building with cute gable windows protruding like eyes, light grey walls, dark grey roof tiles, and tall trees framing the property. It looked every bit the old-fashioned haunted house, especially when we neared the front porch. I gulped. There, sitting on the steps and waving with such enthusiasm I thought her hand might fall off, was Ghost Woman.

CHAPTER 4

'Is it wine o'clock yet?' Mel asked, as she plonked her short self on the three-seater velvet couch and rested her feet on the coffee table.

Hear, hear. I wasn't much of a drinker, but with the guest house looking more like a ghost house I was in dire need of something to take the edge off my anxiety.

'No, not till dinnertime,' Georgie replied as she put away the results of our shopping expedition. 'Cocktails will be served at six, along with hors d'oeuvres. You'll have to use your willpower to wait till then.' She looked like a Stepford Wife, expertly busying herself in the kitchen with a smile, her golden blonde locks tumbling over her shoulders as she bent down.

'I left my willpower back home, it's lost somewhere in the mix of Lego, talking dolls, and dirty towels.' Mel yawned. 'How about some chocolate? Wait, *after dinner*, is that right, Miss Black Belt Chef?' she teased, and our beloved celebrity chef-slash-karate guru came out of the kitchen to give her a pretend kick.

'Spot on. Now get up off your arse and lend a hand.' Georgie winked. You wouldn't know by looking at the tall, slim, model-beautiful Georgie that she could knock out a man twice her size if she wanted to. She looked like she belonged in a hair or skincare commercial, which had probably given a helping hand to her television cooking career.

Mel sighed and twisted her dark hair into a loose, haphazard bun at the nape of her neck. 'Five minutes into my holiday and I'm back in the kitchen.'

As Mel unpacked the wine and did her best not to pop the cork then and there, the ghost tried to pick up the bottles but her hand went straight through.

Oh no, please don't do that, I urged silently as though she could read my thoughts. Well, maybe she could, who knows? She eyed me with a pout then tried again, but instead of succeeding she knocked over the bag of fruit and vegetables and they scattered on the floor.

'Yep,' Mel said, bending to retrieve them. 'Now I really feel at home. Picking things up off the floor. Except I'm the clumsy one instead of my children.'

Ghost Woman (I really should find out her name) circled her arms and wriggled her torso in a happy dance at her slightly off target victory, but victory nonetheless, and 'whooped' out loud. 'Yeah, baby, Ghost Mama is in da howse!'

Great.

'Shame I couldn't lift the wine,' she said. 'I could really do with some in my state. Not that I can drink it. Oh well, I shall practise like mad this weekend to strengthen my... my... powers, or whatever they are.'

'Oh no you won't!' I said. Out loud. Which meant of course that everyone was now looking at me strangely, even Lorena who'd been busy rummaging through some secret bag I wasn't allowed to look in.

'What? Who won't what?' Mel asked.

My brain tried to urgently extract an answer. 'Um, you

know exactly what I mean.' I crossed my arms authoritatively and gave a sharp nod, my bottom lip poking out, as though they were the strange ones by not understanding what I said.

'Huh?' she frowned.

'The, um, the... wine! I saw you looking at it like you were about to cart it off to a secluded corner of the house and guzzle it in one sitting.'

'No I wasn't.'

'Yes you were.'

'Um, no. I was looking at the...' she held up a white and green vegetable. 'What the heck is this thing?'

'Fennel,' Georgie said, looking as though she'd been asked what an apple was.

'Oh, right. Never had it before. Thanks, you learn something new every day.' Mel high-fived Georgie.

'Fair enough. But you were *thinking* of opening the wine early, weren't you? And you heard the expert, no wine till dinner.'

'Hun, I'm always thinking of wine. That, and sleep.'

'What about sex?' Lorena piped up, raising her perfectly arched eyebrows.

'Well I would, but who has time or energy to think about that?' Mel huffed.

Trust Lorena to move the conversation from fennel to sex. Must be all those pregnancy hormones. Then again, she was always a cheeky girl. If it wasn't for Lorena and the Dolly magazines she smuggled into my magazine-forbidden house when we were pre-teens, I wouldn't have known anything about the subject at hand.

'My husband does, apparently.' Georgie closed one of the wooden cupboard doors and paused, a secretive look in her eye. Ghost Woman's face strained as she focused on the door, no doubt trying to open it with her mind. She grunted, but that didn't work either. She flung her arms up in the air in defeat then disappeared. Her disappearances brought relief but also apprehension. Relief that she was gone but, with her habit of dropping in suddenly and scaring the life out of me, I actually wondered if I'd prefer her to be a constant presence. If I had to choose one or the other.

'All men do, but is there something you're not telling us?' Mel nudged Georgie in the ribs as a sneaky grin crept up Georgie's cheek.

'Yes, what *are* things like with Mr Mason?' Lorena perched on a kitchen bar stool and leaned forward.

Georgie's husband was thirteen years older than her and had provided her with an instant family; twin teenage stepdaughters to call her own.

She flicked her hand. 'Oh nothing. I shouldn't talk about this stuff with you guys. It's between me and Phillip.'

Okay, now even *I* was curious. And I wasn't one for gossip.

'Girls, let's promise that whatever we do or discuss this weekend at Barron Springs, stays at Barron Springs,' Lorena said. 'It's been forever since we've all been together, just the four of us. Like the old times.'

'Ah yes, whatever happened to The Housewives Club we pledged to create?' Mel asked.

'Um, I think we left that sexist terminology back in Year Five, along with our Barbie dolls and toy tea sets,' Georgie scoffed. 'Can you believe back then we actually aspired to be like the women in those old sitcoms? How times have changed.'

I twisted my lips to the side. Yes, I was a working woman, but when it came to the household duties, I did them all. Greg wasn't any good at them so it was simply quicker and easier to do them myself.

'I'll have you know I'm quite proud to be a super-dooper domestic goddess, thank you very much.' Mel took on the same posture I'd displayed before when trying to pretend I'd been talking to her and not the ghost.

'Oh, c'mon, I didn't mean it that way,' Georgie said. 'And besides, you're not only a stay-at-home mother of five, you're a businesswoman too. I don't know how you do it.'

Mel softened. 'Oh, I only do what any woman would do in my situation, and eBay is my outlet, I need it.'

Any person overhearing our conversation might have thought she was a shopaholic, but shopaholics kept her in business. And them in debt, more than likely. Her popular humorous T-shirt store was growing, much like her family. *And my anxiety*, as I scanned the house for our unwelcome visitor. Where *does* she disappear to? Heaven? Hell? Or some kind of transitionary place for ghosts who can't decide whether they actually want to rest in peace?

'Anyway, stop getting off topic and tell us the goss, Georgie.' Lorena rubbed her hands together.

Georgie leaned forward on the kitchen counter as though afraid her husband might hear her from fifty kilometres away. 'Phillip has been having some, ah... problems.' She cleared her throat. 'And I caught him jotting down the phone number on a late-night TV commercial.'

'You mean, one of *those* commercials?'

'Yes. Something about *"making loving last longer"*.' Georgie covered her reddening face.

'Well, it's good that he's making an effort to improve things. Go him, I say!' Lorena pumped her fist.

'What's with all this *longer lasting loving* business? I don't have time for that,' Mel said as she leaned back. 'Personally, I'm all for time efficiency.'

'Mel!' Lorena slapped her arm.

'Please don't say a word, you guys,' Georgie said.

'We won't.' Lorena held out her hand, palm facing

downwards. 'C'mon, girls. Say it with me: "What happens in Barron Springs…"'

'"… Stays in Barron Springs,"' we chorused, and my stomach fluttered a little. Was it wise to have put Lorena in charge of my bridal weekend? Something in her mischievous smile told me she had something more than a simple, relaxing, dignified weekend in store.

※

'I think I'll get unpacked. Who's sleeping where?' I picked up my overnight bag and peered behind the kitchen.

'Sal, you're upstairs. Bride-to-be gets the luxury suite,' Lorena said with a smile. 'I'm over here,' she pointed to a room near the front of the house. 'And Mel and Georgie, you're sharing in the room next to mine.'

'You better not snore, Georgie, I've been looking forward to a weekend without Michael's blocked sinuses.'

'Nothing to worry about, Mel, I'm as quiet as a mouse.' Georgie followed Mel into the bedroom.

'In my state, even a quiet mouse would probably wake me up,' Lorena said. 'Which is why I brought these.' She plucked a container of earplugs from her bag and held them up. 'Pregnancy does weird things to you. All my senses — heightened. Taste, smell, it's all so strong.'

But her hormones obviously hadn't heightened her sixth sense. For some reason that was allocated to me. Plain, practical, non-believing me. Maybe this was some sort of brain malfunction. A tumour? A mini stroke? A surge of apprehension shot through me. If it wasn't for all the trouble Lorena had gone to in organising this weekend, I'd be back at the hospital in a flash, but this time as a patient. At least to rule out anything sinister. Maybe I could do my own neuro obs every hour? Check if there were any other signs of neurological abnormalities? No, that wouldn't work. I'd need someone else to do them to be accurate.

'Are you okay, Sal? You look like you've seen a ghost.'

'Huh? No. Of course not. What, why, how, why would I look like that? I haven't seen a ghost. Ghosts don't exist.'

'Yes they do!' Ghost Woman jumped in front of me, her eyes piercing mine with their glare. 'How would you feel if I acted like you were invisible, huh?' She planted her hands on her hips.

I covered my eyes with one hand and leaned on the wall with the other. 'This can't be happening.'

'Oh, hun, what's the matter?' Lorena placed her arm around me, then gasped. 'Oh! Are you pregnant too? You can tell me, remember: what happens in Barron Springs…'

I straightened. 'No, I'm definitely not pregnant. I think I'm… getting nervous about the wedding, that's all. You know I don't like being the centre of attention.'

Lorena dropped her arm and stood in front of me, displacing the ghost. She held her finger to my chin, raising it, and I looked into her big, dark eyes. 'Listen to me, Sally Marsh. If you're lucky, you only get to experience one wedding in your whole life. Don't waste this special time feeling worried or scared. Enjoy it. Savour each moment in the build-up to the big day. No need to be nervous. All the guests will be there for you and Greg, they won't be there to judge you in any way. Where's that confident young woman I met when I was ten? The one who showed me how to climb the huge tree so we could spy on the boys next door?'

She disappeared when my mother had her accident and I transformed overnight from a carefree girl into a carer. Dad had to make ends meet and I had to take on Mum's role as cook, cleaner, and general housekeeper. Until she'd gotten used to being in the wheelchair and we adapted the house to make it easier for her to do things.

'I'm sorry. I hope I didn't sound ungrateful. I'll try to lighten up and enjoy the weekend.' This time I placed my arm around Lorena. 'And you,' I jabbed her in the collarbone with my other finger, 'make sure you put your feet up sometime over the weekend, okay? Nurse's orders.'

'Feet? What are they? I don't see any feet.' She peered over the protrusion of her belly and laughed. 'Okay, you try to have fun and let your hair down, and I'll make time for rest. Deal?' She held out her hand.

'Deal.' I shook it and smiled, and Lorena waddled into her bedroom while I headed for the stairs.

'And you'll help me have some fun of my *own*. Deal?' the ghost asked, with her hand outstretched.

I glared at her and walked up the staircase, the wood creaking with each step.

After doing my best to ignore the intruder singing in my bedroom while I packed my belongings away, I thought for a moment about who she could have been. If she was a real ghost, that is, and not an hallucination.

I eyed her curiously.

'Finally! What do I have to do to get some attention around here?'

'What's your name?' I asked.

She diverted her gaze and looked at my clothing. 'Let me guess, you're wearing white trousers on your wedding day instead of a dress?'

'No, of course I'm wearing a dress, if you must know. And why don't you answer my question? What is — *was* — your name?'

She glanced at me briefly. 'I'm not telling.'

'Am I supposed to keep calling you Ghost Woman?'

'You can do better than that.'

'The Girl in the Purple Polka Dot Pyjamas?'

'Bit of a mouthful.'

'Casper?' I grinned.

'Oh, ha-ha, you're hilarious.'

She slumped on the bed and leaned her elbows on her knees, her hair falling about her face. Bright, red curls, like flames, dancing and tickling her face.

'I know. If you won't tell me your real name. I'll call you: Red.' I gave a firm nod.

'Red? I always hated my red hair.'

'Yes. You're officially Red until you tell me who you really are, or were. Take it or leave it.' I crossed my arms.

'Fine.' She sighed and walked across to the window, trying unsuccessfully to open it with her laser focus.

'So, Red, there must be a reason you're here. Why me? What do you want?'

She turned around, and for the first time her expression held a look of seriousness. 'I can't tell you yet.'

'Why not? Tell me now and then we can get whatever it is over with so I can get on with enjoying my bridal weekend.'

She turned back to the window.

'First sign of insanity.'

I spun around to face the owner of the voice; Lorena, her light chocolate skin glowing in the afternoon light streaming through the window.

'Talking to yourself, first sign of insanity, hun.' She winked. 'Don't worry, I do it all the time, gotta get things out of my head sometimes.'

She walked to the wardrobe. 'So, what are you wearing tonight? You did remember I said to bring something a bit glam, right?'

'Yes, I remembered. I'm wearing this.' I pointed to my black slacks and a mauve cotton shirt with a slight frill around the collar.

Lorena eyed me as though I'd said I was wearing my wedding dress to go scuba diving. 'Honey, that's more office wear than glam. Didn't you bring something a bit snazzier? A dress perhaps?'

'Ha!' Red exclaimed, turning around from the window. 'See? Now that's what I'm talkin' about.'

I diverted my gaze back to Lorena. 'That's about as snazzy as I've got, I'm afraid. And we're just having dinner here at the house tonight, aren't we?'

'Yes, we are, but you'll need something dressier than this.'

'Why?'

'You'll see.' Her mischievous grin returned. 'Hang tight, I'll go see if Georgie has something you can wear, she's about your size, though a bit taller of course.'

Floorboards creaked as she went downstairs, and I dashed towards Red. 'So you *are* here for a reason. Tell me. Tell me now,' I urged. 'Am I supposed to tell Greg something? What is it?'

I stepped closer and she vanished with a swirl of colours left behind, until they too disappeared into the ether.

'Red!' Geez, right when I wanted to talk to her she goes MIA.

'What?' Lorena yelled from downstairs.

Oops.

If I was going to get through this weekend without telling my closest friends there was a ghost joining the bridal party, I'd have to try and keep my outbursts silent.

'Um... I said, red! Does Georgie have a... red dress?' I called out feebly. I didn't really want to wear red, it didn't suit me. Overpowered my pale skin and light brown hair.

'That's the spirit!' Lorena replied.

Ha. *Exactly.*

'But no.' The clicking of footsteps grew louder. 'Phew! I

think I *will* need to put my feet up if I have to keep going up and down these stairs. Hence you have the upstairs room.' She held up a small dress in front of me, its silver sequins shimmering slightly in the fading light.

'That's only the top, right? I'll wear it with my black pants?'

Lorena laughed. 'No, this is the whole outfit. You've never seen a shift dress before?'

I scrunched my face. 'Will it even cover my lower half?'

'It ends just above your knees. Gives you a chance to show off those slim legs of yours.'

I flicked my hand. 'Oh, but my knees are knobbly, and my legs look like they belong to a twelve-year-old boy!'

'Don't be silly, or would you rather have my legs with their varicose veins and cellulite? Happy to swap.' She chuckled. 'Now, get into this sexy number and then I'll do your hair and make-up.'

'What about you? Don't you have to get ready?'

'My hair and make-up is already done, I only have to get into my dress. Though I might need some help with the zip!'

I didn't even bring make-up. The most I wore was a swipe of tinted lip gloss and the occasional flick of mascara for a work function, but that was it.

'Should I be worried?' I lifted my limp ponytail.

'I'd be worried if you kept your hair the way it is now, girlfriend,' Red said behind me, and I spun around. Damn it, I couldn't talk to her with Lorena here, and she knew it.

'Sal?'

'Oh, I thought I felt a spider on my neck.' I brushed my hand around my skin and clothes to make a show of it.

'Lucky you bought all that bug spray then. Rightio, get dressed, and I'll meet you in the downstairs bathroom.'

I turned around and Red was gone. Bloody impulsive, fiery,

redhead. I bet she was an Aries too, not that I believed in horoscopes.

I'll show her, I thought, as I stepped into the shimmery dress. I'll show her I can be a sassy, sexy, woman. I'll show her I can have some fun too. No ghost of my fiancé's ex-girlfriend is going to stop me enjoying my one and only hen's party.

&a.

'Lorena, you're a miracle worker,' Georgie said, as I walked on wobbly high-heeled feet out of the bathroom and met my bridesmaids in the living room.

'Gee, that fills me with confidence about myself, Georgie,' I said.

'I didn't mean it like that, sorry! You're gorgeous in your own natural way, but wow! You look a million bucks. You should dress up more often.'

'Yeah, I can hardly recognise you,' Mel added. 'Those curls look amazing. Totally suits you.'

Lorena hadn't let me see the final result until she'd finished, and when she'd swung my chair around to face the mirror, at first my instinct was to rub the gunk off my face and pull my hair back into a comfortable ponytail as usual. But something twinged inside. Whether or not it was the desire to show Red I could pull off sexy and glam like the best of them I wasn't sure, but part of me felt excited. Different. And I liked it. Lorena was right. I needed to let my hair down literally and metaphorically this weekend, make the most of it and create some fun memories to look back on. Maybe I should even dress up like this for Greg occasionally, put a bit of spice into our relationship. I giggled at the thought of him seeing me like this. Plain Jane, Sensible Sally; all bright and shiny and sparkly.

Ding-dong!

I turned to look at the front door. 'Who's that? Are we expecting someone?' Curiosity tickled my nerves.

Lorena flashed a grin and waddled in a sexy way to the door. She opened it to reveal a man and a woman holding bags and what looked like photography equipment.

'Paparazzi at your service,' the man said. 'I'm guessing this is our star for the night?' He gestured to me.

A wide-open smile grew on my face as I glanced at Lorena.

'Sure is,' she said. 'Come on in. Sally, it's time for your glamour photo shoot! I thought it would be nice to get some shots of all four of us to commemorate the weekend, and of course, some of you before the wedding. I bet Greg will love it, you could give him one as a wedding present!'

'Wow, thank you. I never would have thought to do this.' Probably because I didn't know if I *wanted* to do this, though it was a lovely thing for Lorena to think of. But getting my photo taken always felt uncomfortable. And Greg would probably prefer gold-plated golf clubs as a present, but we won't get into that now.

After setting up their equipment and lighting and taking a few snaps of us together, it was time for my solo shoot. They got me to sit seductively on the velvet couch, though I probably looked more awkward than seductive.

'Oooh! I'll be the fan!' Red jumped in front of me, blowing with all her might to try and make my hair waft backwards. She sucked in deep breaths and expelled them like a blowfish, and if she wasn't already dead she looked like she was about to pass out from hyperventilation. My newly curled hair lightly wafted backwards. 'Woohoo! Did you feel that? Finally, some action!' She kept blowing, and I fiddled with my hair to avoid anyone else noticing.

'Sally, now, keep your hands crossed on your knees like I

showed you. Your hair looks perfect, no need to adjust,' the photographer said.

'Phoooo!' Red blew harder and my hair lifted up. My hand flew to my head to catch the rogue strands.

I pretended to shiver, 'I think there's a draught in here, I'm a bit chilly, are you chilly?' I eyed my friends.

'We'll put on the fireplace tonight, Sal, don't worry.'

'Phoooo!'

And we have lift-off again. My hair flapped upwards and I shrieked.

'My, oh my, we do seem to have some sort of draught in the room.' The female photographer's assistant glanced around the room, but my bet was that she wouldn't find the source of the draught.

I glared at Red and tried to mouth 'stop it' while keeping my lips still, as though I was a ventriloquist. One of those dodgy ones who audition for *The X Factor* and think they're fabulous.

'Why is your mouth going all weird?' Lorena asked.

'I'm, ah, just stretching it out after all the smiling. Who knew one's mouth could get so sore from a photo shoot?'

'Wait till your wedding day, hun,' said Lorena. 'You'll need an intensive mouth massage by the end of it.' She slapped Mel's nearby thigh. 'And she'll probably get one later that night, hey!'

'Girls! Not when we have company, please!' I urged.

'Keep thinking of something funny,' the photographer said. 'It'll make the smile more natural and won't ache as much.'

Funny, funny... what on earth could I possibly find funny about this situation?

I glanced at Red. She pulled her top lip inside out and made her eyes bulge.

Nice try, ghostie.

Okay, funny stuff... um, that Friends *episode when Ross gets a fake tan on one side of his body. That was quite funny.* I smiled, but not enough to make me laugh.

'Getting there, now relax and flash us a great big laughing smile.' The photographer snapped photos while I kept adjusting my facial expressions and pose, and Red kept pulling faces, none of which triggered a burst of laughter. Until she gave up directing them at me and pulled them at the photographer instead. She stood right next to him, shoved her face next to his and grunted, looking like a deformed monkey. A bubble of laughter tickled my throat. She then sat in front of me on the floor and squished her face together with her hands till she resembled a chubby baby crossed with an alien, and that did it. My stomach heaved and laughter burst forth, and *click, click, click* went the camera.

'Bravo! That's what I'm talking about,' said the photographer. 'Now I'll just check some of these before we change location.' He fiddled with his camera and frowned. 'That's odd.'

The assistant approached him and peered at the screen. 'Hmm.'

'Hmm what?' Lorena asked.

'It's okay, but we might have to shoot a couple more to replace a few of these. There's a strange light imbalance in a few pictures.'

'Can I have a look?' I asked, launching from the couch and up to the camera.

'Ah, sure,' he said, holding the camera in front of me.

Oh my God. Right where Red had been sitting in front of me was a warped stretch of light, like a smear of something on glass. He flipped through the images and each photo where Red was in the shot had a 'light imbalance' or whatever they called it. I gulped.

'I don't know where that came from. Look, the one before is

perfect, and then an instant later the shot is disrupted.' He fiddled with the settings on his camera and I looked towards my friends and shrugged. But inside my heart flip-flopped. This was evidence. Proof that Red wasn't just in my imagination or a manifestation of some disease, she was *really* here. A ghost. In this house, with me.

'C'mon, you sexy housewife you,' said Lorena. 'Let's touch up your lipstick while they adjust the equipment.' She led me towards the bathroom, and Red followed alongside us making *The Twilight Zone* sound effects and wriggling her fingers.

Oh dear. I may not be sick or mad, and I wasn't too sure about the sexy part, but I was definitely one very *haunted* housewife.

CHAPTER 5

'I've never felt so glamorous. Thanks for organising the photo shoot!' Mel hugged an arm around Lorena.

'I figured this would be the last chance I get for a while.' She rubbed her belly. 'Had to take the opportunity before sleep deprivation takes the healthy glow from my face.'

'I don't know if I ever had a healthy glow before kids, but the only way I get one nowadays is with some extra help. Now gimme.' She wiggled her fingers near Georgie who was making cocktails.

'Patience, Mel, patience.' She expertly mixed and shook and poured, and eventually placed a tray of cocktails on the large kitchen counter where we sat on bar stools.

Red approached, rubbing her hands eagerly together, and I shot her a 'don't you dare' glare.

'So, do your creations have a name?' I asked Georgie.

'One of them does, but I thought I'd get your creative input on the others. I made them all especially for you guys.' She handed me a drink of luminescent green liquid with a hint of pink at the top, and a white straw. 'This is the Gresally.' She chuckled. 'For Greg and Sally. Made with specially chosen ingredients to complement your caring nature, Greg's love of golf courses, and the love you both share.'

I smiled. 'Oh, that's so lovely. Thank you.' I picked up the glass and Lorena took a photo of me as I sipped. 'If you weren't my bridesmaid I'd have you cater the drinks and food at the wedding!'

'I'd do both if I could.'

'I know you would.' Georgie was known for taking on challenges.

'Now stop chatting, girls, which one is mine?' Mel was practically salivating at the tray of brightly coloured drinks.

'Here.' Georgie handed her a purplish mixture with one of those tacky paper umbrellas sticking out of it. 'And here,' she handed Lorena an orange mixture, 'Non-alcoholic of course.'

'Not fair.' Lorena pouted. 'But only a few months to go.'

Georgie took hers, a fairly plain-looking cocktail with a greyish-silver appearance. 'Cheers!'

'Cheers!' We clinked glasses and sipped.

'I think I'll call mine the Thank God I'm Finally Drinking cocktail,' Mel said as she sighed in relief, and Georgie laughed.

'Or what about... A Night to Remember?' Lorena proposed. 'And mine could be...' She eyed her orangey concoction. 'The Fruit Tingle? The Fruit Loop? The Tingling Touch?'

'Citrus Craving?' I suggested. 'Or something sort of, um, motherly?'

'What, like a Leaking Nipple?' Mel guffawed, her drink half gone.

'Ha ha, Mel. No need to get me *excited* about things to come. How about I call it The Glow?'

'Nice.' I smiled, and clinked her glass with mine.

'What about yours, Georgie?' Lorena asked.

'Don't know. Maybe something in honour of this weekend.'

'The Country Getaway? Girl's Best Friend?' Lorena suggested.

'I'll drink to that.' Mel raised her glass.

'Mel, you'll drink to anything.' I winked.

'True.' She downed the rest of her drink and took another from the tray.

'Hmm, let me think of another name...' I tapped my chin.

'The Dead Chick!' Red exclaimed from beside me, and I forced myself not to look her way. 'The Dead Chick. Go on, say it!'

'Hmm,' I repeated, as though I was putting a lot of thought into it.

'Say it! Say it!' Red jumped up and down next to me.

'Um, what about...'

'The Dead Chick, The Dead Chick, The Dead Chick!'

'Oh all right, The Dead Chick!' I said with a little too much frustration in my voice.

Red burst out laughing, her piercing tone making me lift my free hand to my ear.

'The Dead Chick?' Georgie furrowed her brow.

'Oh, is that what I said? I meant the um, the... The Best Chick! Yep, that's you!' I punched her lightly in the arm in a 'you're such a great pal' way. 'You're the best chick, for making these drinks for us.' Oh God. That was pitiful.

'I'll drink to that too,' Mel said.

'Mel, go easy, we haven't started the hors d'oeuvres yet,' Georgie said, then looked at me again. 'Well, thanks, Sal. I'm glad you think I'm the best chick.' She gave me a confused smile.

'It could be a Dead Chick too, though,' said Lorena. 'I mean, the drink is kinda dark and gloomy looking. Not in a bad way, I mean, I bet it tastes fantastic, but it has a kind of mysterious appeal.'

'Hey, you're right. I reckon Dead Chick suits it,' Mel replied.

'Or even The Haunted House,' Lorena added. 'We are in an old, creaky place after all. Beautiful, but it does have that look of a haunted house, don't you think?' She glanced around.

I scratched my cheek. Then my head. Then my arm.

'Are you allergic to The Gresally?' Georgie asked. 'I hope not!'

'Oh, no. Not at all. Just get itchy sometimes, from all those anti-bacterial hand sanitisers I use at work, I think.' I stole a glance at Red who was in hysterics at Lorena's suggestion for calling it a Haunted House.

'If only she knew, ha ha! Tell her, Sally, tell her I'm here. I dare ya!'

Never in a million years.

'What about The Ghost?' asked Mel.

My eyes darted to hers. 'What? What ghost?'

'What about calling Georgie's drink The Ghost? It has a spooky look to it.'

'Oh.' For a moment I thought they were all in on the ghost situation and were waiting for me to finally admit I could see her.

'Is that what I look like? All spooky?' Red asked, her hands waving about her body, then she laughed.

Thankfully, Georgie served up some nibbles, and conversation steered away from naming cocktails to 'ooh's' and 'ahh's' at her cooking prowess.

'This is so unfair!' Red kept screaming. 'I want some!' She chucked a childlike tantrum and pounded on the floor and I tried my best to ignore her. She was like a hyperactive child high on red food colouring. I wouldn't have been surprised if she'd died from overexcitement.

As darkness fell, Lorena lit some candles and refused my

attempt at turning on the main lights. She checked her watch. It was the third time she'd done it in the last ten minutes.

'Why do you keep looking at your watch?' I asked.

'Huh? No reason.'

Liar. Five minutes later when I got settled on the velvet couch with another cocktail, the reason rang the doorbell.

❧

'Surely not the photographers again?' I asked, twisting sideways to peer over the back of the couch to the front door.

'Nope. You sit right there, hun, I'll get it.' Lorena said with a cheeky grin.

What did she have planned now? Maybe it was a limousine driver to take us to a fancy club? Only there weren't any fancy clubs out here in the country, unless you counted the Barron Springs Pub, which was probably a few points shy of fancy.

Lorena opened the door slowly, and a man stepped in and placed his black winter coat on the coat rack. He was wearing blue scrubs and a surgical mask.

Huh? Someone from work? Maybe we were really having a surprise party and Lorena had invited all my work colleagues.

'Are you okay, Lorena? It's not the baby, is it?' I asked, suddenly concerned that maybe there was some problem she hadn't told us about.

She laughed. 'Oh, hun, there's no problem with me at all. This is Ty.' She ushered him further inside. 'That gorgeous young thing over there is Sally, the bride-to-be,' she said, pointing my way.

Oh God. Was this an intervention? She *had* caught me talking to myself in the bedroom. Though it wasn't *really* to myself. And I had been acting a bit strange and saying weird things thanks to Red. But maybe Red didn't really exist after all and I was actually hallucinating and they could all tell, and Dr Ty was here to whisk me away to the psych ward.

Although the room was dark, apart from the ambient glow of candlelight, I could see strong cheekbones above his surgical mask as he walked towards me. He was also wearing protective goggles, like the ones I wore when I had to assist in a delicate potentially blood-spattering procedure at work. Maybe I, or all of us, were infected with some rare virus and he was here to quarantine us.

Confusion and a bit of fear raced through me. Ty stood dominantly in front of me. Golly gosh. They probably sent the strong one to carry me away and prevent me from resisting. Maybe there was a whole team of elite, muscular doctors waiting outside to ensure we didn't escape. Or to move in if we retaliated. Like a medical SWAT team.

'Sexy Sally,' he said in a low, growl of a voice.

What on earth? What kind of doctor speaks to someone like that?

His mask shifted slightly, as though he was smiling underneath it, and he turned away and pulled something from the medical bag he was holding. Lorena assisted him with God-knows-what in the corner, and when he turned back around, music blared from the bluetooth speaker and I jumped in fright.

The catchy, rhythmic beat pounded in my ears as Ty strode towards me, and slowly, a realisation grew inside. Then it hit me like a whack to the head when he bent forward slightly and pulled at his surgical pants, ripping them off.

'Woohoo!' Lorena yelled, and Mel clapped and started dancing.

Oh my God. Ty was no doctor. He was a stripper! Lorena hadn't listened to my requests to have a dignified hen's party and had cheekily gone out and booked some raunchy entertainment! My eyes darted in her direction and I gave her a look that said 'You didn't!' and she returned it with one that said 'I sure as hell did, honey bunch!'

My mouth gaped as the candlelit glow reflected off the tight cords of his muscular thighs. He moved seductively in front of me and swung his stethoscope around in a circle like he was a cowboy about to lasso a criminal. Or me.

I covered my burning face with one hand, trying not to look at the fine specimen in front of me. What would Greg think! This was *so* not me, and wasn't this sort of like... *cheating*, just a little? He'd promised he wouldn't have a stripper at his buck's night tonight and I'd agreed the same.

Ty grasped one of my artificial ringlets and extended it, then let it spring back to my face. I kept my hand hovering across my eyes, only slightly peeking through so as to not be completely anti-social. He was only here for a quick performance, right? Five, maybe ten minutes, and then he'd be on his merry way and I could get back to the normality that was my bridal weekend, with a ghost in tow?

The beat of the music picked up and the room took on the ambience of an intimate nightclub. Mel was now dancing barefoot on the coffee table, and Ty moved and swayed next to her, which only made her dance more. Georgie stood nearby with a drink in one hand, fanning her grinning face with the other.

I took a deep breath, though it only enhanced the sensation of tension in my chest. My heart beat faster as Ty came back towards me. He did some dance moves along to the music that were actually quite good. He had rhythm and speed and power. Shame he had to waste his dance ability on a career as a stripper. *I bet he has an ego the size of his...*

Whoa! He tugged at his shirt and it ripped right off, exposing a six-pack that Mel would probably give up alcoholic six-packs for. And the pecs, oh my God, the pecs! I could bounce coins off them! Not that I would ever do such a thing. But wow. My Greg wasn't in bad shape but he wasn't exactly Thor either. But this guy... was he even human? Surely no one's body could look that good.

Ty moved with enough confidence to give Georgie a run for her money. He was practically naked except for his skin-hugging black trunks, surgical mask and goggles, and surgical shoes, which looked weirdly out of place on a body like that. His body gyrated and popped and locked in a stylish, sexy way that dancers did on music videos. With each rhythmic pop of his pelvis he jumped closer, his body a few inches from mine as I huddled with a cushion on the couch.

'Oh yeah, work it, Doctor!' Mel yelled, and for a fleeting moment I wondered where Red was. Why wasn't she getting in the way? Surely she would have a field day with this!

As I became aware of a masculine scent of expensive cologne, my face burned hotter, and Ty finally kicked off those sensible shoes with their protective plastic cover that looked like a shower cap for feet. I looked at his feet to divert my eyes from his, um, the rest of him, and my heart skipped a beat. It was dark, but not dark enough that I couldn't make out the slight swelling and discolouration of bruising on his left toes.

Oh my goodness gracious me.

I cautiously glanced up at his face and he lifted the goggles from his head, followed by the mask, revealing the perfectly proportioned face of the man whose toes I'd run over with the trolley in the supermarket.

CHAPTER 6

'You!' I flung my hands over my face.

He stopped dancing and pulled my hands away, peering into my eyes, then turned. 'Would you mind turning on the light for a sec?' he asked Lorena, who obliged, and also turned the music down.

The dim, ambient environment switched to the harsh awkwardness of reality, as recognition hardened Ty's face. 'You're the dangerous shopper from the supermarket,' he said, and his stance changed from seductive and confident to stiff and uncomfortable.

'I'm not dangerous. I didn't see you, that's all.'

'That's *him*?' Georgie asked, and Mel laughed like a hyena. It was almost as bad as Red's laugh.

'Um, what's going on here?' Lorena asked.

I stood and straightened my dress, which felt way too short, though I wasn't showing as much flesh as stripper guy. 'I sort of, um...'

'She did this,' he said, plonking his bruised foot on the coffee table, 'with her shopping trolley.'

'Today?' Lorena's eyes widened, and we both nodded.

'It was an accident, but he didn't have the decency to accept my apology.'

'You were practically racing that thing, you're lucky no bones were broken. I might have had to cancel work tonight.' He put his foot back on the ground and crossed his arms over his chest, making his pecs bulge even more, not that I was looking.

I crossed my arms too, but nothing bulged on my end. His pecs were bigger than my tiny buds for boobs. 'Oh, well that would have been a *huge* shame,' I said with a strong tone of sarcasm.

'Yes, if you must know, I had three more parties wanting to book me for this time tonight. I had to turn them down. I'm quite in demand, you know.' He raised his chin.

'I can't imagine why.' I crossed my arms even tighter. What an egotistical idiot.

'I can,' Mel muttered, then laughed again.

Ty grabbed his pants from the floor and reattached the Velcro, then stepped into them. 'I think I should go. Thanks for inviting me, Lorena, but it's best if I end the show a little early.'

Lorena approached him. 'Oh, no need for that! Sally was just a bit surprised, weren't you, Sal? I'm sure you can both forget what happened today and just enjoy the night, yeah?'

'Thanks, but I think the mood has passed for this bride-to-be.' He looked at me with strong, brown eyes.

'What makes you think I was even in a *mood*? As if I'm some floozy who goes weak at the knees at the sight of a good-looking, half-naked man with muscles the size of mountains?' *Oh God. What was in that cocktail? I don't normally speak like that!*

Ty smirked. 'Ah, so you think I'm good-looking, eh?'

'No, it was just a figure of speech, I didn't mean it!'

'You said good-looking, sunshine. That's pretty straightforward to me.'

I diverted my gaze from his, as my cheeks burned hotter.

'He is good-looking, Sal, admit it,' Mel said. 'You *are* good-looking, Ty.'

He smiled at Mel, then grabbed his top, but Lorena grasped hold of it too. 'Why don't you stay and finish your performance. No need to waste a night of work.' She turned and grabbed her handbag from the side table. 'Here, I'll pay you double.' She held up a wad of cash.

'Go, Lorena!' Mel whooped.

Ty was about to put on his top but hesitated.

'Here, it's yours.' Lorena came over and shoved it in Ty's doctor's bag. 'Now, you two shake hands and forget about your little altercation, and, Sally, let the man do his thing. You only have one hen's night, remember? And what happens in Barron Springs...'

'Stays in Barron Springs!' Mel exclaimed.

'She's right, Sal. No use getting worked up over a little accident.' Georgie shoved another cocktail in my hands. 'Sit back and relax, enjoy the night.'

I looked at Ty and he dropped his top. 'Fine with me,' he said.

I lifted the drink to my mouth and tipped my head back, then held out my hand. 'Fine. But only because Lorena went to the trouble of booking you. You better make it worth her money.' *Oh no, what did I mean by that?* Surely he wouldn't remove anything more than what he already had, would he? That would be plain wrong. I couldn't let him, and I hoped to God he wasn't *that* kind of entertainer. Hopefully he'd just do some fancy dance moves and leave the nakedness part out of it.

Ty grasped my hand and I flinched a little. Despite the chill in the air his hand was warm. Warm and smooth. He gave it a firm shake.

'Truce?' he said.

'Truce.' I nodded.

'Yay!' Mel flicked off the lights and took the liberty of turning the volume up on the music.

Ty gently pushed me onto the couch, as though he was about to climb on top of me. 'Does somebody need an examination?' he asked, and my friends cheered. 'Or mouth-to-mouth resuscitation?'

I flicked my hand as if to say 'no thanks, I'm good', but in an instant his stethoscope was on my chest.

'Breathe in,' he whispered in my ear. 'Breathe out...' He moved the stethoscope around the top of my chest, and then put it down the back of my dress, and I shivered at the cold touch of metal. 'Don't worry, I'll warm you up.' He knelt in front of me and lifted a high heel from my foot.

'What... what are you doing?' I stiffened.

He ignored my question and put my bare foot against his bare chest, rubbing and massaging it with his firm hands. 'I could get you back for the trolley incident, but I'm not one to hold a grudge.' He winked.

I wasn't going to let a petty incident ruin my evening but I couldn't quite get rid of the embarrassing sensation crawling up my spine. *A complete stranger is rubbing my foot!* Barring a professional masseuse, this shouldn't happen to an engaged woman, should it? What would Greg be doing right now? Probably enjoying a super-expensive bottle of wine at the golf retreat and chatting business.

No, he shouldn't be getting this personal with me, I should put a stop to it. I'll just politely remove my foot from his hold and... *Oh God... oh wow... how on earth is he doing that?* My foot was practically having an orgasm. A footgasm. Was that even possible?

Ty smiled as he rubbed and pressed, probably knowing too well the magic his hands were casting. He must be using some kind of acupressure technique. Fancy a stripper knowing that. Strangely, my body softened a little and I let him do his thing, even though I felt like a terrible wife-to-be.

When he'd had his way with my foot he placed it gently back in the shoe, then stood and ripped off his pants for the second time that night. His body moved with the music as though his muscles were controlling the tempo. There was no doubt about it, this guy could dance. Whoever said dancing was a girly pursuit for guys hadn't seen Ty. He oozed masculinity, confidence, and — *gulp* — sexiness, and his performance was in no way cheesy. It was classy. And professional. And... I think I've had too much to drink. I shook away the hint of desire creeping throughout my body like a pack of stealthy field agents. *Greg. Think of Greg.* He's my man, he's my fiancé, and Ty is just some light entertainment to satisfy Lorena's urge to create the ideal hen's party.

'Wipe that drool from your face, girlfriend!' My body stiffened as Red sat next to me.

'Go away,' I hissed through pursed lips.

'What, and miss this show? I've been practically comatose back there in the corner from the shock of all this beauty.' She eyed Ty with intense eyes of desire. 'Mmm... Now I *really* miss being alive.' She floated towards him and moulded her body to his as he swayed.

Red, please don't. I tried to send her an instant message via ESP.

'I can almost feel his heat,' she said, leaning in close to his face. 'I wish I could smell him.' She breathed in violently through her nose like she was trying to unclog her sinuses with nasal spray.

I shifted awkwardly on the couch, while my friends danced about to the music.

'Oh yeah, now *he's* got some moves!' She tried to copy what he was doing, failing terribly. Her coordination and speed had nothing on his. She obviously realised this as she changed tack and started to mock his movements, exaggerating his pops and locks, his pumps and thrusts, his spins and twists. She gyrated excessively around him and the corner of my mouth twinged slightly as her face took on a mock expression of lust. Red pretended to fan herself, then pretended to touch his abs, pulling her hand back with excitement and mouthing 'I'll never wash my hand again!'

I clamped my lips to stop from giggling, but when she repeatedly attempted to rip off her pyjamas the way Ty had done to his scrubs, I couldn't help but laugh. I spluttered and held my hand to my mouth, and Lorena yelled another, 'That's the spirit!'

As Red mimicked his movements and made fun of his dancing I laughed harder, and creases formed between Ty's eyebrows. He came close to me.

'Something funny, Sexy Sally?'

'No, nothing. Nothing at...' Another burst of laughter exploded as Red demonstrated CPR on Ty unknowingly.

She blew at his mouth and pumped his chest, then pretended to put something against him. 'Charging to 360. Clear!' she yelled, then jerked as though she herself was hit with the volts of electricity from the defibrillator.

'Please, please stop!' I said, my stomach aching from laughter.

'You want me to stop?' Ty asked, motioning to Lorena to turn the volume down a bit.

'Oh, don't stop, don't stop!' Red moaned, now gyrating next to Ty with her purple polka dot hips.

'Red, you need to go, now! Please!' I held my stomach as I spoke, realising too late it was out loud.

Ty flung his stethoscope around his neck and took a bow. 'I think that concludes the show.'

'What are you talking about, Sal?' asked Georgie.

'Yeah, that's twice you've said "red" today,' Lorena added.

'Oh, um, I meant my red cheeks. I can feel them going red, and I wanted them to go away. I'm shy, that's all.' I looked at Ty. 'Your dancing was really great. I'm just a little embarrassed.' I patted my cheeks then fanned them for show.

'Well, I'm glad to have made you blush.' He winked. 'A true blushing bride.'

Red must have obeyed my orders because she had disappeared again.

My friends clapped and cheered, and Mel gave Ty a high-five. 'That was awesome, dude.'

'Why, thank you.' He caught her hand after the high-five and kissed it.

What a suck.

Crash!

Our heads all turned in the direction of the noise, upstairs.

'What the hell was that?' asked Georgie.

I shrugged. 'Something must have fallen.' Or been pushed by a hyperactive ghost more like it. What had she done now?

A bang sounded, like a door slamming, and I jumped.

'What if it's an intruder?' Mel asked.

'An intruder? In the upstairs bedroom? How would they get in?' Lorena asked.

'Was your window locked, Sally?' Georgie asked. 'That big tree is right outside your room, it's possible someone could climb up and get in that way.'

Georgie's martial arts training had taught her the art of anticipating danger.

Another bang sounded, though softer than the first.

'I'll go take a look,' said Ty. He tiptoed across the floor, still half naked.

'I'll go too.' Georgie crept along beside him like a ninja.

'I'm staying right here.' Mel grabbed a cushion and cowered on the couch.

I'd be scared too, if it wasn't for that fact that I was sure it was just Red causing chaos. She *had* said she wanted to practise her powers, and God help me if they were getting stronger.

Lorena and I stood close together at the bottom of the stairs as Ty and Georgie crept up them, pausing on the creaky one. If it wasn't Red and there really was an intruder, at least we had a black belt chef and a half-naked dance guru to protect us.

They disappeared into the room and I heard the sound of a window closing. Then they emerged, carrying a broken porcelain lamp. 'Must have been a gush of wind, knocked over the lamp and broke it in two. Wardrobe door was wide open too, and a pair of shoes had fallen out,' Ty said.

'Oh, I must have left the window open. Oops,' I said. Though I didn't even open it to begin with. As Ty and Georgie descended the stairs, Red slid down the railing and landed in a heap at the bottom of the staircase.

'Oops for me too,' she said. 'Sorry, didn't mean to break anything. But ooh yeah, this ghost is getting stronger, baby!'

Wonderful. Just wonderful.

'Oh, man, I wonder how much that thing costs to replace.' Lorena held a hand to her head.

'You got any super glue in this house?' Ty asked.

'Ask Sally, she bought just about everything from the supermarket today as though we were preparing for a zombie apocalypse.'

'No super glue I'm afraid.' I held up my palms.

'Hang on,' Georgie called after retreating to the kitchen. 'I think I remember seeing some when I was inspecting all the cupboards.' We followed her voice and she held up a small tube. 'Ta-da!'

'I don't think it'll hide the crack, but it's worth a try,' Ty said. He positioned the lamp fragments on the counter, the electrical cord running through the centre stringing them loosely together. He spread glue on the broken bits, then pushed the two parts together and waited. Both Mel's and Lorena's eyes were practically superglued to Ty's arm muscles, bulging as he applied pressure to the lamp. Of course, I wasn't looking. I was just looking at the lamp and his muscles got in the way.

'There, that should do it,' Ty said. 'But if it doesn't, use the extra cash you gave me to pay for replacing it.' He went to his doctor's bag and extracted the money, handing it to Lorena.

'Oh, don't worry, Ty, that's yours. I can't take it back.'

'I insist.' He placed it in her hands and wrapped them closed before she could object again, then returned the lamp to my bedroom.

'Well, ladies, it's been fun,' he said as he put his clothes back on. 'I should leave you to enjoy the rest of your night.'

Georgie eyed him curiously. 'Ty, would you like to stay and have dinner with us? As a thank you for fixing the lamp?'

What? Like we needed to repay him for that! Any of us could have fixed it, it wasn't rocket science.

'There's really no need, and I don't want to intrude.'

'You wouldn't be intruding.' Mel grasped the side of his arm with a little too much enthusiasm. 'Here, come and take a seat and Georgie will serve up whatever she has planned.'

Ty glanced at Georgie. 'Hey, you look familiar.' His eyes narrowed.

'That's probably because she's on TV,' Lorena said proudly.

'Oh, are you that chef?' Ty clicked his fingers. 'Yes, you're the Black Belt Chef! I love your show!'

Georgie curtseyed then gave a faux rapid-fire punch in front of Ty. 'Thank you.'

'Well in that case, how can I refuse a meal cooked by a celebrity chef?' Ty grinned and Mel led him to the dining table.

Why on earth would they invite the stripper to dinner? What happened to our dignified dinner and girly discussion? Mel slid out a chair and sat me down next to him. Great.

'Water?' he asked, passing the carafe towards my glass.

'It's okay, I'll get it myself.' I took the carafe from him but, from my nerves or my alcohol-induced clumsiness, I didn't grip it tightly enough. It toppled sideways and water spread over the table and onto Ty's pants.

'Oh dear. I'm sorry,' I said, standing and grabbing a napkin.

'Looks like I'll have to take these off again,' he said with a grin. He stood and ripped them off like before, hung them over a spare chair to dry, then sat back at the table in his underwear and rubbed his hands together. 'So, what are we having?'

CHAPTER 7

What does one talk to a stripper about over dinner anyway? *'How was work? Did you have a good day at the office?'*

Georgie served our meals of Chicken Valdostano, and after taking a mouthful and complimenting the chef, Ty directed questions my way, saving me from having to think what to ask him. 'When's the big day?'

'One week's time. Are you married?' I asked. It was so much easier to ask that question when men knew you were taken, otherwise it sounded like you were sussing them out for potential husband material. But anyway, what sort of wife would want her husband to strip semi-naked and have women grope him in order to pay the bills and put food on the table?

He shook his head, took another mouthful, then asked, 'What do you do for a living, Sally?'

'Sally's a nurse,' Mel said.

'I'm sure she can speak for herself, Mel,' said Georgie, her slender fingers wrapped around the stem of her wine glass.

'Sorry, force of habit. Five kids.' Mel shrugged.

'Ah, you must be a very caring person,' Ty said. 'How long have you been nursing?'

'Geez, he asks a lot of questions.' Red sat at the empty chair to my right and placed her ghostly elbows on the table. Such a classy ghost. Crashing my party and bad table manners to boot.

'Almost ten years now.' I smiled.

'I could have been a nurse,' Red said. 'All those smart, hot doctors to drool over. Mmm...' she rolled her eyes back in an apparent daydream.

I wouldn't spoil her assumption and tell her that most of the male doctors I knew were either grey-haired and pudgy men or skinny and awkward young men with remnants of teenage acne. Sure, there were a few lookers, but it's no *Grey's Anatomy*.

'How long have you been, um, stripping?' I asked, as dignified as possible.

'Three years.' He took a sip of wine. 'And did you always want to be a nurse?'

Did you always want to be a stripper? I couldn't imagine him as a young boy at school getting up in front of the class and sharing his career aspirations for career day.

'Well, sort of, I—'

'I want to ask questions too, sheesh! Can't get a word in with this guy!' Red sat on the edge of the table and I tried not to look at her. 'What's your favourite colour, Sally? Wait, let me guess, mauve, right?'

Quit distracting me! I tried the ESP thing again. But what I really wanted to do was push her off the table. So much for being a caring person.

'Okay, what's your favourite band then?' she persisted. 'Favourite food?' She leaned over the table and shoved her face in front of mine. 'Ooh, what about favourite celebrity when you were a teenager? Huh, huh? Answer me, girl!'

I shifted in my seat and pretended I was trying to retrieve the answer to Ty's question, which had been diluted by Red's constant verbal assault.

'Favourite book? Favourite animal?' she continued shooting questions at me like a tennis ball machine, and my head started to hurt.

'Um...' I cleared my throat and rubbed my ear, tension building inside like a boiling pot of water. 'Sorry, what was the question again?'

'I said, did you always want to be a nurse?' Ty repeated.

'Favourite song? Favourite shop?' Red continued. 'Ooh, ooh! Favourite sexual position?'

In frustration, my hand banged down on the table, sending my fork flying across to the floor. 'Missionary, okay? Missionary!' I blurted.

All eyes stared at me. 'What?' Lorena asked, curiosity and concern on her face at my apparent distress.

Oh dear God.

Red had collapsed in laughter on the floor next to me. 'Missionary! Haha, missionary position! I knew it!' she repeated, rolling about.

Just when I thought I'd have to excuse myself from the table, a convenient explanation hit me. I cleared my throat. 'A missionary. I, er, wanted to be a missionary.' I gave a confident nod.

'Um, no you didn't,' Lorena said firmly.

Mel had cracked up as well as Red. 'Since when did you want to become a missionary?'

I pushed my unnatural curls from my face and raised my chin. 'Well, if you must know, since I was a kid. My parents sent me to Sunday school *(true)* and I really enjoyed it *(false)*. I thought it would be great to one day travel the world and spread the good word of the Lord *(also false)*. There. Now you know.'

'Good for you,' Ty said with a nod. 'What stopped you?'

How could I get off the missionary topic? All this quick thinking was doing my head in.

'I realised there was more need for nurses and thought I'd be better off helping people directly who needed it.' It was also ingrained into me ever since Mum's car accident. Caring became second nature, and I sort of fell into it after high school. But no need to get too personal with a man who was practically a stranger. Even though he'd gotten *quite* personal with us. Physically at least.

'What about you, Ty? Is stripping your full-time job?' Lorena asked.

Thank you for changing the subject, my dear friend.

'Nope. But it pays better than my day job,' he chuckled.

'And your day job is?' Lorena probed.

Ten bucks says he's a bartender, a waiter, or a struggling actor or artist, something like that.

'I'm a disability worker.'

Silence.

'I help young adults with a variety of mental and physical health conditions to integrate into society. I take them on outings, teach them skills, things like that.'

Was this the same guy who not long ago had shoved a stethoscope down my dress and asked if I wanted mouth-to-mouth resuscitation?

'Oh wow, he's like the perfect guy: caring *and* hot.' Red sighed. 'Speaking of hot, are you trying to burn this place down with all these candles?' She waved her hand around the flickering flames from the pillar candles on the table. Then she did the whole 'phooo!' thing, trying to blow them out. They only flickered slightly, from her breath or the general movement of air around the table I wasn't sure.

'I'm impressed,' said Lorena. 'Takes a special person to do that sort of job.'

'Thanks. I enjoy it. The people I work with are great. It's often underestimated how much they can contribute to society.'

True. I'd seen a lot of disabilities in my job. The strength of some of the patients was amazing.

'Phooo!' Red kept blowing.

'What sorts of disabilities do you see?' Georgie asked.

'Some are in wheelchairs, some have brain damage, or Down syndrome. A couple on my team are also deaf, on top of other challenges.'

Team. Nice. My opinion of Ty was slowly changing.

'Gosh, must be hard for them. So do you know sign language then?' Mel asked.

Ty did a few hand gestures. 'That means, *I sure do,*' he replied with a smile.

'Impressive!' Mel high-fived him again. 'The only sign language I know involves a certain finger stuck up in a certain direction.' She laughed and snorted, and I shook my head.

'Phooo!' The three candles lined up in the centre of the table went out in a progressive waft of smoke. 'I did it!' Red exclaimed.

'What the hell?' Lorena said, wafting the smoke with her hand. 'How did that happen?'

'Must have been the sheer force of my laugh,' Mel said, laughing again. She really needed to learn not to drink so much.

'How weird. They just went right out, like someone blew them out.' Georgie appeared puzzled.

Ty's face was creased, obviously confused too.

'Oh, it's just this old place. There are some draughts here and there; remember there was one during the photo shoot?'

'Oh yes, true.'

'You had a photo shoot?' Ty asked.

'Yes, we did happen to have a visit by the paparazzi.' Lorena batted her eyelashes. 'To commemorate the special occasion of Sally's imminent wedded bliss.'

'And what else do you have in store this weekend?'

'Yeah, Lorena, spill, woman.' Mel clapped her on the back.

'Time will tell, you'll have to wait and see.' She leaned back in her chair with her fingers threaded over her belly.

'Are you going to the Winter Solstice Festival in town tomorrow?' Ty asked, then dug into his meal again, the visible strength of his chiselled jaw emphasised by his chewing.

I glanced at Lorena. 'Are we?'

'Yes, but that's all I'm revealing.' She made a show of zipping her mouth shut.

'Might see you there, then.' Ty smiled.

'So, Doctor Ty, can I ask something?' Mel said, and I knew even if he said 'no you may not' she would ask anyway.

'Shoot.'

'Why do you strip? Is it the money or the thrill? It's okay, if it's just because you enjoy teasing women and giving them heart palpitations, we won't judge, will we, girls?' She garnered our agreement with her gaze.

Ty rubbed his hand over the back of his neck. 'I won't lie. It's for the money,' he said. 'But only because I'm saving up for something.'

Must be something big if he's been saving for three years.

'A house? A round-the-world trip?' Mel probed further.

'Actually, medical school.'

Silence again.

'I want to be a doctor.' He tugged at his surgical top. 'A *real* one, that is.'

'Wow. Seriously?' I asked.

'Seriously. I already have a uni degree so I'll be applying for the graduate program, which only takes four years to complete.'

'I see a lot of students come through that program at the hospital I work at. They put them straight into hospital from week one.'

'That's right. On the job training, plus all the academic lessons. Best way to learn, I think.' He gave a nod.

'Definitely. So have you applied yet?'

'Sat the entrance exam earlier this year and passed. I have an interview later this year and that will be the decider.'

'Good luck.'

'Yeah, good luck, Ty,' said Lorena.

'So you'll *really* be Doctor Ty soon!' said Mel. 'Maybe you can tell them you've had some work experience, getting into the role for your preparation.' She winked.

Ty laughed. 'Not sure if that would enhance my application, but if they ask about my work history I won't lie. Maybe it'll show how much I want it.' He took a swig of wine. 'And I won't be Doctor Ty. It'll have to be more professional: Doctor Tyler Roxford.' He smiled.

'Consider me your first patient.' Mel chuckled.

'Do many people your age do the program?' Georgie asked, looking both at Ty and myself. 'I mean, not that you look old or anything, but...'

'But I'm no spring chicken,' he said. 'I'm twenty-eight. I'm guessing there might be a few "older" students, but from the people I saw at the exam, most looked like they'd come straight through a uni degree after high school.'

'Yep. Mostly people in their early twenties. We've had a

couple of people in their forties too. They're often the most dedicated, to be honest. Had more life experience.'

'Hopefully my life experience will be an advantage. And if not, well, I'll keep stripping and try again next year!'

'But you do enjoy it, don't you? The stripping?'

Ty grinned. 'It does have its perks.'

Did he just slide a glance my way then? What a flirt. Maybe he gets a thrill out of thrilling engaged women. Not that I'm thrilled or anything.

'Maybe I'll see you in the hospital halls one day, Sally.'

'Maybe you will. By then I'll be Mrs Sally Simons.' Just thought I'd remind him of my impending marital status.

'I might need you to help me learn the ropes.'

'Something tells me you'll have no trouble finding your way around a stethoscope.' Oops, was I flirting? *Sally!*

Ty smiled, and after a dessert of chocolate raspberry pudding, he took our plates to the kitchen for us and placed them in the dishwasher. Crawler. Probably after a tip.

'Best meal I've had in a long time, Georgie. Thank you, my dear.' He lifted her hand and kissed it, and her lips twinged into a small smile. 'I better get home.' He put his pants back on and grabbed his coat, the jingling sound of keys coming from one of the pockets.

We walked him to the door, and Lorena peered outside. 'Where's your car?'

'No car. I walked here. I only live a few minutes away.'

'Convenient.'

'Everything in Barron Springs is in walking distance.' He smiled, shook each of our hands, and did I imagine it or did he hold mine a bit longer than the others?

'I hope you enjoy the rest of your hen's weekend, Sexy Sally.' He winked, turned away, and we all stood there transfixed as his impressive figure walked leisurely down the driveway and disappeared around the corner.

Mel sighed. 'What a guy.'

'I'll drink to that,' Red said, appearing next to me and wrapping her ghostly arm around my shoulders. I couldn't feel her, but a chill made me shiver.

As we closed the door, Georgie pointed to the fireplace. 'Oh, we forgot to put it on. I guess the central heating was enough for tonight.'

'I don't think it was the central heating that kept us warm.' Lorena chuckled.

'Oh, you girls.' I flicked my hand. 'It's like our teenage years all over again. And you're married too!'

'Just because we're married doesn't mean we don't get attracted to other guys. Doesn't mean we can't look, or fantasise a little.'

'But doesn't everyone else kind of fade away into the distance once you're married to your soulmate?'

'Hun, we don't stop being red-blooded women just because we signed a marriage certificate. Not that we'd cheat, no way at all, but there's nothing wrong with appreciating someone of the opposite sex.'

'Yeah, and do you really think our husbands become immune to other women after they're married? One word: no.' Mel plonked herself on the couch.

'Phillip and I have our celebrity free passes. Do any of you and your hubbies have one?' Georgie asked, perching on the arm of the couch.

'What's a free pass?' I asked.

'A celebrity that you're allowed to have a romantic interlude with if the chance arose. It's just a bit of fun. Phillip's is Sandra Bullock. Mine is Matt Damon.'

'Hey, Matt's mine!' said Lorena.

'Have you girls not seen Henry Cavill?' Mel said in disbelief. 'How can your free pass not be Mr New Generation Superman? He's like the best thing since sliced bread.'

'Who's Henry Cavill?' My question was met with Mel's gaping mouth. She got her phone from her handbag and googled him, showing me some pictures.

'Oh, right. Well he is kind of attractive, I guess.'

'Who would be your celebrity pass then, Sal?' Mel asked.

'I've never really thought about it. Um, hang on...' I looked up at the beams on the high ceiling. 'Well, I guess David Tennant has a certain charm to him.'

'Who on earth is David Tennant?' Mel asked.

'You know, he plays Doctor Who?'

Mel laughed. 'Out of all the celebrities in the world and you choose Doctor Who?'

'Why not? He's intelligent, has striking eyes, and an interesting sort of nose.'

Mel googled again and her mouth returned to its gaping position. 'Sorry, you haven't swayed me. It's Henry or nothing for me.'

'Anyway, that's a silly game. I'm going to think of no one but Greg when I'm married.' I smiled, thinking of Greg's face. 'I'm a lucky woman.'

'Well before you commit to never looking at another man again, there's something you need to do first.' Lorena sat me back on the dining chair and turned me to face the side wall. 'No peeking till I say so.'

'What's going on, you haven't hired another stripper, have you?'

'No, Ty was the one and only. But this will be just as fun. C'mon, girls, give me a hand setting up.'

Giggles and laughter ensued and I forced myself not to turn around.

'You really thought of everything, Lorena!' Georgie said.

Oh dear. What embarrassment was I in for next?

'Ta-da!' Lorena turned me around. 'We're going to play Pin the Tail on the Donkey, only there's no tail and no donkey.'

I froze, mouth agape at the sight before me. A large poster of a naked man was displayed on the wall, except he was missing a certain, um, well, you get the drift. 'You can't be serious?'

'I certainly am.' Lorena shuffled my body towards the poster, and shoved something in my hand.

I glanced down and shrieked. 'I can't possibly pin this thing on that thing!'

'Sure you can! Mel, get the blindfold.'

'What? No, I can't! And if Greg could see me now he'd—'

'Forget about Greg for now, this is *your* weekend. Let loose and live a little, girlfriend!' Mel said.

'Yeah, and it's not like it's anything you haven't seen before. You've seen quite a few in your line of work,' Lorena added.

'Yes, but that's in a professional, medical, caring way. This is in a crude and immature way. The human body should not be objectified like this, it's degrading.'

'The guy doesn't look like he's feeling degraded,' Mel said. He had a cheesy, ego-fuelled smile plastered on his face.

'Then you have a go, Mel.' I crossed my arms.

'Happy to!' She put the blindfold on herself and I handed her the... attachment.

'Okay, let's spin you around.' Lorena grasped her shoulders and moved her body around in circles.

'Whoa, go easy. You don't want me to throw up, do you?' She laughed.

'And, action!' Lorena let go and Mel reached in front of her, feeling her way with her free hand.

'I wish this was in 3D.' She held the plastic cut-out shape on the poster and pushed it against the wall. 'How'd I go?'

Lorena burst out laughing and I twisted my lips to one side. Mel ripped off the blindfold and folded forwards in laughter. The attachment was stuck to his backside like a tail!

'Well that's something you don't see every day!' she said, and a whoosh of cold air rushed past me.

'Can I have a go? Pleeeease!' Red urged.

I shook my head discreetly at her. The last thing I needed was for that thing to start flying around the room like an out of control rocket. Knowing my luck it would probably land smack bang on my forehead.

'Sally's turn!' Mel wrapped the blindfold around me and I pinched the attachment tentatively between dainty fingers.

'I'm still not too keen on this,' I said, knowing that there was no way they'd let me get out of doing it.

'Tough. Now spin around, and pin it, girl!' She spun me around three times.

Ding-dong!

'Huh? Who now?' I asked, lifting the blindfold off my eyes.

'I have no idea.' Lorena looked as confused as me. 'I'll have a peek through the window.' She pulled the curtains aside discreetly, and when her face softened in relief she opened the front door. 'Ty, do you miss us already?'

He stepped inside. 'Forgot my doctor's bag. Sorry to intrude.'

'Oh, no problem, come on in.'

I froze again, and he did too, looking at me.

'Is that what I think it is?' he asked.

My hand was poised in mid-air, the thing dangling from my grip. 'No, no it's not.' I shoved it behind my back. 'It's nothing.' Heat flushed my face.

The corner of Ty's mouth rose and he walked around me, his gaze resting on the wall. 'Judging by the fact that this guy is missing a certain vital body part, I'd say it *is* what I think it is.'

Georgie and Mel had their hands over their mouths, their bodies shaking in semi-contained hysterics.

'Show me,' he said, his hand outstretched.

'No, I will not, thank you very much.' I held it firmly behind me.

He reached around my body and tried to grasp it, but I swivelled my body.

'C'mon, let me see.' He grinned.

'Yeah, Sal, show him!' Lorena said.

Ty's left hand grasped my shoulder while the other took the thing from my grip. He laughed in a slow, amused chuckle. 'Looks like you girls are having a *big* night, eh?'

'It was their idea. I had no idea we'd be playing this,' I said, putting on my best expression of innocence.

'You're the one with a cut-out plastic penis in your hand.' Ty crossed one foot over the other and leaned against the back of the couch, clearly amused. 'Don't let me interfere. Continue with whatever you were doing.' He gestured to the poster.

'I can't do it with you watching me!'

'Why not?'

'Yeah, Sal, why not?' Mel said.

'Do it, Sally, do it!' Red yelled in my ear.

'Just do it, Sal. When else will you have a chance to do something like this?' Lorena teased.

'I'm not exactly grief-stricken at the thought of never getting the opportunity to play such a silly game again,' I huffed.

Mel pulled the blindfold back over my eyes and spun me around.

'Hey!' My protests yielded no relief.

'Now pin it!'

'Pin it, pin it, pin it, pin it!' they chorused, Ty included, and overwhelmed by peer pressure I pushed the thing onto the wall, then pulled off my blindfold.

'Holy crap, Sal, you did it!' Mel applauded.

The cheesy model was now back in correct anatomical alignment.

Ty clapped too. 'Well done. I guess you nurses *are* very familiar with the human body.'

I could feel my face turning the colour of the raspberries from tonight's pudding, and I diverted my gaze away from Ty.

'My turn, my turn!' Lorena said. 'Would you like a go, too, Ty?'

Ty grabbed his doctor's bag and straightened up. 'As much as I've always wanted to partake in such a game, I'll get going. I have an early start in the morning and it looks like you girls are in for a *long* night.' He winked, and once again we watched him walk down the driveway and disappear around the corner.

'I like Barron Springs,' said Mel with a sigh.

CHAPTER 8

After we capped off the evening with hot chocolate and marshmallows by the fire, and Red had given up rubbing her hands near the flickering amber flames hoping it would warm her back to life, we retreated to our respective bedrooms. I couldn't wait to have a nice relaxing soak in the porcelain claw-foot bath and drift off to a restful sleep.

'No bothering me in the bathroom, okay?' I warned Red as she hovered in the doorway. 'That would be beyond creepy.'

She held up her palms. 'Okay, okay, I promise. I won't bother you in the bathroom.'

She disappeared and I sunk into the warm, frothy liquid and sighed in relief. What a day! And what a night. A ghost, a stripper, and Pin the Tail on the... well, that silly game. A smile crept across my lips at the memory, even though I tried not to let it. I couldn't believe Ty had caught me with that thing in my hands. How embarrassing! But I had to hand it to Lorena, she sure knew how to plan an event to remember. I was lucky to have a friend like her, even if we were opposites. She'd do anything for me, and I for her.

I shivered and turned the hot tap on a little to warm the water. I wondered whether Red had good friends when she was alive. If so, they were probably grieving for her right now. I shivered again. Maybe I'd been too harsh on her. She was probably only doing all this crazy stuff to cope with being... departed. To distract herself. I'd try to cut her some slack tomorrow, and try to get her to tell me why she was here, so she, and I, could move on.

I breathed in deeply, the scent of rose and lavender filling my nostrils as steam wafted up to my face. For the first time today, my shoulders relaxed and I let the water ripple gently around me as my chest rose and fell. Remembering the fact that I'd be a married woman in one week, my smile returned, and I imagined Greg and I farewelling our guests and heading off to our honeymoon suite for our first night together as a married couple. He'd carry me inside, help me out of my wedding dress, and we'd roll around on the rose petal-covered bed entwined in each other. Ahhh...

What?

How did *he* get in my visualisation?

I shot up and water sloshed out of the tub. I shook my head. A vision of Ty with his perfect pecs on the rose-petal-covered bed flashed in my mind. *Geez, Sally, get a grip! Goodness gracious, girl.* It must be the cocktails, and the wine, messing with my mind. He was a fine young man, that was no lie. It didn't mean I desired him or anything, no way. It was like the others said: all women (and men) still get attracted to others, it's normal.

I grabbed a face cloth and wiped my cheeks, then leaned back and washed the curls from my hair. Lorena would be devastated, but I'd played the glam girl for one night. It'd be back to the normal me tomorrow: a ponytail, jeans, top, and jacket.

I stepped from the tub and dried off, wrapping a towel

around my body, grateful for the heated towel rail that had warmed it for me. I pulled the plug from the bath, and as water gurgled down the drain I walked into my bedroom where my pyjamas were neatly laid out on the bed. Well, everything except...

Where's my underwear?

I narrowed my eyes and glanced around. I was sure I'd put them here on the bed, my light pink pair with the ribbon heart at the front. I opened the drawer but they weren't in there. *Nope, I definitely put them on the bed.*

My shoulders sunk. 'Red?' I whispered. 'Did you move my underwear?' I said in a fed up 'I've had enough games for one day' voice.

A swirl of colours caught my eye near the door and her figure appeared, my undies hanging limply from one of her fingers.

'Looking for these?' A cheeky grin flashed on her face.

'Yes, now hand them over. C'mon.' I gestured for her to come over.

She dangled them above her head. 'You'll have to come and get them!'

I sighed and reached out to grab them, but she moved her hand to the other side. 'Red, c'mon. It's late.'

'For you, maybe. For me, I have all night! Come to think of it, I have eternity!'

I reached for them again but she stepped backwards and hid them behind her body, which was becoming less transparent the more I saw her.

I stepped out of the bedroom and onto the landing, conscious that below the stairs my friends were sleeping, or trying to. 'Red,' I urged in a whisper. 'Please, let me get dressed.' When she failed to hand them over I turned away. 'Well in that case, I'll just get a different pair.' I pulled at the knob on the wardrobe but it was stuck. 'You've got to be kidding me. Red, open this door.'

She shook her head like a naughty child who refused to leave a candy store.

I thought back to my bath and tried to remember what she might be going through. 'I know you just want to make the most of everything right now, but if I could please get dressed and go to sleep, I would really appreciate it. I will see you again tomorrow, I'm sure.'

She lifted the undies in front of her and wiggled them.

I lunged but missed, and she held my undies over the stairwell.

'Oh no, no you won't.' My empathy was wearing thin now.

She stepped onto the stairs, and desperate to get into my warm PJs I followed her, my hand reaching out and urging her to give up her little cotton hostage.

'C'mon, I don't want to wake up my friends.'

She paused at the landing where the stairs curved around, held the undies up, then moved them back and forth as though she was about to fling them down the stairs and into the living room.

'No, Red, no. Enough, okay?'

We stood at the ready like two cats preparing to pounce, and just when she let go of the underwear I reached out to try to grab them but, reaching a little too far, my damp foot slipped on the wooden stair. I landed with a thud-thud-thud down the last three stairs until I arrived on the floor below with an aching butt and a towel that probably wasn't covering as much as it had been before.

'Ouch!' I cried, scrambling to my knees and lunging forwards onto my stomach to retrieve the undies that were a metre in front of me. I grasped them with relief, while Red rolled about on the floor in hysterics.

'What happened?' Georgie's croaky voice asked as she emerged from the nearby bedroom, followed my Mel who had the zombie look going on.

'Um, nothing,' I said, as Lorena hobbled out of her room too.

'What are you doing on the floor, Sal?' she asked, lifting her eye mask. I laughed, as did the others, at the sight of her; earplugs poking out her ears, mask over her forehead, wavy black hair sticking up in all directions, one of those anti-snoring strips stuck across her nose, and...

'What is that thing?' I asked, pointing at the square padded item between her knees.

She glanced down, though probably couldn't see it. 'Oh, that's my Velcro knee pillow. Separates my knees at night so my back doesn't get sore.' At the look on our faces she crossed her arms. 'I guess you're wondering what other strange things I have attached to my body, huh? Well let me tell you, when you get pregnant, Sally, you'll probably do the same.' She plucked out her earplugs, which had obviously not drowned out my cries as I'd fallen down the stairs. 'I wake at the slightest noise, hence these things, not that they do that much. And my sinuses are playing up, okay, with the hormones, so I stick this thing on my nose to open up the airways a bit, and the mask shuts out all light so I can get a deep sleep. Happy now?'

'Sorry,' I said, standing and rubbing my sore behind.

'Anyway, I thought we were asking what you were doing down here in your birthday suit.' Her gaze shifted to what I was holding. 'Are they your undies?'

I scrunched them up into my fist and held them close to my side. 'Ah, yes, I was just um...'

More hysterics from Red.

Lorena snapped her fingers. 'I know, you were inspired by Ty's performance and wanted to try a little striptease of your own, right?' She grinned. 'Practising something for Greg, are we?'

'Maybe I should try that with Phillip,' Georgie mused.

'If I tried that with Michael it'd probably have the opposite effect.' Mel snorted.

'No, I'm not practising any such thing!'

'It's okay, don't be shy. We're married women. We know what lengths couples must go to in order to make the most of their intimate lives.'

'I'm not, I wasn't, I was just... I dropped my undies accidentally.'

'Down the stairs?'

'Uh-huh.' I nodded with wide, innocent eyes.

Lorena scrunched up her face as she eyed the staircase. 'Looks more like you would have flung them down instead of dropped them. Oh wait, were you trying to do a sexy slide down the handrail?' She raised her eyebrows in a suggestive way.

'Gosh, no, that could be dangerous,' I said. 'I dropped them and each time I tried to grab them I dropped them again until they ended up here.' I walked awkwardly towards the staircase, holding my towel tight around me. 'Anyway, it's late, you need to get some rest, Lorena. You too, ladies,' I said. 'And I'm a bit cold and really need to get into my PJs now.' I smiled and stepped on the first stair. 'Night!'

Mel trudged off and I heard a thump from her collapsing onto the bed. She probably wouldn't even remember this in the morning. Georgie said goodnight and returned to her room, and Lorena kissed me on the cheek and whispered, 'I think it's great what you're doing, Greg is going to be a very lucky man on your wedding night.' She winked and pulled her knee pillow back up that had fallen to her ankle, popped her earplugs back in and closed her bedroom door behind her.

I whooshed out a deep breath and, not waiting to get

upstairs first, I stepped into my undies before Red could take them again.

A couple of minutes later I was tucked up in bed in my cosy, checkered, flannelette PJs and my heavy eyelids drooped. Maybe tomorrow things would get back to normal. Red's had her fun, she might leave it at that and spare me any further humiliation.

I spoke too soon. No sooner had I started drifting off to sleep than she started singing 'All the Single Ladies', like she had in the supermarket.

I turned my head and inched it upwards a little. 'Red!'

She continued, and by the light of the moon easing through the sides of the curtains I could see her dancing and wiggling her behind. 'What? You don't like this song? Okay, I'll try another.'

Oh God no. She bent her elbows and marched her arms and legs as she walked on the spot and sang The Proclaimers' song '500 Miles' or whatever it was officially called.

The. Most. Annoying. Song. Ever.

She even put on a fake, daggy, male voice.

I pulled the pillow around my ears. 'Stop!'

She only sang louder. I covered my head with the blankets too, but they failed to muffle her rendition. For a moment I was tempted to creep downstairs and steal Lorena's earplugs while she slept, but she would probably hit me with her knee pillow.

'Red, you are being really annoying!'

'Oh,' she stomped her foot, 'you're no fun.'

'That's because it's after midnight and I want to get some sleep!'

'Hmph!' She crossed her arms. 'But I want to stay up and talk and have fun. I'm not tired at all. In fact, this is the best I've ever felt!' She held out her arms and spun around in a dizzying circle.

'Well in that case, okay. Let's talk, Red,' I said with a firm voice, sitting up and patting the bed with my hand. 'Let's have a good ol' girly chat about, hmm, let me see... oh, I know! Why on earth you're here, for starters.'

She went to sit where my hand had beckoned but hovered at my last words. 'Doesn't matter, I'll leave you alone now.' She flicked her hand and moved towards the door.

'Wait, what is it? Why can't you tell me why you're here?' I stood, moving towards her. 'Does it upset you?'

She turned her gaze away from mine. 'If I tell you, you'll hate me.'

'Well, we're not exactly best buds now, so why not continue your roll and put the icing on the cake, huh?'

She shook her head, then met my gaze and plastered an obviously fake smile on her face. 'You rest up now, you hear?' Nighty night, girlfriend!' She spun around and vanished into thin air.

I shook my head in disbelief and stood on the spot for a moment, before returning to the warmth of my bed. As I tried to relax and get ready for sleep again, an uncomfortable thought floated through my mind. *What if she still loved Greg and was here to break us up? To interfere with my dream wedding and not let the man who got away get away with marrying someone else.* I clenched the blankets tightly around me, hoping I was wrong.

CHAPTER 9

I awoke to the sounds of cutlery clanging and bridesmaids chatting, and I rubbed my eyes as sunlight filtered through the gaps on either side of the curtains. I automatically scanned the room, but Red wasn't there. I hopped out of bed and stretched my arms up high, squeezing the remaining sleep from my muscles. On opening the door, I almost stepped on something. A T-shirt lay folded outside my room, white with black writing. I lifted it and the folds dropped away.

A chuckle tumbled from my mouth, and I called downstairs to Mel, T-shirt designer extraordinaire. 'Um, I take it you want me to wear this today?'

'You bet,' she called back. 'We're all wearing different ones.'

It didn't bother me, I'd be covering up most of it with a jacket anyway.

Ten minutes later I walked downstairs in my jeans and sneakers, my light brown hair in a neat ponytail, and a long-sleeved T-shirt that said: *Sorry guys, I'm engaged.*

I hung my jacket on the back of a chair and sat at the kitchen counter with the others. 'I'm flattered,' I said to Mel.

'That you think someone might hit on me this weekend. This T-shirt will set them straight. Good thinking, Ninety-Nine.' I gently punched the side of her arm.

'Well, you never know. You could get swamped at the festival today so I thought I'd save the poor fellas some time and heartbreak.' She winked, then popped out her chest so I could read her T-shirt: *Think I look good now? Wait till you see me on eight hours sleep. Note: You might be waiting a while.*

I smiled, and looked at Georgie's which said: *I'm not as sweet as I look,* and Lorena's whose made me chuckle: *YES I'm pregnant, YES I know what I'm having, and NO you may not touch my belly.*

I reached my hand across and patted her belly to tease her, then eyed the plates of hash browns, grilled tomatoes, mushrooms, crispy bacon chips, and gourmet omelettes. 'Oh, Georgie, I didn't realise how hungry I was till I saw all this.'

'Dig in, Sal,' she said, handing me a plate.

'Yeah, before I have seconds,' Mel added.

After a hearty feed and a quick freshen up in the bathroom, I grabbed my shoulder bag and met my friends at the door. Things were looking up. No sign of Red, and all I had to do was wear this T-shirt and enjoy the day at the Winter Solstice Festival. Easy.

'Oh, Sal, one more thing,' said Lorena, grasping something from one of her secret bags. 'Here, you have to wear this all day.' She propped something on my head and I looked in the mirror. A glittery, sparkling, blingy-as-bling-can-be tiara with the words: *Bride to Be.*

Aren't friends just the best?

The bustling, colourful, vibrant atmosphere of the festival swallowed us up as we entered Barron Springs Park. There wasn't much diversity among businesses and places in this town; it seemed everything had Barron Springs tacked onto the front of it: the supermarket, the park, the guest house, the post office, the doctor's surgery, the corner cafe, the pharmacy, and even the pub. The addition of the town name seemed redundant, they might as well have called everything according to the nature of what it was: The Park, The Supermarket, or The Pub, and save a bit of time when greeting customers over the phone.

People weaved in between each other in the crowd, some in regular clothes and others in costumes to celebrate the longest day of winter. There were a few witches, a fairy or two, some cuddly bears, some... unidentified strange costumes, and even a kangaroo. I turned around as the man-kanga literally hopped past me, his hands hooked in front of him. He stopped and made a noise with his tongue, like Skippy or something, and hopped away.

'There's one in every town,' Mel said.

'What, a man-kanga?'

'An *eccentric* is a nice way of putting it.'

I didn't feel so conspicuous in my tiara now. In fact, no one had given me a second glance.

Except for a clown who walked towards me blowing bubbles through a plastic circle on a stick, wearing — wait for it — purple polka dot baggy pants. I leaned closer to check it wasn't Red in a different outfit, but no, the stubble showing through the white face paint and a hint of masculine deodorant met my senses, confirming it was a man. A bubble popped on my nose and I blinked away the splash of detergent.

A woman up ahead twirled a long fancy ribbon, her red, curly hair appearing to twirl itself. *Red?* As we got closer I noticed her leathery tanned face, and her hair was obviously coloured as grey roots threatened to burst through the red.

A child nearby laughed and cackled in a high-pitched tone, and once again I was reminded of Red. Geez, even when she wasn't here I couldn't get away from her.

'Miss me?'

I flipped my head sideways at the voice, and there she was, same pyjamas, same curly red hair, same mischievous grin. If everyone else could see her she would blend right into the crowd. No one would think twice about a young woman in polka dot pyjamas on a day where anything went in regard to attire.

'Well, did you?' she asked.

'Did I what?'

'Did you what, what?' asked Lorena, her long mascaraed lashes casting a shadow under her eyes in the morning sun.

'Did you *miss* me?' asked Red.

'No,' I replied, then quickly turned my attention back to Lorena. 'I mean, did I... *what?* Did I forget my, my...' Gosh, what could I pretend to have forgotten? 'Hand sanitiser?' I rummaged through my bag.

'What do you need that for?'

'All these people, you know. Billions of germs just waiting to pounce on unsuspecting victims.' I waved my hand about to the crowd. 'Darn it, I did forget. Oh well.'

I carried on walking, and Georgie stopped at a stall showcasing various antiques. I wondered, if life really *did* exist after death, did spirits, or ghosts, or whatever I was supposed to call them, stay connected to important or sentimental belongings? Did each of these items have its own ghost? I decided not to touch any, especially the gilded hand mirror Georgie had picked up, scared if I looked in it I might be met with the face of its deceased owner. I shivered and pulled my jacket more tightly around my shoulders.

'Psst!' Red whispered, though I didn't know why since it wasn't like anyone could hear her. 'I want to watch the stage show. C'mon, let's go!' She gestured to the right.

'Not right now,' I mouthed, as Georgie was clearly fascinated by the antiques. I felt a slight pull against my jacket, and Red's powers had no doubt increased as I stumbled over my feet as she made my body move sideways. I resisted, trying to move my body back to the stall, but she persisted, so I looked like I was doing some kind of line-dancing.

'Sally, what are you doing?' Mel asked, intrigue on her rounded face.

Red pulled me sideways, and I moved back again, and the tug of war continued so I clapped my hands and did a little twirl, then hooked my thumbs in my jeans pockets so I looked like a cowgirl.

'C'mon, Mel, join me for a spot of line-dancing?' I asked feebly.

Lorena giggled. 'Who are you and what have you done with Sally?'

Mel didn't seem too fazed; she stood behind me and copied my movements, the ones to the right being slightly more awkward and jerky as a result of being pulled by Red.

'Oh, why not?' Lorena said, and joined in too.

Within moments, a crowd had gathered around us and some people in costumes joined the line too, copying my every move. When Red flung my hand up in the air, they did too, and when she yanked me so hard sideways that I appeared to be suffering with some kind of muscle spasm, the crowd laughed and followed. I turned briefly. About ten people had joined in the dance, goofy smiles on their faces as they danced along to my impromptu performance.

To make the most of the situation, I flexed my foot and pointed my toes repeatedly in a heel-and-toe line-dancing movement, then prepared for the tug of war with Red. Her ability to move living objects seemed limited, only lasting a few moments before my human ability to regain my posture overtook her. She growled in frustration, then on seeing the laughter and cheers from the crowd, took it upon herself to make the most of it. She pushed my head sideways so that my ear almost touched my shoulder, then again; push, push, push, as though I had a tic. Amazingly, my tiara stayed put, thanks to the clips on the side of the headband, which Lorena had snapped onto my hair to secure the glittery abomination in place. Red poked my stomach and it tickled, which made me double over, and she kept repeating each movement so it turned into an extremely weird, though original, seizure-like dance.

Ty has nothing on me, I thought to myself with a grin. I may look like a fool, but I was an entertaining fool, and at least Ty wasn't here to witness this strange public show of my dancing ability, or lack thereof. I spun around one way, then the other, then Red flung both my arms up in the air at once, and when they dropped to my side for the third time I saw him. Ty. Standing right in the middle of the crowd with a wide grin on his face.

If that wasn't bad enough, some guy with a microphone came over from a sideshow game to commentate on what seemed to be a flash mob initiated by yours truly.

'Lookie here, folks, step right up! We have a bride-to-be line-dancing guru showing what she's made of, and showing what appears to be a tribal dance of some sort, or perhaps a mating ritual of Amazonian gorillas?'

I rolled my eyes, and Red laughed, and Ty must have seen enough because he gave a small wave and walked off. *Great, more embarrassment to add to my collection.* Red broke away from her puppet master duties and said, 'Okay, I've had enough, now I *really* want to go to the stage show. C'mon!'

I gave an awkward bow to the crowd, who clapped and cheered, though I thought I heard someone say: 'What a strange woman.' Georgie, with a bagful of antiques, approached me and asked if I was all right, and Mel said she reckoned she'd burnt off enough breakfast to have morning tea now, despite having only been at the festival a matter of minutes.

Red urged me with her eyes, and I pointed towards the stage. 'Why don't we go see what's happening over there? I'm sure whoever's on stage will be a bit more accomplished than me,' I chuckled.

'You were tops, hun,' said Lorena. 'You're really coming out of your shell this weekend, good to see! I told you you'd have some fun.' She hung her arm around me and we walked towards the stage where a new crowd had gathered.

Boppy music began playing from the large speakers beside the stage, and a young man in a wheelchair was helped onto the stage. His mouth was wide in a smile, and he clapped his hands in time to the music, encouraging the audience to join in. As hands clapped, a few more people walked onto the stage, clapping their hands and bobbing their heads. One of them simply stood behind the man in the wheelchair and patted his hair affectionately like an animal. The man didn't seem fussed. The music intensified and someone else graced the stage, his body moving in time to the music in a way that oozed rhythm and experience. Ty. He high-fived each person on the stage, then they (or most of them, except the head-patting young man) performed a series of basic dance moves. Some in time to the music, some not so much. But the looks on their faces showed they were having the time of their lives. A serious-looking woman of about twenty was quite good. She never smiled, but copied each of Ty's movements with vigour and purpose, like her life depended on it. She was practically working up a sweat from pure concentration. I glanced at my friends who clapped along, and Mel repeated her statement from last night: 'What a guy.'

The dance crew certainly overshadowed my lame performance; they were delightful to watch, and it warmed my heart to see these people with various challenges overcoming any inhibitions or limitations and putting on a damn good show. So not only did Ty teach life skills and take his 'team' on outings, he also taught them to dance. What a guy indeed. Though I hoped his instructions stopped there and didn't include stripping, that would be taking it a bit too far.

The performance ended with the team's fists pushing high to the sky with the last burst of music, followed by a bow. The audience clapped and whistled, and everyone had a big smile on their faces. Maybe Ty hadn't walked away from my performance in boredom after all, he just had to get ready for his own.

As the team filtered off the stage, some with a bit of help, appreciation drew me towards them. Ty noticed me and waved me over.

'What a great performance,' I said.

'Could say the same thing about yours,' he replied.

I flicked my hand. 'Oh, it was just a bit of silly fun. But yours,' I glanced at a few team members who had gathered around Ty, 'yours was the most entertaining thing I've seen this year.'

One of the young men's faces glowed, and I reached out and shook his hand. 'Well done,' I said.

The other young man, whose specialty was patting people's heads, came close to me. 'Would you like my autograph?' he asked in a nasal voice that suggested he might be hard of hearing, or had had trouble learning to speak.

'Cody!' Ty gently whacked his friend on the chest.

I chuckled and replied, 'Yes indeed, I would love your autograph.' I pulled a pen and notepad from my shoulder bag and handed it to him. He scrawled something illegible on it, then added a drawing.

'It's a tree,' he said. 'I like trees.'

'I like trees too, how did you know?' I smiled at him as he handed the paper back to me.

'Sally, this is my brother Cody. Codes, this is Sally,' Ty said.

I held out my hand and Cody gripped it. A little too tightly, but it was cute. 'Nice to meet you, Cody.'

'You were right, Ty, she is pretty,' Cody said, and Ty's face grew a little pink as he shushed his brother. 'She's like a beautiful tree.'

Ty offered a lopsided smile, and pointed to my T-shirt. 'See that, Codes? It means she's getting married.'

'To you?'

'No, of course not! To someone else.' He ruffled Cody's wavy hair.

Then without warning, Cody wrapped his arms around me in a warm hug. His hand patted my back lovingly, and although I stiffened at first, I soon softened and allowed myself to enjoy this random act of affection.

'C'mon, Codes, we better get everyone together and let Sally enjoy her day.' He turned to me. 'I've got to get everyone sorted out and back to their respective carers, but I might see you and your friends around a bit later. Maybe you can teach me some of your moves.' He hooked his thumbs in his jeans pockets in a teasing mockery, and I covered my face with my hand and lowered my head.

'Have a good day, Cody,' I said, and he waved as he walked off with Ty.

I turned around to find Red with her hand over her heart. 'That was adorable. I think I'm going to cry.' Her face contorted into a slightly exaggerated expression of happy crying. I left her there and walked back to my friends.

'Let's go, Sal, I've found something fun for us to do!' Lorena tugged on my jacket much the same way as Red had done, and out of my newly ingrained habit I considered breaking into a line-dance again, but thought better of it.

She led me towards the stalls.

What surprise would greet me next?

'Palm reading?' I asked.

'Why not?' Lorena shrugged. 'It'll be interesting.'

'Guess so, but you know that stuff is just a load of hocus-pocus, right?'

'Hocus-pocus or not, I'm in.' Mel approached one of the kaftan-wearing women behind the stall and handed her some cash.

'My shout,' Lorena said. 'Ooh, but wait. Do your jacket up and let's get rid of this.' She unclipped my tiara and I buttoned up my jacket, hiding the fact that I was a bride-to-be, unless they'd happened to see my tribal, bridal, mating ritual or whatever that man with the microphone had called my dance. 'Wonder if they can tell you're about to get hitched!'

'Hmm, and I wonder if they can tell you have a baby on the way.' I glanced at her rounded T-shirt poking beneath her long purple cardigan.

'Haha. But if they can predict *what* I'm having, then I'll be impressed.'

'What *are* you having by the way?'

'Ah, nice try, hun. You know I'm not telling anyone.' She winked.

Lorena paid the other woman and I held out my hand.

The woman grasped it gently and gave it a rub. 'Okay, let's have a look, sweetheart.' She pushed her glasses higher on her nose and studied my palm. While I waited for her to analyse it, or make stuff up, Red stood beside me staring at my face with an intense look of concentration. I wanted to ask her if she was giving me a face reading or something, but kept my mouth shut. Instead, I eyed her with a curious 'what are you doing?' expression, and she stopped her staring and said, 'Drats. Oh well, I'll try again later.'

Try what? I narrowed my eyes, but she ignored my silent request and tried to fiddle with the crystal wind chimes hanging from the stall. They tinkled slightly and she smiled.

'You have a good, strong lifeline, sweetheart,' said the woman, running her finger along a line that curved down the middle of my palm. 'Some challenges early in life, but as an adult you have stability and security, and a fairly straightforward direction.'

With a ghost hanging around me I wasn't exactly feeling stable and secure right now, but I didn't want to interrupt and tell the poor woman, who was simply trying to make a living.

'You tend to rule with your head more than your heart,' she said, running her finger down another line. 'You need to learn to be more open-minded.'

'I guess that's why I'm having a palm reading,' I said with a small smile.

She took her focus off my hand for a moment and looked in my eyes. 'We all have to start somewhere,' she said, then returned her attention to my hand. 'There is some conflict between your practical nature and your emotions, and you would benefit from trusting your intuition.'

I nodded, and Red nodded too.

'Interesting, you are both fearful of many things, a bit of a worrier, yet calm under pressure. As long as you follow the rules you feel you can cope with life.'

Hmm, it did sound a bit like me. But I bet anyone could recognise themselves in her description. Maybe she was doing that acupressure thing like Ty had done on my foot, softening me up or something.

She tilted my hand a little. 'I see three main romantic relationships in your life. Three loves.' She smiled. 'You're engaged, yes?'

Wow. Lorena was right, maybe she did have some sort of higher power or intuition.

I nodded.

'Nice ring,' she said.

Oh. In my effort to hide my self-explanatory T-shirt and bride-to-be tiara I'd forgotten to remove my engagement ring!

Not so psychic after all, Kaftan Woman.

'So I take it you were third time lucky?' she asked.

'I'm sorry?'

'In love. Third time lucky, with your fiancé.'

Three loves in my life. Greg, of course, and there were a couple of guys before him but it wasn't exactly love, and then before that there was Mark, definitely love, but after three years his love for travel overpowered his love for me and our relationship took a nosedive. And before Mark, well, there was Stephen, but that was more lust, and Evan, well, that was barely more than a high school crush that never manifested into anything more than getting to school early so I could watch him get off the bus when it arrived.

So... Greg, and Mark. That was it. Two loves, not three. This woman had it wrong.

'Actually, my fiancé is my second real love, and so much more than my first. We're very happy.' I plumped my lips into a content smile.

She smiled awkwardly, and checked the markings. 'Definitely three here. It is *slightly* possible the third could indicate some other significant relationship. But you're sure you haven't had a third love, long ago; high school sweetheart perhaps?'

I shook my head, and glanced at Red who was eavesdropping on Mel's reading.

'Not to worry, then. Now, let's see what else we can find out.' She continued giving her analysis, and when she finished, she gave me back my hand but asked me to put it inside a white box. 'Every palm reading comes with a bonus gemstone lucky dip. Take your time, feel around and pick up the one your hand is naturally drawn to. You might be surprised how appropriate the stone is for you, based on its meaning and properties.'

They were just lumps of rocks to me, but I did as she said and took my time, picking up a smooth, oval-shaped stone that tapered a little. I held it up and the woman clasped her hands together in delight. 'Oh, I've been waiting for someone to get that one! Only one in the whole box. It's very special.' She smiled and nodded.

I eyed the greyish-green stone with its silvery-white shimmery flecks that gave it a feathery appearance, and asked what it was.

'Seraphinite. Comes from Siberia. It's an extremely powerful stone, increases your intuition and communication with other realms.'

'Realms?'

'Yes, the divine feminine power that is all around us, and the angelic realm.'

The divine? Angels?

'Do I have a halo?' Red asked as she shoved her face in front of me, her hand above her head. 'Do I? Do I?'

I wanted to tell her that if angels existed they were supposed to be kind, loving, gentle beings, and not irritating, demanding, pains in the arse. I shook my head with subtlety. But the woman noticed.

'Oh yes, I assure you, it is true. Hold this stone when you wish to connect with the divine feminine, to enhance self-healing, and intuitive abilities.'

'Oh, okay then,' I said, even though without the stone I was quite in tune with the 'other side', thank you very much, and didn't exactly want to tune in even further. Heaven help me if I was surrounded by multiple Reds demanding my attention.

I thanked the woman and moved away from the stall, as the others remained, listening intently to their readings. I held the *saph*, the *sephar*, the *s...* oh what was it called again? Anyway, I held the stone up to the light of the sun. It was quite pretty, with its streaks of green, white, and grey. I could use it as a paperweight.

Red stood in front of me and looked at it from the other side (ha!), and pointed her finger at the stone in deep concentration. She pushed her finger forwards, and — plop! —the stone fell from my grasp and down my T-shirt through the small valley of my cleavage. I shivered at its cold, smooth surface as it travelled down to my abdomen. 'Oh no!' Red laughed as I unbuttoned my jacket and tried to discreetly shove my hand down my top.

'Can I help at all?' I spun around to see Ty standing nearby, my hand still lodged between my boobs and my elbow pointing to the heavens, where I wished Red would toddle off to. I yanked my hand out and straightened my jacket.

'No, I'm fine thanks. Where did you spring from?'

'I saw you looking at something in your hand so I came to see what it was.'

'Oh, it's just a gemstone.' I brushed a non-existent strand of hair from my face. 'It sort of, um, fell down my top.' I could still feel it low against my belly, but I didn't think my arm could reach down far enough to get it. I could also feel an uncomfortable wave of heat rushing across my face, belying the fact that it was a cold winter's day.

Ty tried to hold back a grin, but a hint of it twinkled at the sides of his mouth. 'So, maybe just give your shirt a bit of a shake?' He grasped his close-fitting black ribbed top at the hem and gave it a shake, and a glimpse of his tanned, hard abs brought back flashes of him last night in his underwear.

The heat on my face intensified. 'Well, you see, I sort of can't,' I replied, touching the spot where the gemstone lay.

'Why not?'

Oh dear God. Of all the days, why did I have to wear this thing underneath?

'Because I'm wearing a bodysuit.'

Ty's eyebrows rose. 'Oh, one of those all-in-one Lycra things?'

I nodded.

'So you'd need to, um...'

'Unhook it, below, yes.' Too much information. Why was I telling him this? Surely a man of his 'experience' knew how a woman's bodysuit was structured.

'In that case, I'll let you get on with it.' He gestured behind and turned away, then turned back briefly. 'I'll just wait over here.'

I hid behind a stall and grasped the stone through my clothing with one hand, walking it up my body the way one does with a draw cord lost in the waistband of one's pants, but it only moved slightly. I plunged my hand down my top again and dug around, but the tight-fit of the bodysuit made it difficult. *C'mon, gemstone! Where are you?* It was like the Bermuda Triangle in here. If this failed I'd have to find the ladies bathrooms and do the unhooking, but if I could just get it...

I grunted, sinking my stomach muscles inwards to make more room for my arm, and stretching poor Mel's T-shirt piece of art. My fingers came in contact with cold stone which I grasped, and with my other hand I pushed it upwards, until the stone was in my hand and my arm was finally out of a place I didn't exactly aspire it to be whilst in public, or even private, for that matter. 'Phew!' I breathed out, having held my breath for a little while.

I adjusted my top and jacket and returned to where I'd been, feeling as though everyone was looking at me, even though they weren't. Except Ty.

'Got it?' he asked.

I held up the stone in victory.

He clapped. 'If you were single I would have given you a hand. You know, just to do the helpful gentlemanly thing.' He winked.

Flirt. 'Oh, I'm sure.' I crossed my arms and diverted my gaze from his.

'Hey, Ty!' Lorena said, as she approached with Mel and Georgie, each with their own gemstone.

'How was your palm reading?' I asked Mel, who seemed quite pleased.

'I have a pointy girdle of Venus.' She held up her palm and touched the area under her two middle fingers. 'Something about being emotionally up and down, hot-headed sometimes.'

'And is that true?' Ty asked.

'Are you calling me hot-headed?' she mocked, in an

exaggerated angry voice. Ty held his own palms up, as if to say 'no, not at all', not as if to have his palms read.

'Oh well,' Mel said. 'At least it wasn't a saggy girdle like this one.' She patted the belly that had grown five children.

'So what did she say, Sal, anything about love and marriage?' asked Lorena. 'She said I have two relationship lines, or two loves in my life. Luckily, since I married my second one.' She held a hand over her heart.

I gulped. 'Um, yeah, she said the same about me.' I didn't know why I felt the need to lie. It was all just made-up, new-age stuff anyway. Wasn't it?

CHAPTER 10

'Well that was fun, how cute and quirky is Barron Springs?' Georgie asked, as she closed the door behind us when we returned to the guest house.

'We should come here more often, have a regular girls' weekend every six months or so,' Mel added. 'And we could book Ty again. You know, help him pay for medical school. Would be a nice gesture.'

'Something tells me you'd want to book him even if he didn't need the money.' Lorena nudged Mel in the ribs and she shrugged.

'Maybe we could go somewhere new each time, if we make these girls' weekends a regular thing,' I suggested.

Lorena nodded. 'Good idea.'

'But why go anywhere else?' Mel said with a cheeky smile.

Georgie plated up some antipasto and placed it on the coffee table. 'Dig in, gals.'

'It's also time for us to play a game,' Lorena said, rubbing her hands together.

My stomach dropped a little. 'Not Pin the You-Know-What on the You-Know-Who again?' I asked.

She flicked her hand towards me. 'No, something new.'

I glanced at the old wooden bookcase towering beside the fireplace, which held not only a collection of books but an array of board games. 'Oh good, what about Scrabble? Or Operation?'

'Yeah, like we'd have a chance against you with your large vocabulary and medical precision. Nice try, Sal. We're going to play something a bit more... fun.' She grinned, then disappeared into her bedroom and returned with a large bag. She withdrew a huge lump of newspaper.

'Papier-mâché?' I asked, as my forehead drew downwards.

She laughed.

'God I hope not. That stuff is evil,' said Mel. 'I vowed never to do that with my kids again, such a mess.' She scrunched her face then raised her finger. 'Unless... are we going to fashion a 3D version of Pin the You-Know-What on the You-Know-Who?' Her eyes widened.

'Mel!' I scolded. 'You naughty thing.'

Lorena held up the large lump in front of her own large lump. 'Can't you tell what it is? Pass the Parcel!' She shook the lump in anticipation.

My stomach returned to its normal position. *Phew*. Nothing naughty or embarrassing, just a simple childhood game with gifts inside. Much better. 'Haven't played that for years!' I said, taking a spot on the floor on top of the intricately patterned rug. 'Let's get started.'

'Now that's what I like to see, enthusiasm for my initiative.' Lorena placed the parcel on the floor in front of me and tried to kiss my forehead, but couldn't bend enough to reach me so sounded a 'mwah!' instead.

Lorena sat on the velvet couch with her iPhone and played some music: 'The Wedding March'. She really should leave retail management and go into event management, the woman thought of every little detail.

Mel and Georgie sat on the floor too, in as much of a circle as three people could manage.

'But you won't get any gifts, Lorena,' I said.

'I know what they all are anyway.'

'But still, how can we play so that you get to keep some pressies too?'

'I'll take her spot!' Red exclaimed, leaping onto the floor and sitting between myself and Georgie.

I shuffled a little closer to Georgie to try and nudge her away, then gestured to the gap between Mel and I. 'Why don't we pretend you're here, and place the parcel on the floor during the game. If the music stops before Mel or I get to pick it up then that means you get to open one of the layers?'

'Umm...' Lorena didn't seem overly fussed about playing. Maybe the gifts weren't that great, perhaps only two-dollar lipsticks and other little novelties. I looked at her luscious fuchsia lips and realised that nope, she wouldn't stoop to cheap gifts.

'Yeah, but you have to turn away when you play the music so you can't see who has the parcel when the music stops,' Mel instructed.

'All right then. I officially declare that spot of rug to be my proxy.' She pointed, and when Red looked like she was about to jump over there I glared at her. She pouted and crossed her arms.

I accepted a slice of Turkish bread covered with marinated feta and roasted red peppers, and gulped it down. I passed the parcel to the invisible 'Lorena' then Mel picked it up and passed it to Georgie, then Georgie passed it to me. The situation repeated, until the music stopped when the parcel was in my hands.

'Perfect timing, Lorena!' Mel said. 'Bride-to-be gets first gift.'

I wriggled in anticipation and unwrapped the first layer, revealing a lavender eye pillow. 'Oh, how nice! Thanks,' I said, placing the pillow over my eyes as I leaned back a little. 'I might have to have a nanna nap before dinner so I can try it out.' And maybe it would stop me seeing Red for a while. I rested it on my leg and as the music resumed I passed the parcel again. Next was Georgie who got a decorative metal bookmark, then me again with a small sachet of heart-shaped chocolates.

'I'll swap you,' Mel said.

'But you don't have anything to swap,' I replied.

'Exactly.'

I chuckled and handed her a chocolate, which she wolfed down in one hit. Eventually the music stopped on her turn and she got a small pocket book called *Ten Steps to Happiness in Love* by a Dr Reginald Bloomschneider.

'With a name like that, he must have women falling at his feet,' she joked, flipping through the book and forgetting to pass the parcel. 'Oops, sorry! I'll read this tonight. Wonder if it advises having no more than three kids.' She laughed, as she always did, about anything to do with serious issues. I wondered if she truly was happy with her marriage. Was she just being light-hearted about it or did she really have some concerns? I made a mental note to catch up with her after the wedding, just the two of us, to find out how things were *really* going.

Lorena finally got a gift; a pair of dangly earrings, which I was glad about because they weren't something I would wear. When the music stopped again with the parcel in my hands, I wondered what other treats she had hidden in this bundle of generosity.

I pulled out a slip of paper and read it:

This voucher is for one truth or dare.

I glanced up at Lorena with inquisitive eyes. She shot me a knowing look. 'Truth or dare?'

I nodded.

'Oooh, goodie!' said Mel. 'So which one do you want: truth or dare?'

'Hang on, let's save up the truth or dares till the parcel is all unwrapped,' said Lorena.

'You mean there are more of them?' I asked.

'Yep.'

'I'm up for that,' Georgie said. 'Already spilled my guts to you yesterday about my sex life, why stop now?'

But she never got a truth or dare. By the time the game was complete the four vouchers had been received only by Mel and I, two each. Maybe we could do one truth and one dare. The other gifts shared between us were a heart-shaped silver photo frame (which I would put a wedding photo in), a sachet of gummy bears (which now ceased to exist thanks to Mel's appetite), and various accessories and novelty items. Oh, and a twenty-five per cent discount voucher for an online 'adult' store, which Mel placed next to her on the floor and smiled at.

'Damn, and I was hoping I'd get that one,' said Lorena with a wink.

Apart from the truth or dare vouchers, which were causing an uncomfortable, nervous sensation in my chest, I was quite impressed with my loot. 'You've really put a lot of thought into this, Lorena.' I stood and gave her a hug. 'Thank you. The gifts are perfect.'

She smiled. 'It was fun! I loved putting the parcel together. And it was good to get in some practise before my gorgeous girl is born.' She patted her belly and smiled again, then her jaw dropped.

Mine did too. 'You're having a girl?' I asked, eyes wide, my hands grasping one of hers.

She covered her mouth. 'Oops.'

Mel whooped and Georgie placed her hand over her heart, and that, combined with Lorena's expression which had morphed into something softer, something motherly, made tears pool at the back of my eyes. 'A little girl! I'm so happy for you.' I kissed her cheek and hugged her again, and Lorena wiped a tear from the corner of her eye.

'Please don't tell anyone, we agreed to keep it secret until the birth. My parents don't even know.'

I formed a cross over my heart with my finger. 'Secret's safe with me.' I was used to keeping things confidential; it was second nature, and a legal requirement of my job.

'Don't worry, hun,' said Mel. 'What happens in Barron Springs...'

'Stays in Barron Springs!' we chorused, then collapsed into a group embrace on the couch with a glossy-eyed Lorena.

'Okay, enough, girls, I believe we have some truth or dares to get through?' Lorena ushered us away and we each took a seat, me next to Lorena on the velvet couch, Mel sprawled on the rug, and Georgie in the armchair.

'You go first, Mel,' I said. 'Truth or dare?'

'Well it looks like I have to do both anyway, but let's get the ball rolling with a dare.'

Mel and I were opposites; I'd rather start with truth. I'm an honest person, so that wouldn't be a problem. Except for the little white lie about what the palm reader told me. Oh, and if they asked me if I'd ever seen a ghost, I was screwed.

I racked my brain for a suitable dare, one that would be a bit challenging, or embarrassing even, but not in a totally life-ruining way. I considered telling her to put a cushion down her top and walk down the street and pretend she was pregnant, then go into fake labour in front of people, but that could be tricky if someone called an ambulance. Then again, being a nurse, I could always say I'd take her to hospital and assist her on the way, or deliver the baby myself. Nah, better to do something here, something we didn't have to leave the house for. There'd been enough public excitement for one day.

The pink voucher lying on the floor next to Mel caught my eye, and my mouth curled up at the corner. I whipped out my phone and typed in the website of the adult store. *Aha! Perfect.*

Mel eyed me curiously. 'Do you want me to order something with my discount voucher now, is that it? Because I can do that, no problem.'

'Not exactly. I want you to call customer service and ask them to explain the difference between some of the products so they can help you select the um, toy, or whatever those things are, that's right for you.' I nodded in satisfaction and handed her my phone. Then I pulled it back. 'Actually, better use your own phone, in case they track phone numbers or something and try to call me with special offers.'

Mel took a deep breath and Lorena and Georgie egged her on, chanting, 'Do it, do it, do it!' with Red joining in too, as though she thought she was one of the girls. I was even starting to get used to having her around, and she was behaving a little better at the moment.

'But it's Saturday, they're probably closed.'

I shook my head. 'Customer service open nine to five, seven days a week.' I handed her my phone so she could see the website.

'Okay, I can do this. Sure thing.' But she looked a little nervous and scrolled through the website on my phone so she could prepare herself. Every now and again she'd chuckle, or gasp, or laugh out loud at whatever she was coming across on the site. She rested my phone on one of her crossed legs as she sat on the floor, and held her phone to her ear. She cleared her throat and called the number.

'Ah, yes, good morning. I mean good afternoon,' she said, and I wished I'd asked her to put it on speakerphone so we could hear the other side of the conversation. 'Yes I would like some help actually. I'm trying to, um, choose a... product. Could you let me know what the difference is between The Enhancer and The Illuminator?' She held back a grin as she listened to the voice on the other end. 'Oh, I see. So The Illuminator is an advanced version of The Enhancer?' She waited. 'It has what?' Mel's eyes bulged and she covered her mouth with one hand to restrain a laugh. 'So it actually lights up and plays music when it detects heightened sensitivity?'

My jaw dropped open and Lorena was silent-laughing and slapping her thigh.

Mel cleared her throat again. 'And it glows in the dark? Wow, so that's how it gets its name then.' She smirked. 'But the cost, I mean, it's not exactly cheap, how do I know I'm getting my money's worth?' Georgie clapped her hands towards Mel, quietly, applauding her inquisition. 'I take it you can't exchange it for something else?' More waiting. 'Oh, so you do have a satisfaction guarantee? How does that work?'

My torso trembled in giggles as she spoke, it was as though we were teenagers and she was making a prank call to a boy she liked.

'So you refund my money within fourteen days if I'm... unsatisfied. What happens to the item?' We perched forwards, waiting for each development in the conversation. 'Melted down, sanitised, and recycled? Wow. Talk about environmentally friendly.' Mel was enjoying this now; she'd relaxed back on one hand. 'Is that so?' she continued. 'A bonus instructional video? That *is* a good deal.' She glanced at us and smiled. 'Um, well I'm not one hundred per cent sure I want to order yet, I may need to do some more research... What's that? Put me through to a recording of testimonials from satisfied customers?'

No way. Who would be prepared to do such a thing? The company must have paid them big bucks.

'Okay then, sure. Go ahead.' Mel pressed speakerphone and we listened as a woman's voice talked about her experience and mentioned things like 'most prized possession', 'better than having a husband', and 'my inner goddess has been illuminated'. Her tone was like a normal, everyday, super-happy woman, like those cheesy ones on TV commercials for laundry detergent where they smile and glow as though their life's purpose has been fulfilled because their whites are whiter than ever.

After listening to a couple more testimonials, I couldn't bear to hear the words 'inner goddess' or 'illuminate' again, and Mel ended the call and collapsed in hysterics. 'Oh, Sal, that was a blast!' She slapped her thigh. 'You should have heard her explaining the science and mechanics behind it, as though she was telling me how a new vacuum cleaner worked. To be honest, she spoke so methodically I can't even be sure she was human.' She laughed and snorted. 'Maybe she's really a robot, made of the same technology and recycled plastic and metal. Probably has her own in-built Illuminator!'

Lorena's laughs were audible now, as were all of ours, and as laughter filled the room, tears ran down our faces, and I reached out and high-fived Mel for her efforts. Red raised her hand for a high-five too, and I went to reciprocate. Lorena furrowed her brow between laughs.

'Oh, I thought you were about to put your hand up,' I falsely confessed. 'My bad.'

'Here, hun,' she said, holding up her hand. I high-fived it

and snuck another warning glance at Red. She knew how to catch me off guard and I couldn't let her get in the way of my hen's weekend with my wonderful, supportive, comfort-zone-busting friends.

'Great dare, Sal, how about yours now?' Georgie asked, having recovered from laughing and now digging into the antipasto.

Damn, with all the laughs I'd forgotten I hadn't had my turn yet. 'I think I'll go for a truth first,' I said, though I was only delaying the inevitable.

'Okay, okay, time to think,' Mel said, wiping tears of laughter from her red face and shuffling on the floor to get comfortable. 'Truth time, baby.'

I raised my eyebrows in waiting.

'Rightio, got one.' She cleared her throat. 'Have you ever felt unprofessionally attracted to a male patient in your care?'

I thought for a millisecond and shook my head. 'No.' *Gee, that was easy.*

'C'mon, Sal, think carefully. You've seen hundreds of patients, done countless examinations, administered tons of treatments, there has to have been the odd good-looker. Think!'

I thought. After years of nursing, everything sort of blurs together — time, experiences, and patients. It's hard to remember exact details. Sometimes I see people in the street who look vaguely familiar and I wonder if I've nursed them and forgotten. Had I been doing this too long, become too detached, that I was starting to forget people and see them as just another patient? I hoped not. I liked to treat each as an individual and get to know them a little, so I could help them feel at ease and recover as quickly as possible. Like that forty-year-old man I nursed back to health after he'd broken bones in a motorbike accident. He was in top form, and I could still remember the firmness of his muscles as I tried to find good veins on his tattooed arms. Oh, and there was that nice young swimmer in for an infection who required IV antibiotics back when I'd started nursing. He was always smiling despite the fact he must have felt like death warmed up, and he always had a compliment for me. Oh yes, *him*. Him with his soft, green eyes, his gentle smile, his...

'Sally?' Mel tapped my leg.

'Huh?'

'You've remembered someone, haven't you?'

'What? No. I've never fallen for a patient. It's unprofessional.' His strong, sculpted arms, shaven of course to allow for smoother gliding through water, and that six-pack... it was hard to stay focused on palpating his abdomen when the muscles were so hard I could barely feel any internal organs underneath.

'Sally!' Mel said. 'Earth to Sally.'

'Oh all right! I do remember feeling... a*ttracted* to a guy, slightly younger than me, as he recovered from an infection. I was young, a new nurse, I was just getting used to the whole getting close to patients thing.'

'And?'

'And?' I echoed.

'Tell us more.'

I tightened my ponytail and adjusted my position on the couch. 'He was hot, all right. That's it. It was nothing but hormones.'

'Did you get to know him?'

'Of course. He told me about his swimming training, and how he had come over to Australia from France when he was a teenager.'

'He had a French accent?'

I nodded.

'Swoon,' Mel said, holding a hand to her head.

'He taught me some French, but I've forgotten now. It was too long ago.'

'And did you ever think of asking him out, you know, when he was ready to get out of hospital?'

'No, definitely not. As I said, I was young and new. I had to remain professional and didn't want to risk my reputation or job.'

'Oh, Sally, there wouldn't have been a problem once he was discharged. You would have had his contact details on file, why not call him afterwards?'

'No, that would have been way too embarrassing! You know me; I've never been one to take any sort of initiative. Lucky Greg made the first move, otherwise I'd probably still be admiring him through the window of the cafe on my way to work!'

'You need to learn to take a few risks, girl,' said Mel.

'Why? I have Greg now, I don't need to worry about all that awkward dating stuff anymore.'

'I don't mean with that, although it could have been good for you to take some risks back then, but I mean generally, in other areas of your life. Be spontaneous, adventurous, try new things every now and again.'

'I tried that Pin the Tail game, that was new.' I crossed my arms.

'Hey, don't badger the poor woman,' said Georgie. 'She just likes to do things in her own way, isn't that right, Sal?' Georgie sat on the edge of the couch next to me and draped a friendly arm around my shoulders.

'Yes, not everyone needs to be outgoing and adventurous to live a fulfilling life.'

'Don't you ever wonder, though, what could have been? Like what if you'd asked that patient out? You may have had an amazing, unforgettable love affair.'

'But in the end it doesn't matter, because I'm obviously meant to be with Greg, so it would have led here anyway.'

'True, but it's sort of intriguing to think about things that could have been, that's all.'

'Okay,' I said. 'I think it's your time for truth.'

'Fire away,' Mel said, opening her arms to the side.

Forget about waiting till after the wedding, now was as good a time as any. 'Do you ever regret getting married to Michael?'

There, I'd said it. Asked the difficult question that was playing on my mind for some reason.

'What?' Mel flicked her hand. 'Why would I regret that?'

'Have you ever?'

She clicked her tongue as though it was a stupid question, but kept evading it.

'Mel?' Lorena probed.

She lowered her head and fiddled with the hem of her T-shirt. 'I love Michael, I do.' She took a deep breath. 'But lately, things have been... bland, is the only way I can think to describe it. I'm not talking about the bedroom so much as the overall feeling of our relationship. Maybe it's just the hard work of the kids, I don't know.' She blew air up past her top lip and her wispy dark brown fringe flapped against her forehead. 'But,' she said, then an expression I hadn't seen in a long time creased her face, not since she'd lost her pet dog of fifteen years. Her eyes became shiny and her usual nonchalant confidence disappeared. 'Someone at work, a woman, wants him for herself. She hit on him after work one day.'

'What happened, Mel?' Georgie sat on the floor next to her and touched her forearm.

'They kissed. That's all. Just a kiss. I shouldn't be that upset, I mean he was honest about it and...'

'He confessed straight away?' Lorena asked.

She nodded. 'But I should clarify, it was *her* that kissed him. He pulled back as soon as it happened and told her it wasn't on. At least, that's what he told me.'

'Bitch.' Lorena shook her head. 'Do you trust him?' she asked.

'Yes, of course, I mean, he's my husband, he's, he's... Oh God, I feel sick at the thought of someone else with their lips on my husband.' A tear dripped down her cheek and I leaned forward and wiped it away, then rested my hand on her leg. 'Every time we get close now, I keep thinking of her and him, and then I lose all interest.'

'Oh, hun, why didn't you tell us before?' Lorena patted Mel's back.

'I didn't want to bother you guys with my domestic dilemmas, you've got a baby coming,' she gestured to Lorena, 'and you're about to be married,' she touched my hand. 'I didn't want to worry you or spoil your special time.'

'Mel, we've been friends forever, you can tell us anything, at any time. Promise me,' she glanced around, 'all of you, promise me we won't keep secrets from each other if something's bothering us. We need to be there for each other, help each other make sense of things when problems arise. Deal?'

'Deal,' we all said, though I whispered my response. I was all for it, but there was one thing I wasn't prepared to share. I glanced at Red who sat on the dining table, looking strangely distant.

'Give it time, Mel, I'm sure things will get back to normal,' Georgie said. 'If he was honest and told you what happened right away, then that is what a good man does. He's a good man. He just got caught out in a situation he probably didn't see coming. If you believe his side of the story, that he backed away and then told you, then he did the right thing. Don't let some other woman ruin things for you.'

'You're right.' Mel straightened. 'This is exactly what she'd want. But she's not going to get it. As soon as I get home I'm going to sit down and talk it all out with Michael. We need to work out a solution, a way that they don't have to interact at work. He's in a higher position than she is, I'm sure he can arrange something.'

'That sounds like a plan.' Georgie reached over to the coffee table and plucked a piece of bread and handed it to Mel. 'And don't let her spoil your weekend either. Eat up and enjoy yourself while you're kid-free.'

Mel smiled and accepted the food offering. 'You guys are the best, you know that?'

'Yeah, we know,' Lorena said, then pulled Mel to standing and hugged her.

'Anyway, enough of this truth stuff, it's time for Sally's dare!' Mel's expression brightened, while mine probably darkened in fear. I gulped.

'We can finish up now if you want. After all this deep and meaningful stuff, why don't we go for a nice walk?' I suggested.

'Not so fast, girly.' Mel grasped my arm. 'I called that company about their products, and you can do something challenging too.'

My chest tightened and my heartbeat intensified. There's no way I could have done what she did, so hopefully they wouldn't make me do anything similar.

Mel glanced around the room and her gaze rested on the bookcase with the games. She walked over to it and pulled out a game. Twister.

'I want you to call Ty and ask him to come over for a game of Twister.'

'Twister? But that's a game for flexible young kids who don't mind clambering over each other.'

'Ty is flexible.'

'I'm not! And I'm engaged, it wouldn't be right to get that close to another guy. You'll have to give me another dare.'

'Okay, I dare you to walk down the main street and sing "Tomorrow" from *Annie* at the top of your lungs, and hug random people as you go by.'

I had visions of being captured on video and going viral on YouTube. 'No, no way.' I shook my head vigorously.

'Then call Ty.' Mel handed me back my phone. 'Twister or "Tomorrow". What'll it be?'

I ran a hand over my head. No way could I sing in public, especially after my dance incident. Singing was a completely different thing, and my voice could barely crank out a simple 'Twinkle Twinkle Little Star' in tune.

'So I just have to call him and ask, it doesn't matter if he says no, right?'

'If he says yes, you have to play Twister with him, but if he says no, well, I guess there's nothing you can do about that. But you have to at least ask him.' She shoved the phone into my hand and it shook in my grasp. It was only a simple phone call, but something about being around him made me nervous. Maybe it was his superhuman physique, or the fact that he seemed like some super-caring, kind, too-good-to-be-true angel from heaven sent down to earth to make women swoon and look after those who needed a little extra support. He came from a completely different world to mine, and it felt like I was about to call my teenage celebrity crush.

'Here's his number,' Lorena said, showing me her phone.

I added him as a contact and my finger hovered over his number.

'Press it, Sally! I want to see this!' Red was back to her usual self at the prospect of another embarrassing moment for me.

I pressed it.

'Hello? Ty speaking,' he answered.

'Hi, Ty, I...' *Oh God, I'm rhyming!* 'It's me, Sally.'

'Sexy Sally?'

Heat rushed up my face. 'Well, the one from the guest house.'

'Yeah, as I said: Sexy Sally. What can I do for you? Would you like to book another performance?'

'Oh goodness, no, not at all.'

'Gee, thanks. Glad you're so keen.'

'Sorry, I didn't mean... I just meant, anyway, I'm calling to ask something.'

He was silent for a moment, then: 'You'll have to speak up, sunshine.'

I cleared my throat but my voice remained croaky. 'I was wondering if you'd care for a game of...' I cleared my throat again at the same time as uttering the word, 'Twister'.

'Sorry? A game of what?'

'Twister,' I said more loudly, the painful embarrassment like a red-hot burn on my cheeks.

Mel tipped her head back with a sudden laugh.

Ty's voice held a hint of a smile. 'You want me to come over to play Twister?'

'I guess so.'

He chuckled. 'You girls are an entertaining bunch.'

'It's okay, you don't have to, I know you've had a busy day and you probably have other things to do with your brother, or a job to go to, or—'

'Be there in ten.'

'Huh?'

'The guest house. Ten minutes. I'll warm up on the way there.' And then he hung up.

I kept the phone next to my ear and furrowed my brow, my mouth agape.

'Sal?' asked Mel.

'He hung up.'

'He hung up on you?' Georgie asked.

'No, he hung up after saying he'd be here in ten minutes.'

'Woohoo!' Mel exclaimed. 'I only wanted you to ask him, I didn't think he'd actually agree to it! Ooh, this is going to be fun to watch!'

'Watch? But you have to play too, I can't play it on my own, with him.'

'Nope, the dare was for you to ask him over to play.'

'And I'm definitely out of this game,' Lorena said, holding her belly and convenient excuse. I was sure, though, had she not been pregnant, she wouldn't have minded playing Twister with a stripper.

'And as much as I'd love to get up close and personal with His Royal Hotness, I'd much rather see you in action on those coloured spots.' Mel grinned, and I looked towards Georgie for moral support.

She held her palms up. 'Sorry, I'm needed in the kitchen.'

'But we're eating out tonight.'

'Yes, but someone has to marinate the lamb for tomorrow night's dinner.'

'But—'

'Too late for an appeal, Sal, you better get ready. Warm up and stretch or something. I'll set up the mat. Tick-tock!' She tapped her watch.

Oh my goodness gracious me. I felt like I was about to betray Greg. What had I got myself into?

As Mel prepared the game, I swung my arms around in circles. Probably best if I did warm up a little, it would make it easier to manoeuvre around the mat and avoid bodily contact. Why did he agree to play Twister anyway? He knows I'm taken, so it's not like he's seeing it as an opportunity to hit on me or anything. Probably just wants to show off his... bendiness.

Red jumped on the mat and bent her body in awkward angles, placing her hands and feet on different coloured spots. 'Wow, I'm so much more flexible than I was when I was alive. This is cool!' She moved around the mat and collapsed into a tangled lump. 'Your turn, your turn! Hurry up, Ty.' She checked the clock on the wall.

Ding-dong!

I tucked my T-shirt into my jeans and tightened my ponytail. Thank goodness I was wearing a bodysuit underneath so nothing would hang out. Not that I had much in the dangly department. And then I felt slightly exposed anyway, remembering that Ty knew exactly what I had on underneath my clothes after the gemstone predicament.

He walked into the house and eyed me and the mat with enthusiastic anticipation. 'Well, what are we waiting for? Let the twisting begin!'

'Bride-to-be first.' Mel ushered me to the mat and spun the wheel. 'Okey dokes, put your left foot on a red spot.'

Easy enough. I kicked off my shoes and did as I was told, choosing a red spot in the corner.

Mel spun the wheel again. 'Ty, right foot on a yellow spot.'

Ty's shoes were off too, and he placed his uninjured foot on a spot in the middle. Why didn't he pick the one furthest away? Less chance for us to get tangled.

'Sally, left arm on a yellow spot.'

Rightio, I'll just lean over here... I bent sideways and put my hand on the yellow spot at the end of the mat, aligned with the row my foot was on.

Ty's next move had him put his bruised foot on a red spot like me, but he chose the one right next to mine, so now our toes were touching. I inched mine back a little. My arm ached a bit and I urged Mel to hurry up.

'Right foot, red spot.'

'Red is the best!' the eponymous ghost exclaimed, as she watched on the sidelines.

I moved my foot over to the spot behind Ty's foot, grateful to take some of the weight from my arm.

'Ty, left hand, red spot.'

'What is it with the colour *red*?' asked Lorena. 'Are you rigging this game, Mel?'

I wouldn't be surprised if someone else was rigging it. I tried to sneak a glance at Red, peering between Ty's legs.

Ty eyed the available red spots behind him, and in expert dancer/stripper style he bent backwards and placed his hand on one of the spots, next to my right foot. He was now balancing on one hand, his knees bent and body tilted backwards. I made sure not to look up at the rather intimate view I would have right now.

My right hand gratefully accepted a blue spot near my other hand, my weight now more evenly distributed, until a couple of turns later when I had to move both my hands further along the mat, and the only way to get there was to go underneath Ty, through the gap his legs had created. He dropped his weight a little on my back, his butt threatening to make me lose my balance, but I nudged him back upwards. 'Hey, no cheating,' I said.

A phone camera clicked. 'Who's taking photos?' I asked, unable to turn my head in the direction of the sound.

'Photos? What photos?' Lorena said. 'Do you see anyone taking photos, Georgie?'

'No, no photos being taken here.' Another click sounded.

'You better not put these on Facebook,' I said.

A few turns later, Ty and I were almost in the opposite positions we'd been before, with me straddled over him, his hands behind him, and pelvis in the air.

'Sal, put your right hand on a blue spot.'

'Blue? Oh, I don't think I can do that.' I eyed the spot that was on the other side of Ty and would require me to stretch like an elastic band over him.

'C'mon, you can do it.'

'I don't think my arm is flexible enough.'

Ty chuckled. 'Actually, I think your right arm is *quite* flexible. I have a feeling it could contort into a variety of positions and reach deep into remote locations, if the situation required.'

I was able to catch his eye briefly, and I frowned at him. He obviously enjoyed poking fun at me. It wasn't my fault I got a gemstone stuck down my top and had needed to initiate a retrieval mission.

'See? Ty has confidence in you,' Mel said.

'Yeah, and I'll even make it easier for you by lowering myself down a bit. My triceps are going to burn like hell, but I'll survive.'

'It's just, it could be a little... awkward,' I added, noting that to achieve the required position I would virtually be lying on top of him, face-to-face.

'Honey, awkward would be me doing that with my belly in the way,' said Lorena.

Forgive me, Greg, I said to myself, then extended my right arm over Ty's chest and down to the blue spot, where my hand only just connected with the plastic, and my ponytail landed in Ty's face.

'Pff!' he puffed, trying to blow it out of the way. 'Hey, do you mind tilting your head a bit so I'm not getting a mouthful of hair?' With a quick flick of my head I flung my ponytail off his face, my face now directly in front of his, our chests touching. 'I'm guessing that bodysuit of yours is coming in handy right about now,' he whispered.

'What's that supposed to mean?'

'You know, keeping everything... enclosed.'

I diverted my gaze from his but his breath tickled my cheek, and his scent wafted in the air around me. He smelt different to Greg; spicier, dangerous even.

Ty moved his left foot further forwards, which made me wobble, and when Mel instructed me to put my left hand on the blue spot below Ty's back, Red stuck her face next to both of ours and yelled, 'Boo!'

I shrieked and lost my balance, my hand slipping from its spot and my legs collapsing. Whack! I landed on Ty's chest as he lost his grip too, and my ponytail returned to its original residence in his mouth.

'Pff!' he puffed, but I quickly lifted my head and scrambled to my feet.

My friends clapped and cheered, and Red laughed again.

Ty held out his hand and I shook it. 'Well played,' he said.

'So who won?' I asked. 'Does anyone even win this game or is the sole purpose to collapse in a heap?'

'I think it's a tie,' said Ty with a wink, and after a few moments his pun sunk in and I 'ahhed' in acknowledgement.

I readjusted my clothing and hair and escaped to the kitchen for a glass of water. Sweat had collected on my forehead and my lower back, and my muscles felt strained.

'So what prompted this game of Twister?' Ty asked.

'Sally said she hadn't played it in years and wanted to give it a go. None of us were keen so she said she'd ask you instead, ain't that right, Sal?'

I shot Mel a 'look'. 'She's joking, of course. It was a dare, Ty. They dared me to do it.'

Ty tipped his head back. 'Ahh, I see. And you went through with it, kudos to you. I'm honoured to be the subject of your dare.' He grinned. 'And I haven't played it in years either. Was fun! If you've got an able body, use it, I say. Too many people don't.'

'Ah yeah, I'm guilty of that sometimes,' said Mel. 'But I figure chasing five kids around is enough bending and stretching for me.'

'Coffee, anyone?' Georgie asked, joining me in the kitchen and flipping the switch on the kettle. She was met with four yeses. A half hour later Ty rinsed his mug out and put it in the dishwasher. Still sucking up.

'I better get going. This is the most time I've spent at a hen's party, I'm usually in and out in an hour.'

'You're definitely doing some overtime with us,' said Lorena.

'It's my pleasure,' he replied.

'Big night ahead?' Lorena walked him to the door and we followed.

'Got an early evening booking to get to, then it's back home to cook dinner with Cody, show him how to make spaghetti bolognaise correctly. He likes to mix up different ingredients, and last time he used strawberry jam in place of the tomato bolognaise sauce.'

'Ew, that would have tasted... interesting,' Georgie said. 'Can't say I've tried that combo before.'

'I don't recommend it. He ate it, laughing the whole time, but I ended up with eggs on toast that night.' He smiled.

'So Cody lives with you?' I asked.

He nodded. 'It's just the two of us.'

'Well, I hope the meal turns out right, and um, all the best with your, er...'

'Strip? Thanks.'

And he was gone again. And we stood at the door watching him leave again. This was becoming a habit.

CHAPTER 11

After a few too many yawns in quick succession I retreated to my room for a brief nap. The comforting weight of the lavender eye pillow relaxed me, and the scent reminded me of my mother's hand cream. And that reminded me that I needed to remember to call her on Monday night to discuss the wedding day logistics and timetable. We'd be getting ready at her place so she could share in my special day, as our house wasn't the most wheelchair friendly, though we planned to work on making it so after the wedding. Once Greg's bonus came in we'd be able to pay for it.

I breathed slowly and took solace in the peace and quiet for a change, my body relishing the rest after a busy couple of days and not much sleep thanks to an unwelcome guest. I drifted in and out of sleep, thinking about my future life with Greg. Greg and Sally — together forever. This was it, no turning back, I'd found The One and my new life would begin in a week's time.

'Are you sure you're ready for a lifetime commitment to him?' I thought I'd dreamt the question, but I lifted the eye pillow a tad to see it was Red speaking, softly, seriously, as she sat on the edge of the bed.

'Red, I'm trying to rest.'

'I've given you half an hour; I was a good girl, or ghost. Despite wanting to chat I kept my mouth shut, but now, why don't we talk? Tell me, are you really ready for marriage?'

I shifted my upper body higher on the pillow so I was semi-reclined and placed the eye pillow next to me. 'Of course I am, that's why I'm getting married.' I waved my left hand with my simple and stylish engagement ring in front of her.

'But have you really thought about it? I mean, one guy for the rest of your life. No more new-relationship bliss, no more excitement of that first kiss, no more... you know what... with anyone else?'

'I'm thirty. I've been there and done that. Greg still makes me feel excited and desired and happy, and I'm looking forward to being his wife, thank you very much.' I crossed my arms over my chest.

'But what if a couple of years down the track you meet someone else and think — crap, did I make the wrong decision? Wouldn't you rather stay single a bit longer, just to be extra sure?'

'I'm already extra sure. And why are you asking me all this?'

'I'm being a friend, making sure you know what you're getting into.'

'This isn't a crime syndicate, it's a marriage. I know exactly what I'm getting into.'

Red stood, paced around the room, then stopped in front of the bed. 'Isn't Ty a dream? So gorgeous and nice and charming, don't you think?'

'He's reasonable.'

'I can think of lots of words to describe him but reasonable ain't one of them. Not that he isn't, but it's not exactly the most flattering term to use. Ty is exciting, and generous, and caring, and kind, and talented, and savvy, and dedicated, and determined, and… hot as hell, of course.' She touched her finger to her arm and made a sizzling sound. 'Don't you feel even a hint of attraction towards him?'

'I'm engaged to someone else, there's no need for me to be attracted to him.'

'You're avoiding the question. Are you attracted to him?'

'Red, what does it matter?'

'You are, aren't you.'

'I'm *impressed* by him, he does such good work with those people, and he's aspiring to new heights as a doctor. It's commendable.'

'I didn't ask your opinion on his occupational choices, I'm asking about that inner, natural attraction that comes up of its own accord. Those feelings you can't help but feel. I think he has them for you, but of course, he wouldn't act on them. He's a good man.'

'As if he likes me in that way. He's just a flirt, it's his job to be a flirt. And anyway, regardless of how incredibly beautiful he is and those "feelings", as you call them, they're just silly hormones, they're nothing compared to the love I have for Greg.'

'So it hasn't crossed your mind that maybe, just maybe, you could have jumped the gun a little with Greg and wished you had more time to "shop the market"?'

'No! I don't.' I pulled a cushion onto my lap and squeezed it. 'Are you here as some sort of temptation challenge, to get me to question my commitment to Greg before the big day?'

'I'm here to make sure you make the right decision.'

'I already *have* made the right decision.' I stood and approached her, careful not to raise my voice so loud that my friends would hear. 'And if you ask me, I think you're here for a very different reason.'

'Oh yeah, what's that?'

'I think you're jealous and you're here to try and break me and Greg up.' I jabbed my finger towards her in an accusatory manner. 'I'm sorry that you're...' I waved my hands about, trying to think of an appropriate way to say 'dead', '... in this predicament, and I'm sorry that things didn't work out between you and Greg when you were alive, but that doesn't give you the right to come waltzing into my life in a pathetic attempt to steal my fiancé from me!'

Red planted her hands on her hips. 'I am not trying to steal him from you! How could I even do that, huh? In case you haven't noticed, I'm dead!' She tugged at her pyjamas.

'Then you're trying to stop me from having him. It's like if you can't have him no one can!'

'Sally, Sally.' She shook her head. 'I'm not jealous. I'm just trying to get you to see things from a different perspective, to see whether you really have made the right decision or not.'

'You don't even know me, how can you even begin to know what's right for me?'

'I know what's *wrong* for you,' she said. 'Or more accurately, *who's* wrong for you,' she mumbled, turning away.

'What did you say?'

She turned around, chewing her bottom lip. 'I didn't want to tell you yet, wanted you to enjoy as much of your weekend as possible before you found out the truth.'

I furrowed my brow, waiting for her to continue.

She whooshed out a deep breath. 'Greg's not the man you think he is. I'm sorry, Sally, but he's having an affair.' Red lowered her head.

Oh the nerve of the woman! How dare she make up lies to try and stop me from marrying him so she can get her way!

'Oh, sure he is! Yes, of course, why didn't I see it?' I smacked my forehead. 'Do you really think I'm going to believe this? You've been nothing but trouble since you got here, and now you've gone too far. Greg's mine, Red, *mine*! You need to find that white light or whatever it is and let me get on with my life.' I turned to the wardrobe and withdrew my outfit for this evening's dinner out. I laid the black pants and mauve shirt on the bed, and took out a pair of ballet flats.

'I'm not lying. Things are different here, in this... realm. I can sense things, feel things. Please believe me. I'm only doing this to help you, to stop you making the worst decision of your life.'

'The worst decision of my life was letting you get away with what you've done this weekend, and letting you get on my nerves. And besides, Greg wouldn't cheat, he wouldn't do something like that.'

'Yes he would.'

'Oh really, and how do you know?'

Red sat, resigned, on the edge of the bed and stared at the wall. 'Because he did it to me too.'

It couldn't be true, it couldn't be. As we walked to the Barron Springs Pub that evening, my mind went through everything Red had said; how Greg had gone behind her back to date, guess who? Me. According to her, he left her for me. I was the other woman, the mistress. The one everyone's supposed to hate. But now I was the fiancé, the wife-to-be. Greg chose me.

'You're quiet, Sal, everything all right?' asked Georgie.

'Yes, all fine. Just enjoying the crisp, country air.' I forced a smile. 'And saving my voice for the rowdy pub.' I managed a chuckle.

'Oh yes, good idea.' Lorena draped her arm around my shoulders, whether it was a subconscious act of support or the fact that she was tired and needed support herself I wasn't sure.

If Red was telling the truth, which she wasn't, but if she

believed it to be the truth, then no wonder she wanted to drive me mad this weekend. To get back at me for (unknowingly) stealing her boyfriend, on the pretence of 'just wanting to have fun'. But she seemed genuinely sorry for telling me. Genuinely hurt and worried about me. *Oh, what am I thinking?* She's probably a pro at emotional manipulation, that might be why Greg left her and didn't want to discuss his past relationship with whoever she was, because it was too distressing.

Anyway, I'd told her that if she truly cared about me in any way she'd leave me alone and let me enjoy a nice dinner with my bridesmaids. She'd already gotten in the way enough this weekend, and I wouldn't let her, or the lies she told me, get in the way of this evening.

True to her promise, she was nowhere to be seen at the pub, and I managed to remove the silly thought of Greg being unfaithful from my mind and enjoy a great meal and conversation amid the homely, friendly atmosphere of the establishment. Georgie tried not to critique the simple, hearty meals, reminding herself she had the night off from cooking, and we were even treated to a karaoke performance by a local man who wasn't half bad. Though his friend was terrible. And thank goodness I'd used up my dares because there was no way I was getting up there to sing in front of everyone. No, tonight was simply relaxed and enjoyable. It was nice to be around normal, living people, and not have to deal with the demands of Red interfering every chance she got.

After our main meals were devoured and we sat waiting to decide if we could fit in dessert, I excused myself and went to the ladies' room. When I turned the lock to exit the cubicle a couple of minutes later, the door wouldn't open.

Huh?

I locked and unlocked it again, but it was stuck. *Damn old pub, probably haven't replaced the bathroom fittings for decades.*

'Now that you're alone, I need to speak to you,' a voice whispered, and I glanced up. Red was perched on the dividing wall between my cubicle and the next one.

'Oh great, I should have known it was you. Let me out, Red!'

'Not yet! There's been a development. He's with her now. I thought you should know.'

'What?'

'Greg, he's with the woman right now. I saw it in my mind.'

'Oh, well, then forgive me. If you saw it "in your mind",' I made quotation marks with my fingers, 'it must be true.' I continued to jiggle the door lock.

'Call him if you don't believe me. Call him and ask him who's with him, see if he gets nervous.'

'He's on his buck's weekend at a golf resort, I'm on my hen's weekend, and we agreed to not talk until we see each other on Monday afternoon. I'm not going to disturb him and his friends.'

'Look, Sally, I'm not lying, really I'm not. If you could only see what I see.' She stared hard at my face with the same look she gave me back at the festival, when I was having the palm reading.

'What are you doing?'

'I'm trying to imprint my vision into your mind. Something tells me it's possible, but I've been trying all day and it's not working.'

'Probably because it's not possible, and because your vision ISN'T REAL!'

'You should keep your voice down, you know, people might think you're talking to yourself.'

'I doubt they can hear me, the music's too loud out there.' I kicked at the door and pushed hard on the lock, but still no release.

'Promise me you'll think about what I've told you. That you'll look into this and try to find proof.'

'Oh yes, I'll just ask him: Greg, honey, are you having an affair? That would go down real well.'

'Look, just call him, see if you get any sort of hesitation on his part, some sort of hint that I might be telling the truth.'

'Fine, I'll call him, okay? It will be good to hear his voice. Now let me out of here.' As I jiggled the lock, it gave way. The lock and handle but, sadly, not the door. 'Oh no! Look what you've done now!' I held the broken door handle up to her. 'Now I'm really stuck! Fix it, Red, fix it!'

'Oops,' she said, covering a laugh with her hand.

'Oops? Is that all you can say? C'mon, use your... powers... or whatever they are, and open the door!'

She stared at the door with a strained face. 'I'm sorry, I can't. It's well and truly broken.' She held up her hands in defeat.

'Argh!' I ran my hands over my head and kicked at the door again, then knocked on it with my fist. 'Help! I'm stuck in the toilet!' If only I'd brought my handbag and phone in I could have called for help, but it was sitting safely under the table near Lorena's foot.

'They can't hear you, remember? Music's too loud.'

I glared at her.

'Now if you'd listened to me back at the house you wouldn't be in this situation, would you?'

'No, if you hadn't locked me in here in the first place I wouldn't be in this situation!' I scanned my cramped surroundings, and homed in on the spot where Red sat. 'Move off, I'm going to climb up there and down into the next cubicle.' I shooed her away with my hand and she jumped to the next dividing wall. I placed my hands on the toilet cistern for balance and propped my foot on the toilet seat. Like all great pubs, there was no lid on the toilet. I lifted my other foot up as well, grateful I had not agreed to Lorena's offer to wear Georgie's high-heeled shoes. Flats were comfortable and practical, and had much better grip. I swivelled my upper body to face the side wall and moved my right foot to the other side of the toilet seat, and gripped the top of the wall with my fingers. If I put one foot on the cistern for leverage I should be able to boost myself up enough to bend over the wall, then turn sideways and climb over to the neighbouring toilet seat.

I eyed my target and lifted my right foot to the cistern, then prepared to push against it. As I tightened my leg muscles in readiness and pushed, my left foot, which I had unfortunately not been paying much attention to, slipped off the toilet seat and into the abyss of the toilet bowl. I gasped at the cold water encasing my foot and soaking into my shoe, and winced at the bump my knee had sustained as it landed against the inner rim of the toilet seat.

'Oh golly gosh!' I exclaimed, trying to lift my foot from the bowl. It only sloshed about and dipped further into the hole. 'Oh my goodness, I'm stuck! And, oh no! The germs, the germs!' My foot would need autoclaving at the hospital after this.

Red peered over the cubicle and shrieked in hysterics. 'Is there no limit to your amusement potential? You crack me up, girl!'

'Is there no limit to your insensitivity? Help me!'

'I would, but, it's a bit difficult in my position. Though, if I concentrate real hard, I might *just* be able to make that little button go down and—'

'No! You will not dare flush this toilet!'

'Couldn't I try a little flush?'

'No!'

'Oh, c'mon,' she said, then started singing, 'It's just... a little flush...' in the tune of Jennifer Paige's pop song, *Crush*.

'Argh!' I took my attention away from my wet, trapped foot and focused on my dry, free foot and pushed against the toilet seat, lifting my heavy, soggy foot from the unhygienic depths of this nightmare. 'Urgh! Yuck!' I stood on the toilet seat gripping the wall, only now my foot was too slippery to even consider climbing up and over the wall. I hopped down and yanked off a long length of toilet paper and frantically dabbed at my foot, noticing then that my shoe was still stuck in the loo. 'Why, oh why?' It half poked out the top of the hole like a tiny beached whale, and it looked so pathetic and lonely. Kind of like me.

'Where is my hand sanitiser when I need it?' I dabbed at my foot some more, then banged on the door. 'Help!' I glanced down at the gap between the floor and the door. *Hmm, maybe it's not that small a gap.* I measured it with my hands, then, keeping my hands at the same width apart, held them against my torso to see if I could fit through. It was possible. I was only petite, and thank goodness I wasn't in Lorena's condition.

Note to self: never go into an enclosed space without my phone. Or hand sanitiser.

'Are you really going to crawl under there?' Red asked.

'You got a better idea?'

'Nope.'

'Exactly.' I shook my head at her apparent lack of concern, and knelt on the floor. I placed each foot on either side of the toilet bowl so I could flatten my body as much as possible, and poked my head underneath the door. I wish I hadn't eaten that risotto now; as tasty as it was, it was probably absorbing fluid by the minute and swelling up to ten times its size.

As though I was doing yoga, I concentrated on lengthening my spine so I could *slither* out, but with the lack of space for leverage it was proving difficult. I wriggled under the door, inching my shoulders through. If I could get my upper body out, the rest would be easy. But then I remembered my left shoe was still stuck in the toilet and I wouldn't be able to get back in without breaking the door down. Oh no, why didn't I just pluck it out and toss it under the door? Too late now. The priority was getting myself out.

Slowly, I edged my shoulders through, squashing my boobs as much as possible, not that there was much to squash, and tried not to think of all the bacteria that was multiplying on my hands pressed to the bathroom floor, not to mention my foot, which felt incredibly icky.

Okay, now, I'll just try to push off the bowl with my feet, then I should be out. But my feet wouldn't take, they just slipped around like a bar of soap. So I used all the arm and upper body strength I could muster and grunted, but my body would not budge. I couldn't go any further! *Oh no, oh no...* Panic spiralled within. Maybe I should reverse my movements, get back in and rethink my approach. I pushed in the other direction, but I couldn't move that way either. 'Red! Do something, anything! I'm trapped!'

'Oh, Jesus, hang on, umm... let me think...'

'Speaking of Jesus, have you met him on the other side? Maybe you can ask for a miracle or something. Please?' It was hard to speak through my compressed chest, and my ribs hurt against the cold hard floor.

'I don't seem to have progressed that far yet, I'm afraid, Sal. Could you maybe blow out a long breath to empty your lungs and then quickly push yourself out?'

Actually, that was the most useful thing she'd said all day. I breathed in, which was painful, then exhaled as much as I could and inched forwards. But as soon as I moved a little my need for oxygen took over and I had to breathe in again. 'Damn it!'

My eyes darted to the side as the door to the bathroom squeaked open. *Oh thank goodness! I'm going to be rescued!*

'Sally, oh my God! What happened?' Lorena crouched next to me as best as she could.

'I got locked in, the door handle broke, and as you can see I thought it would be smart to crawl underneath but now I'm stuck!'

'Oh, sweetie, you poor thing!' She patted my head. 'Hang on, I'll go get help.'

Maybe Georgie could get me out of this mess. I could grab hold of the backs of her ankles and she could walk forwards, like a human tow truck. I knew she was strong enough.

Seconds later I recognised her smart, black heels as she walked through the door, followed by Mel's strappy pair (and her riotous laughter).

'Sally, you are such a sight! Hang on...' I heard a click sound.

'Did you just take a photo? Mel, how could you!'

'Sorry, but you'll laugh when you look back on it. Don't worry, we'll get you out, the four of us can manage it, I'm sure.'

'The four of us? As you can see, I'm not exactly much help to myself right now.'

'We brought an extra set of hands,' Mel said.

And feet, obviously, as a pair of strong men's feet shod in black boots walked into the ladies' bathroom. 'I think playing Twister gave you false confidence in your level of flexibility.' The deep voice was unmistakeable. So was the chuckle that followed.

Ty.

I tilted my head a little and glanced in his direction. Could this day get any more embarrassing? 'Can you all quit making fun of me and get me out of here, please?'

'Hey, hey, why the angry tone of voice?' Ty asked. 'It's not the end of the world. Try to think positive. Every difficult situation has a silver lining.'

Silver lining? What silver lining? I'm stuck between a toilet door and a dirty floor with a soggy foot whose shoe has gone for a late night skinny dip in an unhygienic body of water.

'I have one!' said Lorena. 'At least you're not pregnant.'

'Yeah, already thought of that. Try again.'

'Ooh, I know,' Mel said. 'At least you're not a D cup like me. These whoppers wouldn't have a chance in hell of getting through that gap.'

'Gee, thanks for pointing that out, Mel.' Nice to know everyone had my small bra size on their mind right now.

Ty spoke next. 'Okay, what I'll do is I'll climb into the cubicle from the other one, and Georgie, you pull Sally under her shoulders while I push her from behind.' To an eavesdropper, this could potentially sound a little odd.

'But what if you get stuck inside too, Ty?' I asked. The last thing I wanted was to be stuck in here with Ty, and my backside poking underneath the door and on display.

'Then we'll have a lot of time to get to know each other better,' he replied, moving away and stepping onto the neighbouring toilet bowl (which probably had a lid). He grunted, and before I knew it his feet were either side of my thighs, standing above me.

'Will you be wanting this shoe?' he asked.

'Well, I do need to walk back to the house, but after that it's going in the bin.'

A slosh of toilet water made me gag. 'Incoming,' he called, and my gaze darted to the left as my shoe landed on the floor outside the cubicle. He rescued my shoe for me? His hand would need sanitising too.

'Don't worry, Sal. I'll give this a wash and dry it under the hand dryer,' said Mel. 'I've had to clean worse things before.' Her voice was followed by the sound of running water.

'Thanks, Mel.'

'Right, ready, Georgie?' asked Ty. 'On the count of three,

pull. And, Sally? Breathe out as much as possible to flatten your chest.'

'Yep, that's what...' I trailed off when I realised I was about to tell them that's what Red had suggested. '... that's what I thought might help.'

I took a breath in and held it.

'One, two, three!'

I breathed out and as Georgie's hands gripped my armpits and pulled, Ty's hands held firmly onto the sides of my hips and pushed me forwards. And as though I was being born again through the birth canal, my torso was free and the rest of me slipped out easily. Lorena clapped as I scrambled to my feet, shaking my hands violently and making a mad dash for the sink to wash my hands and feet. When my hands were reasonably clean, albeit without the protection of sanitiser, I stretched my foot up and over the sink and under the running water. I lathered soap all over it, while Mel dried my shoe under the hand dryer.

'Yuck, yuck, yuck!' I said, washing as fast as I could.

Lorena disappeared for a moment then returned with my handbag, holding up my hand sanitiser. 'You were right, I guess this did come in handy.' I dried my foot and she squirted some onto my hand so I could rub it into my foot.

'Thanks, Lorena, and thanks guys.' I glanced around. 'I thought I'd never get out.'

In my haste to cleanse myself I hadn't noticed that Ty had climbed back over to the other cubicle and back into the bathroom, and was now washing his hands.

'How did the door handle break, anyway?' he asked.

I glanced at Red, who looked guilty, and said, 'It was just a bit wonky, and when I tried to unlock it, it came right off.'

'I'll have a word to Sam — he owns the pub — tell him it's probably time for a few upgrades in here.'

'Yes, that would be much appreciated, not that I think I'll risk using this bathroom anytime again in the near future.'

With my shoe now back on my foot and my shoulder supporting my handbag (which would need a thorough clean due to cross contamination), we walked out of the bathroom. Finally.

'Where did you suddenly appear from anyway?' I asked Ty. He had a habit of doing that. But it *was* a small town.

'Just popped in for a drink after dinner. Cody's fast asleep back home. Got up too early this morning with all the excitement about performing at the festival.'

'Yeah, Ty's going to join us for a bit, aren't you, Ty?' Mel said.

'I won't say no.'

'You guys go back to the table, I'll just make a quick phone call.'

I missed Greg. I needed to hear his voice, to settle my nerves and remind myself that he was my loving, caring, and faithful fiancé.

'Hello?' he answered on the third ring. A faint sound of someone coughing could be heard in the background.

'Hi, Greg.'

'Sal? How are you? Is everything all right?' The background cough returned, a feminine-sounding cough.

'Yes, everything's fine, I just missed you. How's your buck's weekend?'

'Oh, it's fine too. Great. How's yours?' After he spoke I heard a woman's voice ask for a drink. He must be in a bar with his mates, like me. Except there wasn't the usual background noise.

'Um, pretty good. Lots of fun, you know Lorena, she sure knows how to plan a party.' I chuckled. 'Where are you?'

'I'm out to dinner with the guys,' he said softly.

'I guess they're all filling their mouths with food.'

'Huh?'

'It's quiet. Your mates are usually pretty rowdy.'

'Oh, oh yes. A couple have gone over to the bar, the rest are eating.' More feminine throat clearing, then the sound of someone saying, 'Your water, madam.'

Greg's voice was different. Distant. Reserved. Maybe it was just what Red had said clouding my judgement. Making me anticipate a problem when there wasn't one.

'Anyway, I must get going, but thanks for calling, I'll see you on Monday,' he said. And without his usual 'honey' or 'sweetheart' addition. It was as though I was a business associate and he was confirming a meeting.

'Okay then, say hi to the guys for me.'

'I will.'

'And, Greg?'

'Yes?'

'I love you.'

There was a pause, then: 'Same to you.'

I hung up, and was left with an awful, hollow feeling that something was not right. He always said 'I love you too' whenever I said it first. He never said 'same to you', that was what you said to someone who wished you a good day. Was it just that he was in front of his mates and didn't want to be seen getting all mushy and romantic?

I stood still on the spot for a while, trying to make sense of our stilted conversation and Red's outrageous accusations that, despite my not believing her, had cast a slight shadow of concern in my mind.

'I'll be at the guest house when you're ready to talk,' Red said, and before I had a chance to meet her eyes she'd disappeared.

I put the phone back in my bag and returned to the table, suddenly not feeling like any dessert or conversation.

'I'm having sticky date pudding, what are you having, Sal?' Mel asked.

'Actually, I think I might head back to the house, if you don't mind?'

'Are you okay?' Lorena asked.

'Yeah yeah, I'm fine. Just a bit tired, and the whole getting stuck thing was a bit of an ordeal. But you guys stay here and have dessert, don't let me cut the night short.'

'But you can't walk back by yourself,' said Georgie. 'Do you want me to walk with you?'

'No, I'll be right, it's not far, and I have my panic alert thingy on my key ring.'

Ty stood from his chair at the end of our table. 'I'll walk you back,' he said.

'Oh, I don't want to disrupt your Saturday night.'

'No disruption. I should probably get back home anyway, now that I've had my drink and done my civic duty of rescuing maidens in distress from faulty toilet cubicles.' He winked.

'Good idea, go with Ty, Sal.' Georgie said. 'And text me when you're back inside.'

'Yeah,' agreed Mel. 'We'll see you when we've finished stuffing our faces.'

I smiled and walked out of the pub, and at the bottom of the steps Ty held out his hand for me to grasp it. 'Your chariot awaits.'

I eyed his hand and remembered the shoe-rescuing mission. 'Here,' I said, pulling the hand sanitiser out of my bag and handing it to him.

'Flexible, amusing, *and* hygienic,' he stated. 'You're just full of surprises.' He rubbed the liquid over his hands, returned the bottle to me, then held out his hand again to encourage me off the steps.

This time I took it.

CHAPTER 12

The cool night air engulfed us as we walked up the road towards the guest house. I pulled my jacket a little tighter around my collar.

'You seem a little unhappy for someone who's getting married in a week,' he said.

'It's just been an eventful day,' I replied. 'I'm fine.'

Well, I wasn't, really. My safe, secure, predictable life seemed to be slowly unravelling, and I didn't know what was real now and what wasn't. I hadn't believed in ghosts until now, and it hadn't even crossed my mind that Greg could cheat, and I still didn't know if I believed it. I looked at Ty with curiosity. 'You're a man,' I said, watching the way he walked with confidence and calmness.

'Intelligent observation.'

'I mean, you're a man, so you might be able to help me with something.'

He raised his eyebrows.

'Is it just in a man's nature to want to stray, to not tie themselves down with one woman?'

'You're asking me if all men are cheats?'

'I guess so. I mean, not that they all would, but is it really possible for a man to be happy with one woman, forever?'

'I can only speak for myself, but yes, it is possible. Sure, men are naturally wired to seek out a mate, *multiple* mates, but that doesn't mean they have to act on their impulses.'

'So it comes down to a choice. It's not just an uncontrollable urge that can't be denied?'

'Of course it's a choice. No matter how strong someone's desire is, the mind is always stronger. What's brought this on? Getting cold feet about the wedding?'

I eyed my feet. 'Well, my left foot is particularly cold.' I smiled, and he did too. 'No, I'm not, but it's just something someone said, something I heard, that's...' I ran my hand over my ponytail. 'Oh, why am I telling you this?'

'Because I'm here and I'm listening?'

I smiled again, and stopped on the side of the road. 'It's possible my fiancé, Greg, is having an affair.'

Ty's eyes bulged. 'What? Are you sure?'

'No, and I never would have thought it could be possible, but when I spoke to him just now, it was different, weird, and kind of fit in with what someone said about him.'

Ty shook his head. 'Well if he is, he's a damn fool.' He encouraged me to keep walking. 'I take it you haven't confronted him about it?'

'No, no way.'

'But with only one week till the wedding, it's probably best to sort it out sooner rather than later.'

'Tell me about it.' I sighed. 'Sorry, I shouldn't be dumping all this on you. I haven't even discussed it with my friends.'

'It's no problem. But like I said, better sort the whole thing out as soon as you can. Maybe it's a misunderstanding. And if not, then boy, what a mistake he's made.'

Ty's gaze remained straight ahead, and I watched the side

of his face, the dark shadows from the night sculpting his jaw, the protrusion of his Adam's apple, and his strong, confident posture, and I realised he was paying me a compliment and not just speaking generally about infidelity being a mistake.

'Thanks for walking me back,' I said.

'Ah,' he flicked his hand. 'Walking nice ladies home, rescuing them from toilets, performing some light entertainment, all in a day's work.'

'So does Cody, is he, can he…'

'Are you trying to ask me how independent he is?'

'Yeah.'

'He's better now he's a bit older. Before, I had to be with him all the time, but now he's learnt more skills he can do things for himself. He has his own phone he can call me with too, though he can't hear too well so he texts me instead. His writing is quite good, on a screen that is, not by hand. He knows not to leave the house by himself without someone knowing where he is. He's a great kid. A challenge sometimes, but great.'

'And your parents?'

'They died several years ago. Dad had a heart attack while driving. Unfortunately they both didn't make it.' He lowered his head and kicked a pebble.

'Oh gosh, Ty, I'm so sorry.' My hand found its way to his back for a brief moment.

'We manage. It was a big shock, and Cody didn't cope too well in the beginning. But we've made a new life for ourselves and things are looking up.'

'Do you get any help with Cody?'

'My neighbours are great, they keep an eye on him when I'm out working, invite him over for movie nights… they're hard of hearing themselves so it becomes a big subtitle-fest at their place!'

'Oh yes, my parents are the same. The TV is on either too loud or the subtitles take up half the screen.'

We shared a laugh.

'Where did you learn to dance the way you do?'

'Mostly taught myself from music videos, went to a few classes, and after a while I started getting gigs as a background dancer for singers and performers. I'd travel to the city regularly to do shows. At one stage I thought I might even head to the states and try my luck in the music industry doing music videos and stuff. But then the accident happened. Things changed, I had to change. Being there for Cody became number one priority.'

'Wow. You've done so well. I'm sure your parents would be incredibly proud of you.' If I was saying this a couple of weeks ago it would have simply been meant as a nice thing to say, but now, I think I actually believed it. Maybe those who died were still 'around', watching their loved ones and guiding them from beyond.

'Thanks, hopefully they are, wherever they are.' He glanced up at the sky and held out his hands.

I decided to take the opportunity to ask him something. 'Do you believe that there's something after all this. Afterlife?'

Ty twisted his lips. 'I was never really sure, but after they died, I don't know... Something changed. A feeling, a sense that somehow they were still with me.'

I smiled, even though Ty's focus was straight ahead and it was dark. I didn't feel so out of place, so weird, for what I'd experienced with Red. Not that I was going to tell him about her. 'That's nice. I have a feeling they are too. Still with you.'

Ty turned to face me. 'I have a feeling you're very good at your job. You're really great with all this serious stuff. You know what to say to make people feel better.'

'Well thank you. I'm much better with this stuff than I am with all the social, party-type conversation and fun.'

'Oh, I don't know about that. You did pretty well at Twister and that Pin the Thingy game.' He elbowed me in the ribs.

'You're just being nice. And I'm sorry you had to witness all that ridiculousness.'

'Don't apologise. This is turning into one of the most entertaining weekends I've had in a long time.' He grinned, and I knew he was thinking of the various embarrassments I'd endured. 'Though I'm sorry I bit your head off at the supermarket when you ran over my foot. I know it was an accident.'

For some reason I wished I could tell him about Red. Wished I could release this secret that had been overtaking my mind.

Guess what? I saw a ghost!

Hey, you know how you were wondering whether people live on after death? Well, surprise, they do!

Ty, I'd like you to meet Red. You can't see her of course, but I assure you, she's there.

If only I could.

But despite his apparent openness to the other side he'd still probably think I was a little nuts.

'That's okay, I'm sorry for running over your foot in the first place. And for the awkwardness later that night at the house. You really did put on a good show, I must say.' I was glad it was dark because I was probably blushing.

He made a show of bowing.

'So,' I said. 'A doctor, hey? How does Cody feel about the possibility of you being away every day learning how to save lives?'

'He's excited for me, thinks I'll be able to perform surgery after my first day. But if I get in, I'll have to arrange more help looking after him. There is some respite care available, and various support services, but that's something I'm saving up for too. I'll need to hire somebody to be his carer when I'm not there.'

'Well, I'll be sure to recommend your services to everyone I come across. Got any business cards?'

'Why thank you, I do indeed. Always keep a few in my wallet, you never know when a promotional opportunity will present itself.' He took his wallet from his pocket and extracted a few cards.

Ty Roxford ~ Quality adult entertainer and dancer

It showed his photo, a black and white mysterious looking shot from side on, with one of his eyebrows raised, as though his expression was asking *'You ready for some fun?'*

I popped them in my bag, and shook my head at the situation. Here I was, walking at night with a stripper, having a deep and meaningful conversation, one week before my wedding. What was Greg doing right now? My stomach churned remembering our awkward phone conversation, and I knew I'd have to find out, somehow, whether there was any truth to what Red had said, or if she was, in fact, just trying to manipulate me into leaving him for her own satisfaction.

'Can I get you a cup of coffee, tea, or something?' I asked as we approached the front door of the guest house.

Ty rocked forward on his feet with his hands in his pockets and looked like he was about to say yes, then turned his head to look down the driveway. 'Thanks, but I better get back to Cody. And I take it you'll be keen to have a nice hot shower after your altercation with the bathroom floor in the pub?'

'Are you trying to tell me I need a wash?' I asked with a hint of sarcasm, though I knew too well I did.

'No, but if you carry that anti-bacterial stuff around with

you I'm guessing good personal hygiene is one of your high priorities.'

I shrugged and smiled. 'Your guess would be right.'

I unlocked the door and thanked him again for accompanying me, and we both turned away.

'Sally?' he asked, and I turned to face him. 'Some men may cheat, but real men don't.' He grasped the side of my arm. 'Find out the truth before the wedding. Don't brush it aside. If you have doubts, you have to listen to them.' He dropped his hand and turned away again, but my eyes remained on him. He must have sensed them, because he turned back for the second time. 'And if I was with someone as kind and special as you, no way would I be stupid enough to let anything get in the way of that.'

He gave a single, gentle wave of his hand, a soft smile, and walked off down the driveway, while a part of me wanted to hear those words again.

CHAPTER 13

I went straight upstairs without turning any lights on. Inside, the house had a slight moonlit wash to it. Darkness didn't scare me, not now since the ghost that was haunting me appeared in broad daylight anyway. I took my shoes off, not worrying about putting the left one in the bin just yet, and headed for the shower.

Red stopped me at the door.

'You can't have a shower yet, I have to show you something.'

'You've done enough for one day.'

'But don't you want proof? Don't you want to know for sure if I'm telling the truth about Greg?'

Instead of pushing past — or through — her, I eyed her with curiosity.

'Look, I know you're the sort of person who needs to see to believe. Although,' she chuckled, 'even when you first saw me you didn't believe right away. And I've been practising my mind power technique, you know the one, to try and imprint what I see and sense into your mind?'

'Red, that's all a bit beyond my scope of belief at this stage. Yes, I know you're real, well, a real ghost, but I don't see how—' I gasped. A brief, but definite image flashed in my mind. Greg's car. 'Whoa, what was that? How did you? Did I just...'

'You saw his car, didn't you?'

My guess was she already knew the answer. Red stared at me with sharp, focused eyes.

'Hang on, how do I know you're not putting ideas into my head? How do you—' A tiny jolt ran through my body as I saw it again, but this time, the image lingered, and it wasn't just an image, it was moving, like I was watching something on a TV screen, only in my mind. Greg's car, from the side, getting closer to the driver's side window... Greg! I could see him in the car, driving, a faint smile on his face. And music, some rock ballad was playing through the speakers, and his fingers thrummed the steering wheel.

'Red, what is this, what am I seeing? Is it a memory or something?' I said when the image faded.

'It's happening right now. You're seeing Greg, where he is, what he's doing, right now.'

'No way.'

'Yes way.' She gave a nod. 'Isn't it cool what I can do?' She put her hands on her hips in satisfaction. 'Anyway, back to the issue at hand.' She resumed staring at me, and as though her glare pierced my head, a warm, tingling sensation grew around my temple.

Greg again. As clear as day, as though I was peering through his car window to kiss him goodbye on his way to work. But he wasn't looking at me, he didn't know I could see him. His focus was on the road but only one hand was on the steering wheel. The other...

Oh hell. Oh no. This can't be real.

His other hand was on top of someone else's, his thumb rubbing their skin. The recipient of his affection had her hand on her thigh, which despite the cool night was exposed, as her long skirt had ridden up over her knee. Greg's hand moved from the top of her hand to the top of her thigh, her bare thigh, rubbing and massaging it with his fingers. 'Mmm,' a soft feminine voice said over the music.

My mind tried to shake away the vision but it remained, like a piece of plastic wrapping that sticks to your finger despite all attempts to get rid of it. No, no, I didn't want to see this. Didn't want it to be true. How did I know if it was true, anyway? Red hadn't exactly been my best buddy since I'd known her. She could be playing tricks on me just to break up the wedding.

The view widened and my line of sight trailed up the woman's arm, to her shoulder, her neck, and... her face. Her eyes closed in apparent bliss, a hint of a smile on her painted lips, and her hair... I'd seen her hair before. It had one of those popular colour schemes: dark at the top and light at the ends, like her hair colour was fading but it'd been done on purpose. Light blonde wisps of hair fell around her shoulders, darkening at the top into a caramel brown shade. I'd seen her before, at one of Greg's work functions. What was her name? Kylie? Kathy? Kitty? K something.

Get your hand off my fiancé! I urged in silence, as she covered his hand with hers and guided it higher up her thigh. *Greg! What are you doing? I can see you! Greg!* I shook my head from side to side and clamped my eyes shut, and eventually the vision dissipated like a clearing fog.

'I'm sorry you had to see that,' said Red.

I kept shaking my head. 'No, no, no. It's not real, it isn't.' I held on to the doorframe for support and stared at the floor. The alternating black and white tiles in the bathroom appeared to move and switch places, their discordant repetition jarring my eyes.

I looked up when a cool, airy sensation brushed across my hand as it rested above my head on the doorframe. Red's hand, on top of mine, in a comforting gesture. The coolness transformed to warmth the longer she left it there, and although I couldn't feel her hand directly, I felt its effect, its energy. I looked her in the eyes.

'It's the truth. I swear on my grave,' she said, then crossed her heart with her other finger. 'I knew the only way was for you to see it, however shocking, in order to believe. I'm here to stop you making a huge mistake. Don't marry Greg.'

'I'm not totally convinced. I'm confused, I don't know what to believe anymore.' My head continued shaking side to side as though that in itself would erase what I'd seen or make it not true. 'So if that really happened, where is he? Where are they? Right now.'

'On the freeway heading to Pebble Creek.'

'But Greg's supposed to be at his buck's party. At a golf resort.'

'He was, but it was only for yesterday and today. The guys have gone home now, it's just him and her for the rest of the weekend.'

'But Pebble Creek, that's a pretty boring place, not much to do or see, why...'

'Exactly. Less chance of bumping into someone they know.'

'And it's only about a half hour from here. Do your "powers" or whatever they are tell you when they'll get to Pebble Creek?'

She nodded. 'In about forty-five minutes they'll arrive at Pebble Creek Motel. I'm sorry, Sally, but you had to know what he was doing behind your back.'

I turned away from her, the sight of her only bringing me pain. Even if she wasn't lying and was only here to help me and prevent a mistake, I couldn't hold eye contact with her. 'This is all too much. I... I... don't know what...' I ran my hands over my head and down my face, then a surge of adrenaline sped up my heart rate and my shoulders straightened. 'I have to go there. Now. I have to see for real.'

'Sally, no, you don't want to do that to yourself,' she said, but I was already putting a clean pair of shoes on. 'You've seen all you need to see, just trust that it's real. Don't go rushing off in this state.'

'I will decide what I will and won't do, thank you very much. I don't need you dictating to me.' I dashed down the stairs, then checked the little pottery bowl on the kitchen bench. Lorena's car keys. *Yes!* I snatched them up, wrote a quick note for Lorena telling her not to worry and I'd be back in an hour or two, and headed for the front door.

'Wait! So you're going to drive there and wait for him? And then what? You shouldn't drive when you're upset, it could be dangerous!'

'Didn't you hear me before?' I yelled, a bit louder than was normal for me. 'I'm leaving now, and I don't want you coming with me. And most of all, I don't want you here when I get back. I can't take it anymore!'

I locked the door behind me and got in the car, moving the driver's seat forward a few notches, and left a flurry of dust behind me as I drove off down the road.

I checked my watch again for the fifth time that minute. The car park of the Pebble Creek Motel was quiet, only a few cars sat parked in the lot, frost forming on their windscreens. I'd parked next to another four-wheel drive, at the outer edge of the lot, where there were only the two spots, to seem less conspicuous, and to prevent him parking right next to me. And anyway, Greg probably wouldn't recognise Lorena's car. Thank goodness it had dark tinted windows you could barely see through, though I could see out and had a view of all the motel room doors in the plain, rectangular motel.

The vacancy sign flashed its muted neon, the last 'C' missing its light. If Greg was indeed bringing a woman here, I couldn't believe it was to such a tacky place. We only ever stayed in nice hotels or B&B's. Then again, if my fiancé was having an affair, I much preferred it to be in a place like this, with rooms that probably had mould on the walls, horrible floral bedcovers, and a creaky mattress. I hoped they'd get bitten by bed bugs, or trip over a loose corner of carpet, or get poked in the ribs by a damaged mattress spring. I nibbled on my nails as I waited. I never nibbled on my nails. Terribly unhygienic.

A car drove past on the quiet country road parallel to the motel, but didn't stop. What if they decided to go somewhere else? A few minutes later another car drove by, then swung into the parking lot, its headlights lighting up the pale oyster colour of the walls of the building. A silver Audi. Greg's car.

God in heaven she was right.

I sucked in air through tight gaps between my teeth and the seat underneath me felt cold and uncomfortable. His car door opened and he got out. It was dark, but when he walked in front of the headlights his profile was illuminated. It was definitely Greg. But *only* Greg. He went into the reception office and returned a few moments later, got back in the car, and moved it closer to where I was, but not close enough that he would have to look in my direction. I sunk a little lower in my seat, and kept perfectly still. He got out again and shut the door. Then the passenger door opened, and out stepped Miss I Can't Decide What My Hair Colour Should Be. A low growl may have escaped my mouth but I barely noticed it; my eyes were glued to the sight in front of me.

They walked towards the second last room of the motel, and as Greg put the key in the door he dropped it, and laughed. The woman laughed too, and placed her hand on his back as he picked up the key. He positioned his face close to hers and ran his fingers through her hair.

How dare you... I hoped the remnants of blonde in her hair would all fall out. Actually, I hoped all her hair would fall out as he combed it with his touch. My stomach twisted inside as he leaned in and pushed his lips against hers. Urgently. Impatiently. Aggressively. I wanted to throw up. He finally opened the door and they practically fell through it, entwined in each other.

That's it. I shoved the keys into my pocket and got out of the car. I marched in the direction of what I could now see as room number seven, and raised my chin in preparation. For what, I didn't know. I had no idea what I'd say when he opened the door, no idea what I'd do, or what he'd do. I'd caught him, he couldn't lie his way out of this one.

Oh boy, when I get in there I'm going to... What was I going to do? What could even be done about this situation? He kissed her. He's obviously not planning to just switch out the lights and fall straight asleep. Oh God. I stopped, my breath coming fast and shallow. My hands shook and dizziness unsteadied my legs. I gulped but it didn't relieve the lump situation in my throat.

I can't. I just can't. I can't go in there and see him again with her. Can't see... her. What if their clothes were off? The sight of them kissing and groping was traumatic enough, I didn't want to add another unerasable sight to my memory. No. That was it. I'd seen enough. Going in there may stop them going ahead with whatever sick plans they had for the night, but it wouldn't stop the damage that had been done.

I turned and dashed back to the car, revved the engine, and drove away as quickly as I could, anger and sadness clambering over each other in my chest. I put the radio on a noisy alternative rock station and turned up the volume, hoping like hell it would somehow overpower what I'd witnessed.

CHAPTER 14

Katy! That was her name. By the time I took the turn-off back into Barron Springs, it hit me. My chin quivered and my eyes blurred with hot tears. I was here for my bridal weekend, with my bridesmaids, to celebrate my upcoming wedding to a lying, cheating, bastard. *Congratulations, Sally!*

Sadness replaced my anger and I cried, out loud, enclosed within Lorena's car with no one to hear me. Yesterday I was a bride-to-be, but now, how could I possibly go through with the wedding? I knew that some people moved through the trauma and regret of infidelity, but right now, the thought of him and her together brought a sick feeling to my stomach. How could I ever speak to him, or look at him again? How could he do this to me?

All my emotions poured out, and I slowed the car a little. The Barron Springs roads were mostly deserted, only emphasising the abandonment and pain I felt. I quickly wiped my eyes, trying to clear my vision as I turned into Redwood Road. Not long and I'd be home. Well, not home, but back at the guest house where my friends would no doubt hound me about my whereabouts this evening. I couldn't believe I'd have to tell them about this, tell Lorena that her organisational efforts this weekend were in vain. That made me even more upset, that my best friend had gone to all this trouble. For nothing.

My chest shuddered with additional tears, and suddenly, the dark, grey monotony of the road broke when something flashed in front of me. I blinked and widened my eyes. *Red?* A blur of white and purple shot past me, right in front of the car, and even though I knew I could not hit her, instinct made me swerve the car to the side. I screamed as the car mounted the sidewalk and onto the front lawn of a property. I slammed on the brakes, almost hitting another person, who seemed to appear out of nowhere. His hands landed on the front of the car, as though his effort would stop it, then he stumbled backwards.

Oh my God. Oh my God. I didn't hurt him, did I?

I put the gearstick in park and scrambled out, rushing to his side.

'Ty! Oh my God! Are you all right?' I touched his arm as he got to his feet.

'Sally? Yes, I'm fine. But, boy that was close!' He glanced briefly to the road, in the direction Red had run to. 'What are you doing here? What happened? Did you almost hit that woman?'

'I'm just... *that woman?*' I asked, following his gaze to the road again.

'Yeah, ran past here a second ago. Red hair, wearing pyjamas. Where is she?' He walked to the roadside and glanced around.

'You saw her?' *He saw Red?* Oh my goodness, this night was playing havoc with my emotions. I didn't know if I could take much more of this upheaval.

'She was snooping around outside my house, so I went out

to confront her, but she ran off. I chased her across the lawn and she ran right onto the road. Where the heck did she go?'

'I don't know, but she's obviously not hurt, she must have gone through the bushes.' I eyed the thick collection of trees across from us that led into a valley.

Ty shook his head, confusion creasing his brow. Then he looked more closely at me. I rubbed my head, half because it was aching in my fragile emotional state and half because I realised my face must be red from all the crying.

'Are you okay? You're not hurt, are you?' He touched my arm this time. 'What's wrong?'

At his question the floodgates opened again and I couldn't hold them back. I covered my face as I sobbed, and he grasped my shoulders gently.

'Sally, what is it? Your fiancé?'

I nodded.

'Here, come inside.' He led me towards his house and I managed to get a glimpse before my tears further blurred my vision. It was an unassuming red brick house with stepping stones leading to the front door. I felt strangely comforted, even though I barely knew Ty and had never been here before. I wiped at my tears as he led me into the warm embrace of a cosy living room that had a gas heater glowing bright orange next to the TV.

'I'm sorry, sorry for almost hitting you and for losing it like this, it's just—'

'Hey, don't worry about that. I'm fine, and you're going to tell me what happened. Would you like a hot drink?'

'No thanks.' I shook my head, and he handed me a tissue. I breathed in deep and sat next to him on the couch, and he placed a cushion behind my back. 'I went for a drive, as you can see, and... oh gosh, I can't believe I took Lorena's car without asking her! What was I thinking?' I shook my head. 'Anyway, I drove to Pebble Creek and found Greg.'

'He was having his buck's weekend at Pebble Creek?'

So I wasn't the only one who thought it was a seedy place.

'No. His buck's weekend was already over, but he failed to tell me it was only going to be for one night. Tonight he had other plans.' I urged my tears to stay inside. 'I saw him get a motel room, with a woman. They kissed passionately and went inside. I went up to confront him but chickened out. Chickened out! Why didn't I march in there and tell him off? Why didn't I make him explain himself?'

Ty ran his hand over his short mussed hair. 'Because you'd already seen enough,' he said quietly. 'Oh, Sally. I'm so, so sorry.' He rubbed my back and I sniffed, dabbing at my eyes with the tissue.

'I just can't believe it's true. How could he do this? Why? And only a week before the wedding. Why would he even marry me if he's not ready to settle down?'

'I wish I had all the answers, but I don't. All I know is he's made a huge mistake.'

'I feel so stupid, you know?' I shook my head.

'Hey, you're not the stupid one, he is. He let you down.'

I nodded, then a thought hit me. 'What about the wedding! What am I going to do? We have people travelling from interstate, everything's booked, and my parents! What am I supposed to tell everyone?'

'Don't worry about that now. It'll all work out. And your friends and family will understand. Sort it all out tomorrow. It's late now, you just look after yourself.' The warmth of his arm on my back increased as he drew me in close to his side, his other hand grasping my hand.

I softened at his touch and allowed it to comfort me,

surrendering to the exhaustion of grief, hurt, and sadness, as he held me close till my tears dried up.

'Ty, your brother, where is he?'

'He's asleep, out like a light.'

'I hope I haven't woken him up.'

'No, good thing about being partially deaf, you sleep like a baby. He'll be up at six am though, no doubt.'

I looked at Ty. 'But don't babies wake up a lot and cry and generally cause havoc?'

He smiled. 'Ha, true! It's one of those sayings that don't really make sense but people say anyway.'

I managed a chuckle. 'Thank you,' I said. 'For listening to me and putting up with my emotional outburst.'

He gripped me tighter. 'Like I said earlier tonight, all in a day's work.' He turned my chin with his finger to look at him. 'But seriously, I'm more than happy to listen to you when you need an ear. And that Greg, geez, does he need a talking to.'

'I guess he'll get it, once I've calmed down and can think clearly about what to say.'

'It's lucky I wasn't with you at the time, or he would have got what's coming to him then and there.'

'Thanks for your support, but a couple of men beating each other up is probably not the best solution.'

'I wasn't talking about violence. Though I sure would be tempted to hit him where it hurts. I just meant that I'd make sure he knew what an arsehole he was to betray you like that. And hopefully I would have thought up a witty one-liner to really drive it home, but I can't think of one now!'

'You, stuck for words? I'll believe that when I see it.'

The jagged edges of my sadness had smoothed out now; I was still shocked and hurt, but a sliver of hope wriggled its way into my heart. I'd get through this, somehow. But there was no way I was taking him back, no matter what excuse he would try to manipulate me with when I told him I knew about his indiscretion. I could never trust him again.

My phone jingled. Lorena. Oh dear, I should have told them where I was going, not just that I *was* going. What if I'd had a car accident and they wouldn't have known where I was? I wasn't used to acting on the spur of the moment, and they were probably worried about me.

I typed back:

> I'm so sorry. I'm fine. Will be back soon, you guys go to bed and I'll explain everything in the morning. Love you all xx.

'So your friends don't know yet?' Ty asked.

I shook my head. 'And to be honest, I don't think I'm up for explaining it all over again, tonight. I'm... tired. And shocked. And I don't want to keep reliving it.'

'Then don't. It can wait till morning. For now, Doctor Ty would like to write you a prescription.'

I gave him a curious look. 'Valium?'

He laughed. 'No. Give me a sec...' He went to the nearby kitchen and scribbled on something. He returned with a Post-it note and stuck it to my forehead with a pat. I peeled it off and read it:

Dr Ty's prescription for Sexy Sally - 30 minutes of moderate laughter in the company of the nearest available man.

And he'd drawn an arrow pointing towards him.

A wide smile healed my despair and I stuck the Post-it to his forehead. 'Nearest available man, huh?'

He shrugged.

'And just how does Doctor Ty expect me to laugh for half an hour in a situation like this?'

'I could tickle you.'

I covered my arms over my chest. 'You wouldn't.'

'But I could.'

'But you won't.'

'But I will.' He reached towards me quickly and tickled my ribs, and I wriggled and laughed as I tried to get away.

'Stop, stop!' I laughed, trying to tickle him back but trying to cover my ticklish spots at the same time.

He gave me a reprieve. 'See? Laughter comes easy when Doctor Ty prescribes it.'

'But you can't exactly tickle me for half an hour.'

'I could, but I won't. I have a backup plan.' He stood and studied the collection of DVDs on a shelf next to the TV. 'Do you have a favourite sitcom?' he asked.

'Oh, um, let me think...'

'I have a large selection. Cody is addicted to them, watches one every night.'

'Do you have *Friends*?'

He looked at me like I was an idiot. 'Do I have *Friends*? It's only the best sitcom ever made. That and *Seinfeld*. I have the whole series.' He pulled out a DVD. 'Any episode requests?'

'Surprise me.'

'Random episode coming up.' He withdrew a disc and slotted it into the player, and the familiar theme song lifted my spirits and brought back memories of watching this with the girls when we were younger. 'How about that hot drink now?'

'Actually, that would be nice. Thank you.'

'Tea? Coffee? Hot chocolate?'

'I think this situation calls for a comforting hot chocolate.'

'As you wish.' He winked and flicked the kettle switch, and a couple of minutes later handed me a steaming mug and plonked some cookies on the coffee table. I munched and drank, and decided to forget about Greg, if only for the next twenty minutes.

'Oh, is this the one where Ross gets those leather pants?' I asked.

'Yep. I love this one!'

A smile stayed put on my lips in anticipation, and when the scene came where Ross tried unsuccessfully to get his tight pants back on by using talcum powder, I had to put my mug down for fear of spilling my hot chocolate from laughter.

'I thought this weekend had been embarrassing, at least I didn't have a leather pants incident,' I said.

'Lucky. They are tricky things, those leather pants.'

I glanced his way. 'And you know this from personal experience?'

He nodded. 'When I first started stripping I got a pair, and my practice run went okay, but I made the mistake of getting them washed before wearing them to a job. They seemed to have gotten a little tighter, and let's just say the strip was more like a sumo wrestling match than a smooth and sexy display of clothing removal.'

I laughed. 'I might have to call you Ross from now on.'

'Gee, thanks.'

'It's a compliment. Ross attracts the embarrassing situations, but he's a sweet guy.' I bit off a chunk of cookie. 'Oh, and he gets the girl in the end.'

It was only after I'd spoken that I realised what I'd said, and hoped he didn't think it related to us or anything. I didn't mean it that way, and my brain couldn't even comprehend the idea of eventually being with someone else. But a strange feeling arose in my mind, a realisation that I never would have considered had tonight not happened: that there may be someone in this world who's more perfect for me than I ever thought Greg could be.

&

When my episode of prescribed laughter concluded, I stood and took my mug to the sink. 'If Cody's going to be up early I better let you finally get some sleep,' I said, noticing it was after midnight.

'Ah, it's no problem, and I don't have to work again till Tuesday so I can have an easy Sunday.'

'You get Mondays off from your disability work?'

'Every second Monday. On those days Cody goes to a respite centre. Gives him a break from me as much as it gives me a break from him!'

'He's really lucky to have you, have I mentioned that before?'

'Thanks.' Ty interrupted my attempt to wash the mugs and plate with a touch of his hand. 'And you're pretty lucky to have those friends of yours back there.' He tilted his head in the direction of the guest house.

'Very lucky. I'm going to need them more than ever in the coming days.'

He gave a knowing nod. 'And if you ever need a *Friends* marathon, or a reminder of how awesome my hot chocolate making skills are, you know how to reach me.'

I smiled. 'That's good to know.'

I went back to the coffee table and picked up my phone, and my eyes caught sight of the screensaver. Greg and I at our engagement party. All smiles, sparkling eyes, a lifetime of happiness ahead of us. Or so I thought. How did we end up here? What made him forget his promise to me and see another woman behind my back? Or had he been seeing other women all along and I, with my tendency to give everyone the benefit of the doubt, remained oblivious to the whole thing. Red had said he left her for me. Now I knew how she'd felt. I could understand why she had subjected me to a few challenging situations this weekend, and actually couldn't believe she hadn't treated me worse. But I, like her, had not been privy to Greg's infidelity until later. She knew it hadn't been my fault, and I knew it wasn't that woman Katy's fault. Though surely she knew Greg was engaged and that didn't seem to stop her throwing herself at him.

'You okay?' Ty sidled up next to me, and noticed the photo. 'Oh.'

I went to my phone settings and erased the screensaver, replacing it with a photo of me with Lorena, Mel, and Georgie. They would never let me down.

'Nice.' Ty smiled.

I tucked the phone in my back pocket and glanced around for my bag but realised I'd left it and the keys in the car. But I doubted anyone would steal it, there wasn't a soul around this sleepy town at night, except for Red, though I had no idea where she was. I was reminded of the fact that Ty said he'd seen a woman in pyjamas, and I considered asking him about her, or even telling him about her, but bit my tongue. I'd shared enough with him tonight. It was time to go back, get into bed, and cry myself to sleep.

'It'll get easier,' Ty said, as though sensing the return of my sadness. 'Give it time.' He rubbed my arm again.

'I took hold of his hand and squeezed it. 'Thank you. You made an unbearable night bearable. Fun even. I don't quite know how you did that, but thank you.'

'Never underestimate the power of a good tickle and an episode of *Friends*.' He smiled. 'Take care,' he said, pulling me into a hug.

His big, strong arms enveloped me and I closed my eyes as my chin rested against his right shoulder. I went to pull away after the socially appropriate duration but something stopped me. He didn't pull away either. He stood there, embracing me, and instead of relaxing into it my body tensed slightly. My heart rate rose, and the touch of his hands splayed against my back sent an exhilarating sensation shooting through my body. I eased back a little, my eyes slowly gazing upwards to his. He didn't look away, and he didn't remove his arms from around my back. All I felt in that moment was need. Pure, unadulterated need. I recognised the same in his eyes, and before logic and reasoning could pull me back to reality, he moved his face closer and pressed his lips gently to mine. Soft, warm, luscious lips, slowly testing mine, as though he was scared to give in to the full spectrum of desire simmering between us both. My lips told him it was okay, that I wanted him to kiss me, that right now I didn't care what was right or wrong or dangerous, I just wanted his lips, his body, close to mine. His pressure and intensity increased, and his hands moved across my back leaving a trail of blissful warmth in their wake. I had never felt so wonderful, so comforted, so... right. But when my desire for him grew so much it scared me, it felt wrong. I pulled away.

'Ty...'

He let me go and rubbed the back of his neck. 'I'm sorry.'

'No, I'm sorry. I don't know what's got into me. I shouldn't be leading you on like this.'

'Let's forget it ever happened,' he said, standing awkwardly in front of me and avoiding my eye contact.

'Probably for the best.' I moved towards the front door. 'I'll, ah, see you around, maybe.'

'Yeah.' He stayed in the same spot, as if he was scared that if he came closer he might not be able to control himself.

I opened the door, my cheeks burning, my heart aching. But my foot wouldn't step on the porch. In my mind I saw Greg and Katy, tongues down each other's throat and hands all over each other, and a surge of anger and entitlement made my blood boil. I spun around, and a look of surprise graced Ty's face.

I locked eyes with him and confidence straightened my spine. 'If Greg can get it on with someone else then I bloody well can too.' Flames of desire ignited within as I launched myself at Ty. I grasped the sides of his face and pulled him close, planting my lips on his with a fierce urgency.

He didn't complain. He engulfed me with his arms, his mouth, his energy... his body heating mine on contact. Our passionate, desperate kiss was all encompassing; every nerve in my body buzzed with life. It was utterly electrifying.

We moved backwards and fell onto the couch. He eased back and caressed the loose strands of hair that had come out of my ponytail, as though he was sculpting a work of art. His hands twirled them while his eyes looked longingly, and with panting breath he lowered onto me and kissed me with as much intensity as before. It had never been like this with Greg. It had never been like this with anyone. I couldn't believe how much desire coursed through my body for him right now. Where had all this come from? Had I been suppressing my attraction to him out of obligation to Greg, and now that I had no obligation to a cheating fool, it had all come out into the open? I didn't have time to think any further, my hormones took over. I ripped off his shirt and grabbed at his back, revelling in the rewarding pressure of his hard muscles under my hands. As we rolled over I brought my hands to his chest, and they ran across his skin eagerly, appreciating the toned curves of his pecs. His body was absolute heaven. I couldn't get enough, didn't want this to stop.

Ty removed his lips from mine, and panting, looked me in the eyes. 'Sally,' he breathed.

'Yes.'

'I think we should stop.'

My heart plummeted as though I'd been climbing a ladder of ecstasy and it had been taken from under me. I was falling, dropping into the unknown, as Ty manoeuvred to a sitting position and put his shirt back on.

'I'm sorry,' he said, his face red and flustered.

'What's wrong?' I asked, suddenly self-conscious.

'I liked you from the first moment I laid eyes on you, from when you knelt down to look at my foot after running over it.' He gave a brief smile. 'But I don't think this is a good idea. I don't want to take advantage of you, you deserve better than that.'

'But, Ty, it's okay. I know what I'm doing.' I touched his shoulder with reassurance.

He grasped it with his hand and squeezed it.

'I want nothing more than to be with you, to stay here with you, but I can't. It's not right.'

I swallowed a lump that had formed. Deep down I knew he was right. But I didn't want to admit it.

'A couple of hours ago you were engaged. You were preparing to marry someone else. I don't want to be a rebound fling. Don't want you to have more fallout to deal with.'

I nodded.

'Will you be okay?' he asked, his eyes gazing at mine.

I nodded again.

He ran his finger down my cheek. 'You're a special woman. You're not like others I've met.'

'I hope that's a compliment,' I said with a small smile.

'It is. A big, fat, juicy compliment.' He smiled and kissed my forehead, then took both my hands in his. 'Sally, if something were to happen between us, I'd want it to be at the right time, when you've dealt with what's happened, and in the right place, not here with my brother in the next room.'

'I know,' I replied. 'Thank you, for being so respectful.'

'Believe me, it took all my willpower to pull away, but remember what I said before? The mind can always win over the body. The mind gets final say. There is always a choice.'

'You're stronger than me.'

'You're stronger than you think you are.' He squeezed my hands.

I stood and checked my phone was still in my pocket, and he followed me to the door.

'Now go get some sleep, and let your friends be there for you tomorrow. Do what you need to do to handle what's happened, and sort out the next step. I'm only ever a phone call away.'

'Thanks, Ty.' I went to kiss him on the cheek but hugged him, afraid if I felt his skin against my lips I'd be too weak to resist continuing where we left off. 'Sorry for all the drama. And I hope I didn't run over any exotic plants,' I said, gesturing to where the car was parked haphazardly on the lawn.

'Women and parking, huh?' he said with a sarcastic grin.

I smiled and slapped him gently on the arm. 'Let's hope I'm better at pulling off a three-point-turn,' I replied.

'I'll help you,' he said, walking out with me, and little did he know how much he already had.

CHAPTER 15

'Where have you been?' Lorena emerged from her bedroom with her eye mask pushed onto her forehead, breathing strip over her nose, and knee pillow velcroed between her legs. But no earplugs. She'd obviously been waiting for the sound of the car so she could wake when I returned.

'Oh, Lorena, I'm so sorry, I didn't want you to wake up. Are the others asleep?'

'Yes, they went off once I showed them your text that you were okay. Where did you go?'

'I had to deal with... a Greg issue, that's all. Something important.'

'You drove all the way to the golf resort?'

'Not exactly. Anyway, I'm sorry I went MIA, I'll explain everything tomorrow. Right now, you and your beautiful girl need your sleep, and I'm exhausted too. Let's chat tomorrow, yeah?' I leaned in for a goodnight hug.

'Okay, but you're sure? Everything all right?'

I gulped. 'Everything's all right. See you in the morning.'

I only said that so she'd be able to sleep. If I said anything was wrong she'd either force me to tell her and we'd be up all night, or she'd be up all night wondering what it was. I didn't want her health to be impacted by my problems.

I tiptoed up the stairs and hoped Red had paid attention to my wishes and gone away. I wanted to be alone. And sadly, when I opened the door and the room was empty, alone was what I now felt. Very, very alone.

The next morning I got up early and made myself breakfast. Sleep had evaded me most of the night, and I wanted to fill my stomach before the inevitable 'talk' with my friends. I went out the back door and walked around the garden with a cup of coffee, my dressing gown pulled tight around my waist, the sun shining brightly in patches through the trees. Around the country there would no doubt be couples waking up together, reading the Sunday papers in bed with hot buttered toast and fresh orange juice, or toddlers bouncing on the bed and rearing to go for a fun-filled family day. I wondered if there was someone out there like me, someone who'd just discovered their lover was loving someone else. I knew I needed to confront Greg, but not until I'd talked it over with the girls.

'There you are, disappearing again?'

I turned around as Lorena stepped outside, hugging her dressing gown close to her body.

'Just enjoying the peace and quiet of a Sunday morning.' I smiled.

'Without us chatterboxes to spoil it for you, huh?' She winked.

'You could never spoil anything,' I said, placing my mug on the outdoor table setting, sliding my arm around her waist. Unlike Greg. He'd spoiled everything. Not only our relationship, but my friends' time and money for this weekend away, and eight months of planning for this big family wedding. Should I tell the guests that he had an affair and that was why the wedding was cancelled? Or should I spare him the humiliation and just say it was cancelled, and that was it? How does one go about cancelling a wedding? Where to start?

'I have a feeling you've got a lot on your mind,' Lorena said, taking a seat at the table setting.

'I do, actually.'

'Hey, don't like my cooking anymore?' Georgie asked as she brought out a tray of croissants. 'I see you had some toast already.'

'Yes, but maybe I can fit one of these in too.' I picked up a croissant and took a bite.

'Atta girl.' Georgie placed the tray down, and once Mel had woken somewhat we all sat at the table drinking coffee and tea and eating croissants. I told them I wasn't saying anything about last night until they'd all eaten.

'I guess I need to explain myself,' I said, once they had.

'Um, yes.' Lorena turned to face me.

'First of all, I'm sorry about taking the car. I'll pay for petrol on the way home tomorrow.'

'Don't worry about that, just tell us what's going on.'

'Okay.' I took a deep breath, and trying to keep it together, relayed the events of last night. Minus the making out with Ty bit. And the ghost bit. And the nearly writing off Lorena's car bit.

'Oh. My. God.' Lorena's jaw dropped open. 'That total, utter bastard. How dare he!'

Georgie stood, her hand running through her hair and her body alert and ready for attack. Mel came around to my side of the table and wrapped an arm around me.

'So there you have it,' I lifted my palms in the air, 'I'm no longer Mrs Sally Simons-to-be!'

'Oh, Sal. I can't believe this. I'm so angry at him!'

'It's okay, Lorena, I don't want you to get too worked up. It's my problem.'

'Any problem of yours is a problem of ours,' she replied. 'Have you spoken to him yet?'

I shook my head. 'I wanted to wait till I'd spoken to you all. What do I do? What do I say?'

'I know what I'd like to do to him,' Georgie said. 'But sadly my training made me promise to be assertive and defensive, not aggressive. Oh, but if he were here right now...' She paced up and down the patio.

'Men,' Mel said, shaking her head. 'And women who can't keep their hands off other women's husbands.' Since Greg wasn't yet my husband I knew she was reminded of her husband's situation with his colleague.

'Yeah, how dare this Katy woman do this? I'd like to have a "word" with her too,' Georgie said.

'Guys, I know you're all angry, I am too, but what's done is done,' I said in defeat. 'I have to start making arrangements to... to...' The reality of what lay ahead planted its heavy weight on my body and I lowered my chin towards my chest, closing my eyes and trying to shut out the pain that still stung like a burn. The current of grief swept me away again, I was unable to hold on to anything for stability, and tears overflowed from inside to out.

'It's not fair!' I exclaimed. 'Why? Why did he do this?'

'Oh, honey.' Lorena encouraged my head to rest on her shoulder and patted my hair, Mel rested hers on my other shoulder, and Georgie stood behind me, rubbing my back and telling me everything would be okay.

'Don't you worry about a thing,' said Lorena. 'We'll sort out the wedding stuff. Between the three of us, we'll contact the guests and get them to cancel their arrangements, and deal with all the other details, won't we, girls?'

'For sure,' they said, all three supporting my body, which had become weak from emotional overload.

'All you need to think about right now is telling Greg your decision, and then doing whatever you need to do to get through this. And we'll be right by your side.'

This made me cry even more. How could I ever survive without my friends? These three wonderful, amazing women who were there for me no matter what. They were worth ten times what Greg could ever be. 'Thank you, thank you all so much. For everything.'

'That's what friends are for,' Mel said. 'Though don't expect me to start singing that song because otherwise you may not want to be my friend anymore!'

I laughed at this, and hugged her close, tears of sadness and joy combining as they escaped down my cheeks. Sadness at what I'd lost, joy at what I'd gained: a deeper, closer relationship with my friends, and a certainty that I wasn't really alone. I never would be, as long as they were around.

I sat up straight and wiped my eyes with the tissue Georgie had given me. 'I guess I'd better get this over with.' Georgie went inside and returned with my phone, handing it to me. 'I don't think I can speak to him. Not yet. I'll text him.'

A thought flashed in my mind that it was bad form to break up with someone via text message, but then I realised it was even worse form to sleep with someone else while engaged. So stuff it. Text message it was, and Greg wouldn't even see it coming.

Greg — I know about you and Katy. Don't deny it. And don't tell me 'it's not what you think', because I saw you with her at the motel. There is no excuse for what you've done, and I am officially cancelling our engagement. It's over. Sally.

I waited for my friends' nod of approval before pressing send, though Mel asked if there was an emoji I could add that could give him the finger.

I held my breath for a moment, aware of the finality of this message. I shook my head at the last text messages between Greg and I that were displayed above.

Home soon, stuck in traffic.

No problem, see you soon. Can you pick up some milk? S xx

Bizarre how quickly and dramatically things could change. He would never be picking up milk for me again. He would never kiss me goodbye in the morning and hello in the evening. We'd never discuss our workdays again, nor our ideas for what to do on our days off. No more. Greg and me — finished.

The phone rang and Greg's caller ID appeared on the screen.

I froze, my eyes widening. I looked at my friends. 'I can't do it, I can't talk to him. Not yet.'

'Then let him wait. Let him suffer for a while,' said Lorena.

I allowed the call to ring out until it stopped. It rang again. I didn't answer.

'I've told him my decision, there's nothing to discuss, right?'

Lorena shrugged. 'Well, there will be, eventually, but you don't have to do it now.'

'Oh, what about our house, our mortgage?' I covered my mouth.

'You'll sort something out with the help of a lawyer. One step at a time,' said Georgie.

'Maybe you should send another message and tell him to get his things out of the house by the time you get home tomorrow,' said Mel.

I considered this, then shook my head. 'It was his house first. And anyway, I don't think I can be there anymore. With all the memories. I might go stay with Mum and Dad for a while.'

'Or me. You can stay with us for a while,' Lorena offered.

'I'd offer too, but with seven people in the house it might not be the most enjoyable stay,' said Mel.

'Thanks, guys, don't worry, I'll work something out. How about I stay with you Monday night, Lorena, and go from there. My overnight bag is packed anyway.

'Deal,' she said. 'We'll get popcorn and a chick flick and bitch about men.'

'Sounds perfect.' I smiled, tipping my head to hers. 'I'm sorry about the weekend being ruined, you've organised the best bridal weekend.'

'Ruined? Nonsense!' She flicked her hand. 'We've had delicious meals, girly chats, fun and games, and a stripper. I'd say it's been a rather productive weekend, don't you think?'

The others agreed. Especially Mel. If only she knew I'd kissed the stripper last night, she'd probably have a heart attack.

'But maybe I'll cancel this morning's activity,' Lorena said, getting up.

'Oh, what did you have planned?' I asked.

'Oh, nothing much. Just a guided rainforest walk. It's nothing.' She went to get her phone.

'Wait,' I said. 'I'm not going to let Greg spoil the rest of this weekend. I may not be requiring your bridesmaid duties anymore, but this can still be a bonding weekend. Just without the bridal bit.' I stood too.

'You sure? Because we can always laze around here and eat and drink and talk, it's completely up to you,' she said.

'No,' I said firmly. 'We're going to continue as planned. I want to go to the rainforest. I want to walk, and breathe in the fresh country air, and look at... leaves, and stuff.' I gave a sharp nod.

Lorena chuckled. 'Well, leaves are such fascinating things.'

'Yes, let's go,' said Georgie. 'Getting into nature will do us all the world of good.'

'Shall I bring wine?' asked Mel.

An hour later we stood at the start of the rainforest walking track with our tour guide, Randalf Watson, a quirky-looking guy in his early twenties who spoke with a lisp. He wore rugged outdoor boots, khaki jeans, a shirt and jacket, and — a tie! On his tie was a jungle print. I admired his enthusiasm for the natural world. There were four other people joining us for the walk; young, Chinese newlyweds on their honeymoon, and a couple in their late sixties with leathery, tanned skin who were, in their own words, 'seeing as many interesting things as they could before they die'.

'Well then, my dear nature travellerth, are you all exthited?'

Lorena and I shared a smile and we nodded.

'Fantathtic! Follow me, pleathe.'

He led us downhill, along a cute little path that fed into the rainforest.

'Now, ath you can thee here, there are theveral engraved plaqueth along the pathway. Each plaque hath a quote to provide you with inthpiration on your journey into the heart of the wilderneth. I implore you to take the time to thtop and read each one, in order to have a fulfilling and enriching exthperienth.'

We each stopped to read the first one: *Nature does not hurry, yet everything is accomplished. ~ Lao Tzu*

'I wish nature would take over my role sometimes. Hurrying is the only way I can get half my to-do list done,' said Mel.

'Ah, but duth the hurrying really make everything go fathter?' asked Randalf.

'Who knows? I haven't tried going slowly,' she replied.

A couple of lizards scuttled past, and after Randalf gave us a botany lesson on various plants and fauna as we walked along the winding path, we came across another plaque.

We must be willing to get rid of the life we've planned, so as to have the life that is waiting for us. The old skin has to shed before the new one can come. ~ Joseph Campbell.

I stood and reread it a few times. I wondered what life was waiting for me, without Greg. 'Could I take a photo of this, Randalf?' I asked.

'Thertainly,' he replied. 'It holdth meaning for you, yeth?'

I nodded.

'Nature ith alwayth rebuilding itthelf, and we mutht too. Whatever happenth, you can alwayth thtart over anew.'

'You're wise for your years, Randalf,' I said.

'My grandfather taught me about the world'th greatetht philothopherth. I've retained much of what I've read over the yearth.'

I must have started a movement, because the others copied my initiative and took a photo of the plaque too.

Randalf continued walking us deep into the rainforest, and a clean, fresh, cool scent hung in the air, the moisture from the surrounding plants and springs enriching me. I felt removed from the outside world, as though in here, problems from the outside world didn't exist. Randalf pointed out some of the wildlife, both on the ground and in the trees. We all sat for a moment in a clearing, spread out, but in our respective groups, to take a break. Randalf encouraged us to keep an eye out for some of the wildlife he'd educated us about, and promised one piece of candy for each correct identification. Mel had never been so keen to learn something new.

As Randalf chatted to the retired couple on apparent death row, Lorena asked me how I was feeling. I relayed my thoughts about being here, and suggested maybe I move in and set up camp to avoid the pain of going back home to the upheaval of my life.

'So how did you know where to find Greg, anyway?' she asked.

A ghost imprinted her vision into my mind. God, it sounded crazy. I couldn't believe it had even happened, could hardly believe any of last night had happened; the vision, the affair, the kiss with Ty...

'Oh, just something he mentioned when I spoke to him on the phone at the pub. And a strong feeling that I had to go there.'

'It's lucky you trusted your instincts,' said Georgie. 'They are hardly ever wrong.'

My instincts had gotten me into the embarrassing mess with Ty though. I'd listened to them and acted on the spur of the moment, and on looking back, I shouldn't have allowed myself to get carried away. But oh... *wow*. Despite my embarrassment at my hormones taking over, a smile softly grew on my face at the memory of his kiss.

'Sal?'

'Huh?'

'You were off with the fairies for a moment.'

'Sorry, um, just thinking about the *Friends* episode I

watched last night. It was funny.'

'When did you watch *Friends*? You said you drove off pretty soon after getting back to the guest house.'

'I did? Maybe I was thinking of another night then.'

'You sure you're okay?' Mel asked. 'Your face is a bit red.'

I touched my cheeks; they were warm, and grew warmer the more I thought of Ty and tried to hide the fact I'd been with him last night.

'Is there something you're not telling us?' asked Lorena. 'Remember, what happens in Barron Springs stays in Barron Springs.'

I looked at each of my friends in turn, trying to decide whether they would think I was a hypocrite if I told them I'd kissed Ty. Here I was, upset about Greg kissing someone else when I'd done the same thing. Granted, I'd officially broken up with him and never would have done it had I not seen Greg with another woman, but still. I felt like I'd broken some sort of rule.

'Okay. I might as well tell you.' I cleared my throat, and leaned in close so the other people wouldn't hear. 'I watched *Friends* at Ty's house last night. On my way back I passed his house and he was outside, um, doing something, so I stopped the car. I was in a bit of a state after seeing Greg, so he brought me inside and made me hot chocolate and tried to cheer me up.'

'Why didn't you just say so? Nothing wrong with that. What's the big deal?' Mel asked.

'The big deal is that we kissed. A lot. And it could have become something much more had he not stopped it from going further.'

There. All out in the open. Like my failed engagement would be, soon enough.

'Wait, what?' Lorena held up her hand. 'You kissed?'

'Did he try to take advantage of you in your vulnerable

state? Because I'll have words with him,' said Georgie.

'No, no, it was nothing like that. He was a perfect gentleman. I was about to leave and we hugged. I thanked him. And then it just sort of happened. I'm quite embarrassed really.'

Mel's eyes were wide. 'Wow. Holy... wow.'

'And he stopped it going further?' asked Lorena.

'Yes, at first I stopped and went to leave again, but then I thought of Greg with that woman, and wanted to, I don't know, get back at him or something. So I kind of threw myself at Ty.' I covered my eyes and lowered my head. 'But he didn't seem to mind. We'd made it to the couch and then he stopped. Said he didn't want to mess me around since I was on the rebound. He thought I deserved better.'

'Better than Greg, that's for sure, but better than Ty? I'm starting to think there's no such thing!' Mel said. 'Oh! I'll have to make you a new T-shirt that says: *I Kissed the Stripper*!'

My friends laughed and I shook my head.

'So, was he a good kisser?'

'Mel!'

'Well, was he?'

I tipped my head back and closed my eyes. 'Fantastic,' I whispered with a cheeky smile.

'Don't you mean, fantathtic?' asked Lorena, and Mel burst out laughing.

'Lorena! Don't be mean!' I whispered. 'Randalf can't help the way he speaks.'

'I'm not being mean, I think he'th abtholutely adorable.'

'Stop! You're making my belly hurt!' Mel laughed.

'He is adorable, isn't he?' I said. 'You can tell how passionate he is about what he does. It's great.'

'And what are you girlth dithcuthing over here?' Randalf asked as he walked over to us.

'We were just saying what a fabulous tour guide you are,

Randalf,' I said. 'We'll be putting in a good word with your boss.' And for some reason I stood and kissed him on the cheek. I was a right old flirt these days.

The guy turned bright red and touched his face. 'I'll never wath my fathe again!' he said in an exaggerated tone, and we all laughed.

We continued our walk and Mel continued shaking her head in amazement at the whole kissing Ty situation. Randalf brought us to a small bridge that crossed a narrow spring, and water ran down the nearby waterfall and under the bridge. 'Now, thith bridge ith conthidered by many a very spethial plathe.' He placed his hands together as though about to pray. 'People have been known to have thpiritual awakeninths here. It ith conthidered a portal to the other world, if you believe that thort of thing.' He raised his eyebrows.

'Well, I do, but I don't think Sally believes in all that life after death stuff, do you Sal?' Mel said.

'Me?' I fiddled with my bag strap. 'Oh, well there's a lot we don't know. I guess I'm... open to the possibility.'

The retired man joked that he'd find out soon enough and let us know.

'Ath you croth the bridge, take a moment to thtop and reflect on any feelingth or awareneth you feel. You may have a thpiritual experienth if that ith part of your dethtined journey.'

Oh great. After Red leaving, now she'd probably come back as soon as I crossed that bridge. I considered asking if we could turn around and go back the way we came but Mel was already on the bridge, excited.

Randalf crossed to the other side, and Mel closed her eyes for a moment as she walked across. 'Well, I think I felt something. Some sort of cold sensation. It could have been something spiritual.' She seemed reasonably pleased. The Chinese couple crossed together and kissed as they stopped in the middle, then smiled. Spiritual experience or no spiritual experience, we all knew what sort of experience they'd be having later tonight.

The retired couple crossed one at a time, the woman saying she felt at peace as she crossed, and the man asking how long it was to the nearest toilet since all the flowing water was stimulating his bladder.

Georgie crossed and performed some kind of martial arts gesture, which she said was to show respect for the natural world, and Lorena crossed with one hand on her belly and a smile on her face.

'Your turn, Sally!' They beckoned from the other side, but I was wary. Now that I knew I could see ghosts, or one of them at least, what if this supposed portal opened the floodgates and a stampede of pyjama-clad, song-singing ghosts bombarded me? It was silly, and probably not going to happen, but after this weekend, *anything* was possible.

I took a breath and stepped onto the bridge, walked a few steps, then stopped. My senses seemed to heighten, the air was rich with the scent of nature and the embrace of cool winter air, and the green hues all around seemed stronger and more vibrant. But that was it. I couldn't see or hear anything otherworldly. I half-expected Red to jump in front of me and say 'boo!' but she didn't.

'Anything, Sal?' asked Mel.

'No, nothing at all,' I replied, and although I felt bad for Red having died young, I was relieved that I didn't have to deal with her hanging around anymore. I crossed the rest of the bridge with confidence in my stride. There'd be a lot more bridges to cross and paths to travel when I started my new life without Greg, but at least I could do it without a ghost by my side. *Yep, I thought, glancing around, only living people and plants surrounding me.* It appeared she was gone for good.

CHAPTER 16

'I'm glad we went,' I said as we arrived back at the guest house after our walk and a nice lunch at The Rainforest Cafe (people around here didn't seem capable of coming up with unique business names). 'Thanks for organising it, Lorena.'

'My pleasure.' She plonked her bag on the kitchen counter. 'Rest of the day we'll take it easy I think. Might put my swollen feet up for a while.'

'Sounds good to me,' Mel agreed.

'I might do that too, then I'll get started on the lamb roast.' Georgie grabbed a glass of water and headed for the couch.

'I better put away all my goodies.' I picked up the gifts from the coffee table that I'd received during Pass the Parcel. My eyes lingered on the silver heart-shaped photo frame and a wave of sadness rolled through my body.

I was going to put a wedding photo in that.

Over two years of my life with Greg and it had come to this? An empty photo frame, never to hold the memory of what would have been our special day. The other gifts fell from my grasp as both my hands held on to the heart. In an instant Lorena was beside me, followed by Mel and Georgie.

'Leave that,' Lorena said. 'I'll put it away.'

She took it from my hands but I stayed where I was, as though the heartbreak had zapped all my energy and my brain had forgotten how to move my muscles.

'C'mon, sit over here.' Mel led me backwards to the couch and I sat, my gaze fixed on my palms where I'd held the frame. Then it started all over again. The pain and hurt built up and rolled out like a wave onto the shore and, once again, my friends held me until I could cry no more.

I needed a sleep, to shut out the world for a while, so I went upstairs and buried myself under the covers. When I awoke, for a moment I forgot all that had happened. That temporary amnesia you sometimes get on waking up was a relief. Then reality shoved all that aside and took centre stage. I switched my phone back on. There were three messages from Greg. I still didn't feel like talking to him.

When I rolled over and sat on the side of the bed, preparing to return to the land of the living and be with my friends, someone cleared their throat.

I flipped my head to the right. Red was back. She stood in the corner of the room, holding her arm awkwardly with her hand and nibbling her bottom lip.

What? 'Why are you still here?' I asked. 'You've done what you came here to do, you can go now.'

'I can't.'

'Why not?'

'There's something else.' She walked towards me slowly. 'I need your help.'

I stood and shook my head. 'You've just helped my marriage break down and now you want *me* to help *you*?'

'Hey, I did you a favour!'

I turned away. 'It's just that... every time I see you I'm reminded of Greg and what he did.'

'Well *excuse* me for helping to stop you from making a huge mistake!'

'I have enough to deal with now, I can't take anymore. You've done your bit, so could you now, please, leave me be?' I went for the door. 'Goodbye, Red.' I pulled the door open.

'Nancy.'

I turned my head slightly. 'What?'

'Nancy. That's my name. Nancy Silverton.'

Although I wanted to close that door behind me and join my friends, hearing her real name triggered the part of me that needed to help people. Nancy. She'd been a real person. A human being. Sure, if it wasn't for her I would have enjoyed this weekend, blissfully unaware of Greg's true nature, but I knew in reality that wasn't preferable. She was right. She *had* done me a favour, as much as I hated to admit it.

'Nancy is your real name?' I asked, sitting on the bed.

'Yep. Named after my grandmother. Who I'm yet to meet over here, not until I... you know... cross over, or whatever it's called.'

'What do you need help with?'

'I need you to get a message to my husband.'

'You have a husband?'

She nodded. 'Well, *had*. I tried to get through to him, but every time I got close all this pain would come hurtling back at me and it was too overwhelming. Besides, he's never really believed in an afterlife. I can't do it alone. I need you to come with me, to go to him.'

'Where does he live?'

'Wattle Falls, it's only twenty minutes or so from here.'

I picked up my phone and opened a web browser. I wasn't looking up Wattle Falls, there was something else I had to find.

I typed 'Nancy Silverton died' into Google. A few results came up that looked like the right ones, and I clicked on the first link, a news website.

I gasped at her photo on the screen. It was her all right. My eyes tried to read as fast as they could, needing to know what happened to her. I got halfway through the article and gasped again. My gaze slowly met hers. 'Suicide?'

She stood and shook her head violently from side to side, her hands covering her ears. 'No, no, no.'

'Red — *Nancy* — you took your own life?'

'No!' she yelled, and I flinched. 'They've got it all wrong. It wasn't suicide. I swear.' She rubbed her forehead, clearly distressed.

I returned to the article to read the rest, and my heart plummeted. 'Why didn't you tell me you had a baby?'

She looked about ready to burst into tears. 'I had to help you first, before I could tell you about me. And...' She pulled at her red curls. 'Oh, it hurts so much! Knowing I'll never get to hold her again, that she'll never know me. And worse, that she'll grow up thinking I left her on purpose. I didn't!'

The article had reported that twenty-eight-year-old Nancy Silverton had taken her life by jumping off a hotel balcony. I rarely watched the news, so I hadn't seen this report, and I doubt Greg had either since he'd been away when it happened. I could understand why they'd concluded it was suicide:

Nancy's husband, Chris, and Nancy's doctor both confirmed that she had been suffering from postnatal depression since the birth of her daughter, Ruby, ten months ago. She seemed to finally be recovering, and was staying at the five-star hotel by herself as a present from Chris. "I wanted her to have a break from her responsibilities, catch up on sleep, have some pampering, but I never considered she'd be suicidal. If I'd known, I wouldn't have let her out of my sight," he said in an interview yesterday.

'He blames himself now. And I worry how he'll cope on his own with Ruby. I need you to tell him the truth, please?'

I put my phone down and moved closer to Nancy. 'What is the truth? What happened?'

She closed her eyes for a minute and took a deep breath. 'I was about to go to bed, and had been thinking about the state of my life. I went out on the balcony to feel the night air on my face. I never told Chris this, but I had been considering leaving him. I didn't think I could cope anymore and had an urge to run and hide, to save them from my depression. But during my stay at the hotel I realised that was stupid. I convinced myself that I was strong, that I could get through this, and as I stood on the balcony and thought about my marriage, I fiddled with my wedding ring. It reminded me of what I'd committed to, and I cried, as memories of our wedding day came to my mind. All the happy things had been invisible to me because of the depression. I couldn't see through the fog, but that night, I finally did. I held the ring up to the moonlight and watched it sparkle, and knew that when I got home things would be different. I wasn't going to give up: on myself, on Ruby, or my marriage.'

I listened intently and hoped none of my friends would come in and disturb us. I was finally seeing Red, *Nancy*, as a person and not just a ghost.

'And then I sneezed. One stupid sneeze and I dropped the ring!' She shook her head. 'It fell and landed between two narrow slits of metal on some sort of pipe or guttering below. It wasn't far, but I wished it had at least fallen onto the ground below so I could have gone downstairs to get it before someone else did. I should have called the hotel reception and asked for help, but silly me thought I could retrieve it myself. I always was a bit stubborn like that.' She managed a brief smile. 'I leaned over the balcony and reached for it, I almost had it, but it had rained earlier that day and the railing must have been a bit slippery. Before I could get my balance my legs were in the air and I was falling. I don't remember much more, only that...' her voice croaked and she cleared her throat, 'only that in an instant I knew that was it. I knew I was going to die.'

Tears worked their way to my eyes as she spoke, and I wanted to hug her, to hold her close and say how sorry I was, but when I put my hand on hers it went straight through.

'I have a vague memory of my funeral, but the next thing I knew I was in your house, looking at that photo of you and Greg. I don't know how I knew, but I just knew what I was there to do. I also knew it wouldn't be pleasant, so I distracted myself with fun things. I felt so free, and all the depression was lifted from my heart. I wanted to experience that joy while I had the chance.'

'Hence the spinning incident in the dryer and on the clothesline?' I offered a lopsided smile.

'Exactly. And I have to admit, I was a bit jealous. Even though I knew Greg was cheating behind your back, I was jealous of you and the whole life you had ahead of you. I guess I wanted to have a bit of fun at your expense. Sorry.' She shrugged.

'You're forgiven,' I said, wiping a tear from my eye. I didn't care anymore, my suffering was nothing compared to her and her family's. I would do whatever I had to do to help her husband discover the truth.

'What's the address?' I picked up my phone and opened the notes app.

'It's 15 Bentley Street, Wattle Falls.' An expression of hope brightened Nancy's pale face.

'I'll do my best, I promise.' I gave her a reassuring smile, then remembered my friends. 'A car. I need a car. What am I going to tell Lorena? I've already disappeared once in her vehicle. Should I tell them about you and explain everything?'

Nancy looked worried. 'Mel will believe you, I think, but I have a feeling Lorena might take a bit of convincing. It could take a while.'

'Hmm, and I don't want to give her any shocks, with the baby and all. Maybe I could just tell her I need some time alone, go for a drive to clear my head?'

Nancy twisted her lips to one side. 'I have a better idea. While you were out with your friends I was working on a backup plan, in case you refused to help.' She raised her finger. 'Wait here. Give me a few minutes, but get yourself ready to go.'

I did as she said and put on my shoes, changed into a different top and jacket, and freshened up in the bathroom.

Nancy returned soon after with a smile on her face. 'I brought the backup plan.'

I furrowed my brow, not understanding what she meant. Then the doorbell rang.

CHAPTER 18

I rushed down the stairs. Ty stood at the front door, Georgie having just opened it. They turned at the sound of my feet clomping down the stairs.

'You have a visitor, Sal,' she said.

I approached the front door, wondering what Nancy meant by 'backup plan'. Ty was shifting from one foot to the other, his eyes wide as though on high alert and he was scratching his arm and his cheek, like I do when I'm nervous or trying to hide something.

He saw her, I remembered. He saw Nancy last night, if only for a brief moment. Had she appeared to him a few minutes ago and freaked him out?

'Hi, hey, how are you? I'm ah...' he said, then gestured behind him with his thumb. 'Could we have a word outside?'

I turned briefly to my friends and motioned out the door with my hand. They seemed curious but understanding. Probably thought we needed to discuss our kiss last night. Which we probably did, but that would have to wait.

I closed the door and we moved to the side of the porch where we weren't visible through the windows, unless my friends were hiding beside one of them with their ears to the wall.

Ty couldn't keep still. 'This is going to sound really weird, and you can tell me to get lost if you like, but... you don't happen to need a lift to Wattle Falls by any chance, do you?' He shoved his hands into his pockets then took them out again.

My mouth gaped open and a surprised sound escaped. 'Oh my God. Yes, I do,' I said, and he exhaled in relief. 'You've seen her again, haven't you? The woman in the purple polka dot pyjamas?'

'Huh? What? Who?' he spoke in short sharp bursts, consistent with his highly confused and agitated state.

I turned to make sure no one was eavesdropping then moved closer to him. 'It's okay, I've seen her too. I was just as shocked as you are now.'

'You don't seem shocked.'

'That's because I've been hanging out with the ghost all weekend. I'm kinda used to her now.' I smiled.

'Whoa, this is...' He ran his hands through his short, dark strands of hair. 'Is this for real? Did someone put something in our drinks last night, or maybe that hot chocolate was a bit dodgy, I don't know.'

'Ty, it's real. Her name's Nancy and she's, well, she's not like us.' I gestured to our bodies. 'Only we can see her.'

'That's because you two are the most receptive.'

We both snapped our heads to the direction of the voice that had suddenly appeared beside us.

'Argh!' Ty flinched and stumbled backwards a little, regaining his balance and taking hold of the column attached to the porch. I'd never seen him so freaked out; all his confidence and certainty was gone. 'How is this possible? What's going on?' Confused mumblings kept launching from his mouth.

'I think it's because you're both in the caring professions or something, I'm not sure. Or that you've both had a big impact on your lives by death. Makes you more receptive to other energies, like mine.'

'What? I haven't lost anyone,' I said.

'I mean your patients,' she explained. 'You've been around death a lot. And, Ty, I'm sorry about your parents.'

He eyed us both and mumbled an awkward, 'Thanks.'

I spoke to Ty. 'Nancy was the one who told me where to find Greg last night. If it wasn't for her I wouldn't have found out the truth.'

'So, you were, like, sent here to help Sally or something?' Ty asked.

'Something like that,' she replied. 'But also because I...'

'She needs our help,' I said.

'Right. And I take it this has something to do with Wattle Falls? She wouldn't leave me alone until I drove here to offer you a lift. Kept freaking me out and badgering me with flying objects.' He slid a slightly annoyed glance in Nancy's direction.

I held back a chuckle, I could imagine her doing that. She'd freaked me out too at first, but now things had changed I could look at the situation more objectively. Ty was still in the processing stage, trying to decide if he was hallucinating or really seeing the spirit of someone who had died.

'Sorry about that,' she said. 'I had to get you here today, before Sally goes home tomorrow.'

Ty and I exchanged a knowing glance. Today, that's all we had. Not much time to make sense of what had happened last night or decide where to go from here. Though I knew there was no way I could start anything with him with all that had happened. Like he'd said, I was on the rebound, very *freshly* on the rebound, and last night was a mistake. Enjoyable and extremely pleasant, but a mistake nonetheless. I dropped my gaze when it strayed to his lips and I remembered what they'd felt like.

'Wattle Falls is where I lived. Where my husband still lives.' Nancy dropped her gaze too.

I explained everything to Ty. I kept it fairly brief so as to not upset Nancy with the memory, but gave him enough detail so that he knew how important it was to set things right. Not that he was obligated to meet Nancy's husband with me, but a lift and some moral support would be welcome.

Ty looked at Nancy with less fear and confusion in his eyes and more sympathy. His posture straightened a little and his fidgeting had stopped. 'I'll help. We'll both help you.' His eyes garnered my agreement.

Nancy smiled. 'Thank you, so much.'

Ty smiled too. 'All in a day's work.' He glanced at me and I grinned. His job description was becoming more varied by the minute. 'Nice PJs by the way,' he said to Nancy.

A warm feeling grew inside me. *Now that's the Ty I've come to know!*

❧

After telling the girls Ty was taking me for a leisurely country drive (and winking at them so they assumed we wanted to be alone to discuss last night), we left for Wattle Falls. Nancy said if she disappeared occasionally it was only because she was nervous. But she promised she'd be there when we met her husband.

'Thanks for doing this,' I said to Ty. 'I'm guessing it's not every day a woman asks you to drive her to a widower's house to tell him his dead wife has a message for him.'

'Doesn't happen that often, no,' he replied. Every now and

again he'd shake his head in disbelief and say, 'I can't believe it. I can't believe this is happening.'

I was relieved someone else knew about her. I didn't feel so weird anymore.

'So she was here this whole weekend? Even when I was at the house?' Ty asked.

'Yep. All the time.'

'During my strip?'

I chuckled. '*Especially* during your strip. If only you could have seen her then. Her dancing was nowhere near as good as yours though.'

Ty clicked his fingers. 'That's why you laughed. I'm right, yes?'

'Yes. She was mocking your movements and I was having trouble keeping my composure. That's why I said out loud that I wanted it to stop.'

'You said 'red', what was that about?'

'That's what I called her up until this afternoon, when she finally revealed her name.'

Ty tipped his head back in understanding. 'Red. Good nickname,' he said. 'The candles on the dinner table that night, was that her?'

'Correct.'

'And what about the Winter Solstice Festival, was she there too?'

I cringed at the memory. 'My little performance? Courtesy of Her Royal Ghostness. She was tugging me sideways and I had to keep resisting, to stay with my friends. Before I knew it I'd camouflaged the awkward situation with line-dancing. Got into the spirit of it and thought, "what the heck?"'

'Ha! I knew there was something more going on with you. And the gemstone down your top?'

'Red's fault.'

Ty laughed. 'Sounds like she's been the life of the party.'

'Ironic, hey? Oh, and you can also blame her for the bruise on your foot. I was trying to dislodge her from my shopping trolley.'

'Aha, so that's why you were going so fast around the corner.' He slowed as a car ahead stopped to turn off the road, then resumed normal speed. 'And let me guess, she's the reason you got stuck in the pub toilets?'

'Oh God. I'm so embarrassed about that.' I shook my head. 'She made the lock break, and well, I made my own trouble from then on.'

Ty laughed again. 'What a sight that was, seeing you stuck under that door. Barron Springs has never been so entertaining.'

'Gee, thanks. I'll probably go down in history as the "toilet woman" or something.'

'Nah, to me you'll always be Sexy Sally.' He smiled, and our midnight rendezvous jumped to the front of my mind again. It must have jumped to Ty's too, because he didn't say anything further for the next few minutes.

'Ty,', 'Sally,' we both spoke at the same time.

'Sorry, you go,' he said.

'I was going to say... last night, it was... well, I don't ever do things like that. I'm not normally like that. I don't want you to think...'

'I don't think anything bad about you. I was concerned for you, and I let my attraction to you take over. I'm sorry.'

The idea that a hot-as-fire stripper thought of me as attractive was as difficult to believe as the idea of seeing ghosts. I never thought someone like him would be drawn to a Plain Jane like me.

'Don't be sorry. I'm extremely flattered.' I could feel my face becoming pink as we spoke. 'And it was... amazing, last night.

But you were right. It all happened too fast, and we should probably just leave it in the past.'

He clamped his lips together and nodded.

'Wait, you two did the hokey-pokey last night? How did I not know this?' Nancy suddenly piped up, sitting in the back seat and leaning forward between us in the front.

'Oh, hello again,' I said. 'And no, we didn't do the "hokey-pokey" as you call it, not that it's any of your business, you nosey thing.' I shot her a teasing look.

'Oh, so you like, just kissed or something?'

'Gee, you are a nosey thing, aren't you?' Ty said.

'Well there's a slight shortage of gossip on my side of the world and I could do with a fix,' she explained. 'So was it good? Is he better than Greg, Sally?'

'Nancy!' I exclaimed. 'I think that's enough of this topic. Discussion over.' I glared at her in embarrassment, but when Ty's focus turned back to the road I eyed her and gave surreptitious thumbs-up sign. She bounced up and down in satisfaction.

'I think you two would make a great couple,' she added. 'Ty and Sally. Sally and Ty. Tysally. Has a nice ring to it.' She tapped her chin.

'Enough,' I said, though I knew she was just trying to distract from the upcoming task. The distraction was temporary, though, and she gulped as we slowed and turned into Bentley Street, Wattle Falls, then pulled up outside number 15.

CHAPTER 19

The cute, white, weatherboard house screamed 'family home', a place to raise kids and live a happy-ever-after. But this homely facade concealed a deep grief within and a secret that would have remained hidden had Nancy Silverton not haunted me.

'Here goes,' I said, drawing a deep breath and walking to the front door, flowers and chocolates in my hands, and Ty by my side. Before knocking, I turned around. Nancy hung back, her ghostly body seeming tense and unsure. 'C'mon,' I encouraged. 'It'll be okay.'

She came to my side and breathed deeply too, though how ghosts could breathe I had no idea. Maybe it was a residual habit from living almost thirty years in the human body.

'It hurts,' she said. 'I can feel his pain. The emptiness, the guilt, the sadness. I'm not sure I can handle it.'

'You can. Just think how much better it will be when he knows the truth. I mean, not *better*, but he'll have closure. He'll be able to move on.'

'You're right. I know. Okay, let's do this.'

Ty knocked on the door with a firm rap of his knuckles, and

despite my nervousness I noticed how masculine and strong his hands looked. Somehow they gave me a feeling of strength, an assurance that I could handle this. That *we* could handle this.

Ty was about to knock again when footsteps sounded inside. The door opened inwards and the doorway framed a tall man with a slim build, light brown hair, and a pallor that I'd seen many times in my career. The pallor of grief. Of loss. Even if I didn't know who he was, I would have deduced that he'd been through something traumatic or lost someone close to him.

I offered a kind smile.

'Can I help you?' he asked, and the sound of a baby's mumblings could be heard within the house. Nancy made a sound, a cross between a gasp and a cry. Her daughter was inside, and she wouldn't be able to hold her.

'Hi, Chris?' I said. 'My name's Sally, I knew your wife, Nancy.'

'Oh,' he said.

'I wanted to offer my condolences, and give you these.' I handed him the flowers and the chocolates.

'Chocolate macadamia nuts,' he said, eyeing the box Nancy had picked out when we stopped at the service station for petrol and gifts.

'She told me they're your favourite.'

Chris's gaze connected with mine, and this seemed to comfort him a little.

'She did? Yes, they are. Thank you, that's very kind.'

'If you like I can come in and put the flowers in water for you?' I peered beyond him, hoping I wasn't being too forward.

'How did you know Nancy, exactly?' he asked, obviously unsure whether to invite a stranger into his house.

Oh gosh, we hadn't thought this through properly. I didn't even think! We should have come prepared with a list of possible questions and answers, like a FAQ list. If Lorena was here she would have thought of it.

I glanced surreptitiously at Nancy, whose hand was over her mouth at the emotional impact of seeing her husband again. She quickly composed herself, and said, 'Tell him you were my nurse a few years back, when I broke my arm.'

'I was her nurse, a few years back when she broke her arm. We got along well and kept in contact ever since.'

'Oh. Right. I don't remember her ever mentioning a Sally. Then again, we only knew each other for about two years. Marriage and a baby happened so fast. There's probably a lot I never got to find out about my wife.' He lowered his head and appeared to go deep into thought, then snapped his head up. 'Sorry, yes, I'd be grateful if you could put these in some water.' He stepped back to allow us to enter, and Ty put his hand out for a handshake.

'I'm Tyler, a friend—'

'Say boyfriend! No, say fiancé,' Nancy directed.

'I'm, ah, Sally's fiancé.' He cleared his throat and I scratched my head. Maybe Nancy wanted us to look as together and normal as possible.

Chris shook Ty's hand. 'Hi.'

We stepped into the house, and Chris ducked his head into another room, obviously to check on his daughter who sounded like she wanted company, then returned to us and led us to the kitchen. He lifted a vase from a high shelf and handed it to me. 'You can bring them into the living room through there,' he pointed, 'I better check Ruby.'

I turned on the tap and filled the vase with water, and Ty took the paper from the flowers and placed the colourful display into the vase. I raised my eyebrows at him as if to say 'so far so good'. Ty carried them into the living room and placed them on the dining table at the end of the room, next to the bay window that had a picturesque view of the street outside.

'Thanks,' Chris said, picking up Ruby from her walker. 'Have you met Ruby?'

I stepped closer and smiled at the chubby baby with a light layer of red curls on her head. 'No, I haven't. Hello little one,' I said in the usual accent reserved for speaking to human beings under the age of three. I took Ruby's small hand and gave it a wiggle. She gripped my finger and giggled. 'She's gorgeous,' I said to Chris. 'And has her mother's hair.' I regretted saying that last bit, as Chris' expression became sadder.

'She's a real cutie,' Ty said, offering his finger too. Ruby swapped mine for his, her whole hand barely wrapping around it.

I turned to look at Nancy. She stood at the entrance to the living room, her arms hugged tightly around her body, her face filled with despair. I wanted to comfort her, but I couldn't. We had to pretend she wasn't here in order to have a chance of building up to telling Chris the truth.

'She's a good girl,' Chris said. 'I just wish she'd sleep through the night. Ever since... it happened... she's been extra wakeful.'

The poor guy. Grief and sleep deprivation to add to the mix.

'A back massage can sometimes help,' I suggested. 'Baby's usually love it. A warm bath and a gentle massage before bed might make a difference.' I hoped he didn't mind me offering my advice, I often found myself doing that when anyone presented their problems.

'Thanks, I guess I've been too tired to do anything but the essentials. Might give it a go.' He returned Ruby to her walker. A small advantage of losing her mother so young was that she wouldn't feel the same grief as her father. Sure, I bet she missed her mother, but babies at that age were adaptable and generally warmed to whoever warmed to them, whoever fed and changed and comforted them. Later, when she grew up, when she transformed into a young woman. That's when it would really hit. That's when she'd need her mum the most.

'Can I get you a coffee or tea?' Chris asked.

I eyed Ty, whose expression said 'it's up to you'. 'Um, thanks, but I don't want to put you to any trouble. I was just hoping to, ah, discuss a few things about Nancy if that's okay. I was so shocked to hear the news, but I wanted you to know how much I admired her.'

Chris gave a small smile. 'Take a seat,' he said, gesturing to the couch. Ty and I sat there while he sat on the armchair next to it.

'Nancy is — *was* — such a vibrant, funny, friendly person,' I said, aware that there was no way I would have said that before, after what she'd put me through. But now I meant it. And I was starting to understand how she must have been in real life.

'It's funny you say that, because that's what I miss about her most. Her energy. Her enthusiasm.' He shook his head and rubbed his temple. 'I missed it even when she was alive, though, ever since the...'

'The depression,' I finished for him.

'Yes. It took all that away. She lost that spark that made her who she was and it was heartbreaking to see. It's not how I want to remember her.'

'Then don't.' I leaned forward in support, like he was a relative of a patient who'd died. 'Remember the energy, the enthusiasm, the joy she had. She'd want that.'

He nodded, and I hoped he wouldn't start crying, because I didn't want to upset him, and I didn't want Nancy to lose it and run off.

'Did you know her too?' Chris asked Ty.

He opened his mouth but didn't speak right away, obviously

formulating an answer in his mind. 'No. I never met her, but from what Sally told me, I know she must have been a great person. Someone who was fun to have around, and very... determined, I think.'

'She did like to get her own way,' Chris mused with a smile. 'Always liked to be right. And she was such a practical joker.' He eyed the side table, which displayed a photo of her pulling a funny face.

'Oh yes, I'm sure she was,' I replied.

Nancy seemed to be coping better, and came closer, perching herself on the arm of the couch between Chris and us. I shifted on the spot and tried to think how to steer the conversation to where it needed to go. 'And I'm sure she's at peace now, watching over you and Ruby.' I swallowed a hard lump.

Chris seemed unsure. 'Well, I hope she's at peace, if that's even possible. Everyone says she must still be with me, in spirit, but that seems a bit far-fetched to me. I know they're just being nice. She's gone, and we have to get on with life as best as we can.'

'But I'm here, honey, I'm here!' Nancy cried, by her husband's side.

My heart ached, and Ty spoke up. 'When my parents died, I thought that too, that they were just gone. But after a while I felt more,' he circled his hands, 'I don't know, *open*, that some small part of them still existed. It gave me strength, believing they might still be with me in some way.'

The ache in my heart turned to overwhelming gratitude for Ty. That he was here, and that he was actively trying to help me get through to Chris. I wanted to squeeze his hand but hesitated, then remembered we were supposed to be a couple. I put my hand on top of his and squeezed it, his warmth radiating up my arm. He glanced at it with raised eyebrows, then must have remembered the facade too because he lifted my hand and kissed it. Softly, tenderly. Nancy noticed our moment and a brief smile flashed on her face.

'I guess it can make things a bit easier, having some sort of belief like that,' Chris said, his gaze hovering on our entwined hands. 'Don't ever take what you have for granted,' he said. 'Make the most of your life together, and talk about life when it gets hard. Don't push things under the carpet or assume everything's all right. I wish I'd been able to help her more,' he added.

Nancy sat back down on the edge of the couch, shoulders sinking.

'You did the best you could, I know she loved you, and by the looks of things you're doing a great job with Ruby.' I watched her play with the various buttons and amusements on her walker.

'She keeps me going, to be honest. I have to keep going strong, for her.'

I eyed Ty and we exchanged a knowing glance. He needed to know, and soon. We couldn't outstay our welcome and had to make progress.

'You know, after reading the news report about Nancy, there's something that just didn't feel right about it,' I said.

Chris looked me in the eye. 'What do you mean?'

'The Nancy I knew, she was so excited about her future, about becoming a mother. I just can't believe it's true.'

'Well, the depression obviously took its toll. It took all that desire for life away. I thought she was getting better, but I guess I was wrong.' His voice quivered on the last word, and Nancy moved away and hugged her chest again.

'I don't think you were wrong. I think she *was* getting better. It's possible she could have just... fallen.'

Chris straightened in the chair, and I knew things were getting awkward but I had to try my best.

'I agree,' said Ty.

'No,' Chris said. 'She'd given up. She didn't even have her wedding ring on when they found her. I had a feeling she was considering leaving me, and this confirms it.'

'But I changed my mind, Chris! I wanted to start over!' Nancy urged him to hear her.

'What if she dropped the ring and tried to get it? Did the police consider that as a possibility?'

Chris seemed to consider this seriously, then as though the effort in believing it was too much, he returned to his denial. 'No, they concluded that it was clearly suicide, with her history. It makes sense.'

I bit my lips in frustration.

Ty fidgeted on the couch.

'Chris, I know you hardly know me, but I knew Nancy. And I believe that she didn't take her own life.'

Chris stood. 'What does it matter? She's gone, and there's nothing I can do about it.' He held his arms to the side. 'I thought we were going to discuss memories of Nancy, not how she died. I've gone over this way too many times in my head and I don't particularly want to do it again.' He stood closer to us, as though subtly telling us it was time to leave. We stood.

'Oh yes, I understand. I'm sorry, I didn't mean to upset you.' We walked to the entry foyer. This was it, our last chance.

'You know,' said Ty. 'I work with disabled people, and one of them is in a wheelchair from a fall. When he was unconscious in hospital, they thought it had been a suicide attempt as he was going through a hard time. It was only when he woke up and told them that he'd fallen from the roof of his double-storey house because he wanted to get a better view of the local fireworks that the truth was revealed. If he'd never woken up, they never would have known.'

Wow. I mouthed a 'thank you' to Ty as our eyes met.

Chris raised his eyebrows. 'Interesting. I wish Nancy could come back for a minute to tell me what happened that night. Then again, if it was indeed suicide I don't think I could cope with hearing the details.'

A spark of resolve shot through me. Enough. He had to know. 'It wasn't suicide,' I blurted. 'I know that for a fact.'

Ty cleared his throat and Chris stepped backwards a little. 'And how do you know that?' He crossed his arms.

I glanced at Nancy and she nodded.

'Because she told me herself.' I approached Chris carefully, ironically like someone would approach a person who was about to jump off a building, my palms facing him in preparation. 'I know this is hard to believe, I didn't believe it at first, but I've seen your wife. I've seen her spirit. She came to me so I would come to you and tell you the truth. She wants you to know it was an accident.'

Chris held up his hands and shook his head repeatedly. 'Oh no, no way. And I thought you were genuine, coming here and telling me nice things about my wife. No, that's not on. Why make something up like this?'

'I'm not, I swear. It's real.'

'It's true,' said Ty. 'Yesterday I wouldn't have believed her myself, but today I saw her too. She's here now.'

'Oh my God, I can't believe it. Both of you, as deluded as each other! I think you can go now.'

'But, Chris, she *is* here. She told me what happened. She took off her wedding ring because she was admiring it in the moonlight and was planning to start fresh with you and Ruby, but she dropped it.'

'Please go.' He opened the front door and gestured outside.

'She dropped it and tried to grab it, but fell. It's the truth!'

'Please believe her, Chris! I'm here!' Nancy stomped her foot.

'C'mon,' Ty whispered, hooking his arm with mine. 'We tried.'

'But!' I tried to resist but Ty led me outside. 'Nancy, do something, make something move, show him you're here!'

'Oh for God's sake! Go, now.' Chris exclaimed, ushering us out and closing the door behind us.

Nancy had gone outside too and was now crying, hunched on the front steps and sobbing with such heartache that tears welled in my own eyes.

It was too late. We should have planned this better. Should have had solutions ready for the disbelief that would be expected when confronted with something so hard to believe.

I turned to Ty and he wrapped me in his arms. 'Why can't he just believe me? Look at her! You see her too, right?'

'Yes, I see her,' Ty replied. 'Give him time. He might come around to the idea at another stage, once he's had a chance to think.' He rubbed my back and I gripped the backs of his shoulders.

'C'mon, we better leave in case he calls the police or something.'

We walked, arms around each other, back to the car. 'I'm so sorry, Nancy, so sorry,' I said. Nancy slowly followed us, her body trembling with tears.

She sniffed and looked at me. 'You did your best, I know that.' She tried to compose herself. 'God, why does he have to be so stubborn?'

'Men can be like that,' said Ty. 'But like I said, give him some time and he may come around.'

I nodded. 'Yeah, you're right. I'll come back. I'll come back,

Nancy, after a while, and try again. I'll keep coming back and keep trying until he believes.'

'You will?' Nancy asked.

'You bet your purple polka dot pyjamas I will.' I offered her a smile.

A hint of hope brightened her eyes.

'Maybe you could write a letter first,' suggested Ty. 'Get it all out on paper, send it to him. He might be more open-minded when there's not some stranger in his living room.'

'Yes, can you do that, Sally?'

'Absolutely, and maybe you can tell me things about your life, things that only you two would know, so he's more likely to believe me.'

Nancy whacked her forehead. 'Why didn't I think of that? I was so overwhelmed with emotion and grief it didn't cross my mind.'

'Nor mine,' I said. 'Do you think we should go back in and try now?'

'Not now,' said Ty. 'He won't let us back in. A letter would be perfect.'

'You're probably right. Okay then, I'll do that, I'll write a letter. I'll write ten if I have to.'

'If you need me to help, let me know.' Ty patted my back then unlocked the car.

I stood and looked at him, and realised how far off my first impressions of him had been. 'I don't know what I would have done without you this weekend,' I said.

He turned from the car to face me. 'You would have been fine, I'm sure.' He wiped a tear from my cheek. 'But things are always better with someone by your side.'

I smiled and got into the car, and when he slipped into the driver's seat and put his hand on the gearstick, I grasped it and gave it a firm, appreciative squeeze. He looked at me with beautiful, deep, hypnotic brown eyes, interlocked his fingers with mine and squeezed my hand right back.

***

Despite not needing vehicular transportation to travel, Nancy sat in the back seat for the trip back to Barron Springs. She didn't speak the whole way, and had her eyes closed like she was sleeping.

Ty drove into the driveway of the guest house and parked his car behind Lorena's.

'Coffee before you go back home?' I asked.

'Mmm, it's tempting.'

'Consider yourself tempted,' I replied.

He smiled as he got out of the car.

'The runaway medicos are back!' Lorena said as we walked through the front door. 'Have fun?'

Ty and I exchanged glances. It was by no means fun, but despite Chris' unwillingness to consider my revelation, a calm sense that all would eventually be okay had washed over me during the drive back. 'Not as much fun as you all had by the looks of things!' I gestured to the coffee table that was laden with afternoon snacks; chocolates, potato chips, dips and crackers, though half of everything had been devoured.

'You'd think I starved you all up until now,' said Georgie.

'Bottomless pit,' said Mel, rubbing her stomach.

The aroma of roasting lamb, garlic, onions, and fennel filled the air and brought with it a comforting, safe feeling. 'How will you fit in a roast dinner after all that?' I asked.

'As I said, bottomless pit.' Mel said, then yawned.

'And one can always work up an appetite for good food, isn't that right, Georgie?' said Ty.

'That is true,' she replied. 'You want to stay for dinner, and bring your brother over too?'

Ty opened his mouth and was about to speak, when the loud crunch of car tires on the pebbled driveway turned our attention outside through the open door. The pull of the handbrake sounded, and I walked to the entrance to see who our visitor was. Parked in the driveway was a very familiar silver Audi.

CHAPTER 20

'Greg! What are you doing here?' I said, as my now ex-fiancé got out of the car.

'What do you think? I've come to take you home so we can sort out this situation,' he said gruffly, inviting himself in. 'Better get your bags.' He stopped when he saw everyone looking at him, Georgie's arms crossed and Lorena and Mel eyeing him with disgust. Ty stepped next to me with an air of authority about him.

'Who's this?' Greg asked, looking Ty up and down.

'This is someone you'd do well to look up to. Could teach you a thing or two about being a real man.'

'Sally! Don't speak to me like that.' Greg's brow furrowed.

'She can speak to you any way she wants after what you've done,' said Georgie, stepping closer.

Greg held out his hands. 'Calm down, everyone. Sally and I need some privacy to work a few things out. It's all a big misunderstanding. C'mon, grab your bags and we can go.'

I planted my hands on my hips. 'I'm not going anywhere, thank you very much. But you, you can just go back home and leave me alone.'

'I came all this way; you can't turn me away.'

I shook my head. 'You are unbelievable.' I glanced at my friends and gave them a nod, telling them to give us a minute.

'Ah, Ty, want to help me get those coffees?' asked Georgie.

He caught my gaze, and his expression said 'will you be okay?' I nodded.

Lorena and Mel stepped back into the living area near the couch, giving us some privacy at the front entrance, but still close enough that they'd be able to hear anything said in a raised voice.

'Look,' I said. 'I know there are things to discuss, practicalities mostly, but as for us, our relationship, there's nothing to discuss. You broke my heart, Greg.' I said with a strained face. 'There's no excuse for what you did. I could never trust you again.'

'But, Sal, sweetheart, it all just happened in the excitement of the buck's weekend, I wasn't really thinking.'

'You told me your buck's weekend would last for both Friday and Saturday night. But obviously you failed to tell me that the Saturday night agenda was a rendezvous with a willing woman. Sounds like that was planned ahead of time to me.'

He shifted onto his other foot and leaned on the doorframe. 'If you must know, I did plan that night with her, but only so I could end things.'

'From what I saw it looked like things were just getting started.' I shot my words at him like an arrow.

'Look, after all that, I told her I needed to put a stop to things. It's not going to happen again, I promise.'

'That's not the point!' I fumed. 'The point is you did it. You knew full well what you were doing and didn't have the willpower to control yourself. I can't believe you would be so weak.'

'Weak? Weak!' He raised his voice. 'If I was weak I would

still be with her. I'd say it was pretty gutsy of me to drive out here and fight for you.'

'Futile, more like it.' I crossed my arms.

'Don't be like that, honey.'

'Don't call me honey or sweetheart, or anything like that. You lost that right.'

Greg sighed. 'Look, I know you're upset, and I know I've been a fool. But we're so good together, you and I. We're all set with the house, and the wedding, and we can't cancel everything now!'

'Yes we can, in fact, my friends are already onto it, aren't you, girls?' I turned back to them.

'Too right. All the arrangements will be cancelled by end of Tuesday,' said Lorena. 'And don't worry, Greg, we won't burden you with anything that might disrupt your schedule or social life. Leave it with us.'

'You can't do that! This is between Sally and me. It's not your call.'

'It's my call,' I said. 'And they're going to help me. Since we've been planning the whole thing anyway without your help.'

Greg shook his head and rubbed his forehead. His voice took on a softer tone. 'Sally. I can't be without you. Please. Let's at least go home and talk properly.'

I shook my head and tightened my crossed arms.

'I'll spend my life making it up to you. And it was just a one-off indiscretion. I'm not a bad guy.'

'Oh really? Well a little birdie told me that you have a thing for dating multiple women. If only I knew beforehand that when you started dating me, I was the other woman!'

His eyes widened as he looked at me.

'Oh yes. That's right. I know all about Nancy.' I nodded my head and raised my eyebrows.

'Who's Nancy?' asked Mel.

I waved her question away, aware that I probably shouldn't bring up the topic of having a ghost in the house.

'What? How did you...'

'It doesn't matter how I found out, only that I did. I know what you're really like now. Now I get you. You're a man that will never be happy being monogamous. You want someone at home to take care of you, and someone else to give you a bit of extra excitement.'

'What I need is you, Sally.'

'No, what you need can be found in the Yellow Pages under 'domestic services' and 'escort services'. And maybe you could add a live-in nurse for variety.'

'You're being ridiculous.'

'Me? I'm ridiculous?' I was aware this was escalating and we probably wouldn't get anywhere, but boy-oh-boy did it feel good to have a go at him!

Greg's face creased with sadness and a little fear, and he tried the whole 'puppy dog' look. Like he used to do after a slight argument about some menial domestic issue. But it wasn't endearing, it was pathetic.

'I can't live without you, Sal, what will I do? You're my world. I need you.'

I eyed him silently for a moment, taking in his words and figuring out how to put an end to our debate. I stood straight, squared my shoulders and said, 'You may need me, Greg. But I sure as hell don't need you.' I grabbed the edge of the door and flung it closed: the last thing I saw was the look of shock and surprise on his face as he stepped back to avoid being hit. I had physically and metaphorically closed the door on our relationship for good.

I stood still, staring at the closed door and processing what had happened. Then I turned around. My friends all walked towards me slowly, preparing to catch me should I fall, looks of concern on their faces. But instead of crying and collapsing at the realisation that my potential marriage had ended, a surprising sensation rose within. A sudden, burst of laughter shot from my mouth. Then another, and another. 'I really told him where to shove it, didn't I!'

Mel burst out laughing too. 'That was movie-worthy, Sal. You even had the slamming door and everything!'

'Yeah, what's gotten into you this weekend?' asked Lorena. 'What happened to prim and proper, polite and courteous Sally Marsh?'

I glanced at Nancy who was sitting on the foot of the stairs with a big grin on her face. 'I've had some opportunities to practise my assertiveness this weekend. Who would have thought telling people off could be so much fun?' I grinned.

Mel gave a few slow claps, then the others joined in, applauding my resolve to resist Greg's apology. If I hadn't met Nancy, I probably would have at least gone home with Greg to discuss the problem in detail, let him explain how things came to this. But it didn't matter. I wasn't interested in finding out, and it wouldn't have made any difference. I wasn't prepared to be with someone who clearly preferred to be with someone else. It was over, and I didn't want to waste any more time in moving on with my life.

'You did good, sunshine,' said Ty, reaching his hand out for a friendly tap on my arm.

'Thanks.' I smiled. Sure, I wouldn't be surprised if the tears came back later. There'd be a process to go through, as there was with any emotional upheaval. But it was okay, I'd be okay. I'd just ride the waves until they settled on the shore and calmed down into a gentle ebb and flow.

'Coffees all round?' asked Georgie.

'Yes please,' I said. 'And hand me some of those crunchy

things.' I pointed to some sort of breadstick-slash-lavash thingy, made to be eaten with creamy dip.

Mel dipped one and handed it to me.

'Dinner will be ready in about an hour or so, so don't eat too much. And will you be joining us, Ty?' she asked.

'I'll stay for that coffee, but then I'll go. I've used up a lot of your fantastic hospitality, but it's your last night here. I think you girls should enjoy it together.' He pressed his lips together and smiled. 'What time do you have to check out tomorrow?'

'We'll leave here at ten am,' said Lorena.

Ty nodded. 'I'll pop over before you leave, to say goodbye.'

Never had that word sounded so uncomfortable. I gulped when I realised something...

I didn't want to say goodbye.

CHAPTER 21

The next morning I stood outside the guest house with Ty, preparing to do the inevitable. Sure, I'd probably see him again sometime — I still had to try to reach Chris Silverton again — but my bridal bonding weekend had come to an end. Along with my wedding.

Last night the four of us (actually, make that five, with our invisible guest) sat by the fire in our pyjamas (Nancy felt right at home), eating food, laughing and crying over a couple of chick flicks. It was perfect. And Nancy behaved, allowing me to enjoy a relaxing night with my best friends, and allowing her a chance to have something she'd never have again: the company of friends. Even though I was the only one who knew she was there. I think it gave her comfort too, after the disaster with Chris. And I was reminded of how important friends were. Men may come and go, but a good friend will always be there.

'Bye, Ty, I...' *Oh no, I'm rhyming again!*

He chuckled.

'I'm glad we met,' I continued. 'Thanks for your help with the situation yesterday.' I glanced towards Lorena and Georgie, putting things in the car, to make sure they couldn't hear. Mel was still inside packing her stuff. 'And thanks for rescuing me from the toilet, for playing Twister, and... for your support during my crisis.' I gave a smile.

'Anytime, sunshine.' He smiled, took my left hand and brought it to his lips. I was sure I was blushing, though the winter sun above us was warmer than it had been the last couple of days. Just before he lowered my hand a sparkle caught my eye. My engagement ring. I'd forgotten to take it off!

I brought my hand close to my face and fiddled with the ring. 'I'm so used to wearing this I didn't even notice I still had it on,' I said.

'Sometimes we don't fully see the things that are right in front of us,' he said, and I wondered if his words had a double meaning. 'Are you going to leave it on for a while?'

'No. I can't. It needs to come off.' I fiddled with it some more and drew a deep breath. 'Here goes.' I slid the ring along my finger, slowly, my last gesture to sever all ties to Greg, until it was free and my finger felt strangely naked. I opened my handbag and popped the ring into the coin holder of my purse. I had every right to sell it for a profit, but I'd give it back to Greg. I just wanted to be free of it.

Ty grasped my hand and ran his thumb over my naked finger. 'You'll have to give this a bit of strategic sun exposure to even out the tan line.'

'Huh,' I said, noticing the white band from where the ring had lived for eight months. 'And I thought I didn't tan much.'

'How do you feel?' he asked.

I twisted my lips and gazed at the sky. 'Tired. Sad. But free, and hopeful.' I looked at my finger again and gasped.

'What is it?'

'The ring. Nancy's ring!' I looked around for her. She was wandering aimlessly around the garden, but caught my eye and I gestured discreetly for her to come over. Luckily, Lorena and

Georgie appeared deep in conversation and were no doubt giving me and Ty some privacy to say our goodbyes. 'Nancy, did they ever find your wedding ring?'

She thought for a moment. 'No, I don't believe they did. Oh, poor Chris probably thought I pawned it or threw it out or something!'

'Tell me again, what date did you, um...'

'Die?'

I nodded, and she told me. I thought back from then to now and couldn't recall that we'd had any rain during that time. The ring could still be stuck between those bits of metal outside the hotel window!

'Oh my God, do you think it's still there?'

'It could be! Are you able to go there somehow, get a glimpse and see if it is?' I asked, unsure of the logistics of her ghostly transport capabilities.

She shook her head. 'I can't, not by myself. Just thinking about it overwhelms me with grief. Like when I tried to visit Chris the first time.'

'Okay, don't worry. What if we could go there and have a look?' I turned to Ty. 'If I could get the ring and return it to Chris, he might believe me!'

'You might be onto something there,' he said, then looked at Nancy. 'What hotel were you in and what was your room number?'

I got a little thrill at the reminder that he could see her too.

'The Renshaw. Room 814.'

'Hang on,' Ty said, plucking his phone from his pocket and swiping the screen.

'What are you doing?' I asked.

'Calling them to ask if we can get into the room.'

'We?'

'Yeah. You don't think I'm letting you deal with this on your own, do you? I know you have bendy and stretchy arms, but I'm not letting you dangle over that balcony.'

I smiled. 'What, now?'

'I'm cool with that if you are.' He tipped his head towards my friends. 'And I can drive there, then drive you home.'

'You sure? If we'll be allowed in, then yes, let's go.'

Nancy jumped on the spot.

Ty moved a bit further away so Lorena and Georgie wouldn't hear. A little while later he slipped his phone back into his pocket and returned to my side. 'All set. They wouldn't let us in without booking a room, so we can have the room at one pm. But no longer than an hour, they have a guest arriving at three or four.'

'Great! Okay, I'll tell the girls.'

Mel walked out of the house at that moment, accompanied by her bags and a slight hangover. 'Ow, too bright,' she said, putting her bags down to withdraw sunglasses and put them over her eyes. 'Hi, Ty. And bye, I guess. Was an absolute treat having you grace us with your presence this weekend,' she said.

'It was my pleasure.' He lifted Mel's hand and kissed it too, then took her bags to the car for her. Still a big suck. But I liked it.

'Um, guys, a slight change of plans.' I threaded my hands together and twisted them nervously. 'Ty's going to drive me home, after he, um, takes me out for a while. Lunch and stuff.'

'Oh, you sure, Ty?' asked Lorena.

Mel kicked her leg gently. 'Of course he's sure, Lorena,' Mel said.

'Well okay then, but you'll come straight to my place later and stay over?' Lorena asked. 'I'm taking tomorrow off work to help you get your things from the house while Greg's at work.'

Oh, that's right. The weight of what lay ahead pushed down on me for a moment. I'd be packing up my things and moving in with Mum and Dad. They just didn't know it yet. 'Sure am. Thanks, hun.'

'Then I'll see both of you later on. Text me when you're close and I'll put the kettle on.'

I smiled and gave her a hug. 'Thanks for this weekend. I know it wasn't exactly as planned. But despite all the drama, I had the best fun with you guys and your silly games. I won't forget it.'

'I won't let you forget it. Besides, we'll have to do it all again. Once this bubba comes out I'll need regular time away to catch up on sleep and goss.'

I hugged Mel, and Georgie too. 'Georgie, what did I ever do to deserve such a great friend who cooks gourmet meals?'

'You became a great friend to me, that's what.' She kissed me on the cheek.

'And, Mel, I'll be waiting on the other end of the phone once you've talked to Michael. Let me know what happens.'

'I will,' she said with a knowing nod. We all had things to deal with when we went back to our regular lives, and now that I'd seen what could happen to someone so young and healthy like Nancy, I vowed to never waste a minute of the life I'd been given.

⚘

'I'll go back home first and sort out Cody, see if the neighbours can keep an eye on him,' Ty said. 'Otherwise he'll have to join us.'

'That would be fine.'

He drove back to the scene of my near-miss car accident and I waited in the car with Nancy.

'I know you have to get over Greg and all, but seriously,

Sally, don't let that one get away.' She tipped her head in Ty's direction.

'Oh, I don't know. We probably wouldn't work. And he lives over an hour away.' It was then that I remembered I wouldn't be living in my house anymore, and would have to find a new place. Maybe closer to the hospital, which was halfway between home and Barron Springs. Not that my nurse's wage would afford me much luxury without Greg's income. But that didn't matter. I didn't need much; I just needed a clean, safe place to live.

'Distance schmistance,' Nancy said. 'It doesn't matter at all, location can always be changed.'

'I think it's a bit early to be thinking about this, I can't just leap into a new relationship when I was supposed to be getting married this weekend.'

'Fair enough, but if I've learned anything from being "dead",' she made quote marks with her fingers, 'it's that time waits for no one. Do what you want, when you want it, and you'll be much happier. You did everything right with Greg and look how that ended, no offence. Why not take a risk for once?'

'I'm a bit risked out after this weekend. But I promise, I'll try to be more spontaneous and risk-taking from now on, in honour of you, okay?' I offered her a smile.

'I'll be watching.'

'Oh, I know you will.'

Ty came back with a plastic bag and something poking out of it.

'What's in there?' I asked, as he got back in the car.

'My old *Inspector Gadget* extendable arm claw. Just in case our human ones don't cut it.'

I laughed. 'You kept that from your childhood?'

He nodded. 'Cody loves it now. He's always picking things up with it, it's actually quite precise. I thought it might come in

— pardon the pun — *handy*.' He winked. 'I also brought a magnifying glass, and a ziplock bag for the ring.'

'Wow, you're well prepared.'

'Well, I *was* a boy scout.' He grinned, holding up the hand sign for 'scout's honour'.

Ty said that the neighbours would collect Cody in about half an hour and take him to town for lunch, then bring him back home. So it would be just the two, er, three of us.

'Since we don't have to be at The Renshaw till one, how about we stop in the city for lunch first?' asked Ty.

'Sounds good.'

'Oh you two are such big teases! I'm dying for a hamburger!' Nancy giggled.

⟊

After eating a burger with the lot in Nancy's honour (not my usual choice of meal), we arrived at the hotel with our high hopes and bag of retrieval equipment.

'Here's your room key,' the receptionist said; a young male with sculpted black hair that looked like plastic. 'Don't forget, it's only for the hour, so we'll see you back here at two pm.'

'Yep, don't worry, we don't need long.' Ty accepted the key.

'Well, if you find you do go over time, I'm afraid we'll have to charge for another hour.'

'I understand, but as I said. We won't take long.'

The young man tried to hide a grin, and his colleague, a blonde beauty, eyed him with a look that told me they thought we were here for something naughty. Great. *They probably think I'm a prostitute!* I pulled a strand of hair from my ponytail and dragged it over the side of my face in an effort to hide myself.

When Ty turned around from the reception desk, a bulky man accidentally bumped into him, knocking his plastic bag to the floor and exposing the *Inspector Gadget* arm. Ty picked it up quickly and shoved it back in the bag, and as we walked away I saw the young guy whisper to the blonde woman and laugh. Wonderful! *Now they probably think it's some kind of bedroom toy!* At least they didn't see the magnifying glass; I hated to imagine what they thought we'd be using that for.

The rising of the elevator matched the rising of my heart rate, so by the time it pinged to signal our arrival on Level Eight, my heart was going overtime. I wasn't the biggest fan of heights, but had forgotten about this until now. Blood I could handle, and burns and torn skin, but not so much heights. Or spiders. And anyway, what if the ring wasn't even there and this was all a big waste of time and further disappointment for Nancy?

We stepped out of the elevator and walked the long corridor to room 814. The shiny numbers on the door gave me an ominous feeling, knowing something bad happened in there. I doubted the hotel staff informed guests of the history of the room... *'Special offer! Come stay in our most sought after room — scene of a terrible accident!'*

Ty unlocked the door with a slide of the key, and light flooded the room as he switched on the overhead light. The afternoon sun was filtered partly through the sheer curtains, the rest hidden by heavy drapes. Ty went straight for the balcony and pushed aside the drapes.

'Nancy?' I asked, turning around. She wasn't with us.

'Where'd she go?' Ty asked.

A swirl of colours appeared and she seemed to float through the door. 'Sorry, this place isn't making me feel too well.'

'It'll be okay, and we have an hour, so no rush.'

Nancy's breathing quickened like she was about to get on stage in front of hundreds of people, then a jolt shot through my heart when the bedside lamp cracked open and collapsed.

'What the?'

Ty went to the bedside table. 'How did that happen?'

'Oops, I'm sorry! I think I did it. Somehow. I'm feeling quite tense.' Nancy looked guilty, and a little terrified.

'Unfortunately,' Ty said, 'I don't think this can be fixed with super glue like the one at the guest house.'

'Damn. We'll have to pay for it. Don't worry, I'll cover it,' I said.

Crash! The light shade on the overhead light exploded, including the globe, shattering all over the floor and partly on the bed.

'Oh no! Nancy, try to stay calm!'

'Sorry! God, what is happening to me?' She held out her hands in disbelief.

'Don't worry, it's okay, let's just focus on what we're here to do and then we'll be out of here. Can you show us where you dropped the ring?' I busied myself cleaning up the shards of glass while she readied herself. Ty picked up a garbage bin and I placed piece after piece in there. The vacuum cleaner would have to do the rest.

Nancy drew a deep breath. 'Okay, the ring. I can do this. Right...' She inched across the room as slow as a tortoise, until she came to the balcony door. Ty unhinged the lock, slid the door back, and a gush of cool air pushed past us into the room.

'Whoa, even I felt that!' Nancy said.

To encourage her, I stepped out onto the balcony, followed by Ty. The junction separating the room from the balcony was like an embodiment of my comfort zone. I steadied my breathing and focused on the task at hand. The railing was high enough for safety, but the builders obviously didn't account for someone leaning over it, trying to extract a dropped wedding ring.

'I was standing here, and...'

Crash! A terracotta pot splintered and broke, spilling soil and plant material onto the balcony floor.

'Oh no! I'm a walking disaster!'

'No you're not, just stay focused, don't worry about that right now.' Though I *was* a bit worried. We could probably have afforded a two-night stay for the cost of what we'd have to replace.

'I leant against the railing here, holding my ring. Stupid of me, in hindsight, but what can I do?' She re-enacted her movements from that fateful night. 'And when I sneezed, it fell from my hands, down there.' She pointed.

Ty and I peered over the railing and down below. Between a narrow slit of metal, a diamond sparkled in the afternoon sunlight.

'It's there! It's still there!' Nancy exclaimed.

Relief flooded my veins and I exchanged a smile with Ty. I took a couple of photos in case we needed proof of where we found the ring. It could be possible to retrieve it. Though there was no way I was leaning over the balcony. Ty was taller, so I hoped he'd be up for the job. No wonder the police hadn't found it, it was slightly underneath the balcony, and not viewable unless you arched your head a certain way. The sneeze or direction of the night breeze must have guided it to its resting place. And with her history of depression, and the fact that camera footage showed no one had been seen entering her room, meant that foul play had been ruled out. To them it was clearly a suicide. To us, it was a sad, silly, terrible accident.

'Maybe I can just grab it myself,' said Ty, angling his body over the railing.

I tugged on his shirt. 'Wait! Let's do this slowly, cautiously. It may look achievable, but as we know, looks can be deceiving.'

'Then let's try our best available option.' He turned to the door. 'Go-go Gadget arm!' His humour at this critical moment seemed out of place, but funny nonetheless, and even Nancy managed a tiny smile.

Ty returned with his extendable arm claw thing.

'Hang on, let's practise!' I dashed inside and took my lonely engagement ring from my purse, and placed it on the floor of the balcony.

Ty lowered the plastic arm and pulled a lever to expand the tiny claw at the end of it. When one part of the claw hooked under the ring he released the lever and lifted the arm, the ring captured by it.

'See? Easy.' Ty handed the ring back to me and I put it away.

'But this is in a trickier spot. Maybe we should just flick it off, then rush downstairs and get it from the ground before anyone else.'

'It could get stuck further down the strip of metal where we can't get it, see how it gets narrower?' He pointed and I gripped the railing tightly as I looked. 'Or it could land in a drain down there, or on someone's head. We're too high up to do it properly.'

'I guess you better take the opportunity to practise your surgical skills then. I'll hold on to you so you don't lose balance.' I gripped his hips as he manoeuvred over the balcony railing and leaned forward.

With Ty in front of me I couldn't see the mission in process, but I heard the sound of Ty extending the arm and pulling the lever. A tinkle of metal followed.

'Damn! Got it but dropped it again,' he said.

'Oh no, can you still get it?'

'I think, I just... need to...' he grunted, and a moment later lowered back onto the balcony, slowly carrying the toy arm over to safety. A diamond ring hung delicately from the claw, and a victorious smile hung on Ty's face.

'You did it!' My eyes widened in happiness.

'My ring, oh, my ring!' Nancy cradled her ghostly hand around it, desperate to touch it.

'Let's get it inside before the breeze wafts it away,' Ty said, holding on to the ring and not activating the claw lever until it was safely on the desk in the hotel room.

I picked up the ring and held it up to the light.

'You're the light of my life ~ Chris'

I read the inscription on the inside of the band. My heart warmed at this simple sentiment, and I looked at Nancy. 'You were very lucky to have him.'

'I know,' she whispered, then reached forwards gently. 'Can I try? To hold it?'

'Do you think you can?'

'I held your underwear and flung it about, didn't I?' she said with a smile.

'What?' asked Ty. 'Just what did you girls get up to before I became privy to your presence, Nancy?'

'You don't need to know.' I slid a glance his way.

'Fair enough.' He smiled.

Using the ring finger on her left hand, Nancy teased the ring as I held it up. A tingle of energy ran across my hand as she tried to grasp it. After focusing intently and gently sliding her finger between the unbroken circle, it took. It stayed there, as though she was really here and it was really on her finger. Delight lit up her face and she slowly rotated her hand around in front of her, admiring the sparkle and solidity of the ring against her semi-translucent hand.

I exchanged a wondrous smile with Ty, who was shaking his head at the miracle. If anyone walked in right now they'd see a ring floating in mid-air.

After a few moments, the ring went straight through her finger and dropped to the carpeted floor. I quickly picked it up, not wanting to let it out of my sight. Ty handed me the ziplock bag and I secured the ring inside, then placed it into my handbag.

'We did it,' Ty said with a smile.

'You did it,' I corrected. 'Thank you.'

Nancy held her hands up to both our cheeks and a cool then warm tingle spread across my face. 'Thank you both,' she said. Ty touched his face with his hand at the remarkable sensation I knew he'd felt. I wondered if his parents were here, somewhere, witnessing this, watching over him.

Nancy seemed restored, and that cheeky expression I'd come to know (and hate, in the beginning) returned. 'Before we go, can I have some fun?'

'Not if it involves causing more expensive damage, but apart from that, knock yourself out!' I said.

She jumped onto the bed and bounced, even though the mattress didn't move much. Her body partially weightless, she jumped and leapt for joy. 'Wheee!' she exclaimed, then leapt onto the nearby chaise longue and rolled over it. A few shards of remaining glass had jumped off the bed with her, and I picked them up and put them in the bin.

As she continued twirling and rolling around the room, Ty glanced at his watch then stepped in front of me. 'Still about half an hour left of our room booking. Maybe we should make the most of it.'

Huh? Was he suggesting... 'Why, what did you have in mind, a private striptease or something?' I joked.

His expression remained straight, and he started unbuttoning his shirt, revealing those incredibly amazing superhuman pecs.

'Ty! Um, I don't think...'

He laughed. 'Relax. I'm joking, sunshine!'

I opened my mouth in relief. Sort of. I wouldn't have minded seeing him in that way again, but now was neither the time nor the place. 'Oh, right. Sorry!' Heat crawled across my face.

'You two are hilarious!' said Nancy. 'Just get a room already, will you?'

I glared at her.

'Oh wait! You already did! Haha!' She went into hysterics, and her shrill laugh gave me a happy feeling instead of an annoyed one for the first time this weekend.

❧

'That was quick,' said the young guy with the plastic hair when we went to pay at the reception desk. 'Did you enjoy your *brief* stay?'

'Definitely,' Ty replied. 'Did what we came here to do.'

'Yep, mission complete.' I looked at Ty. 'Lucky you made use of your... long thing,' I added, and at the look of surprise on the receptionists' faces I realised I should have thought before speaking.

Plastic Hair Guy cleared his throat and pushed a piece of paper across the desk. 'Okay, well then, if you'll just sign here and make payment, that would be great.'

I went to sign but Ty's hand covered the paper. 'I've got this,' he said, and in a jiffy he'd signed his name and handed over his credit card. 'And, ah, sorry, but there were a few slight... breakages.'

'Breakages? What specifically?'

Ty scratched his head. 'Ah, the bedside lamp, a potted plant, and um, the ceiling light shade.'

The receptionist's eyed bulged. 'How did... never mind, not a problem, sir.' He cleared his throat again. 'You understand we'll have to bill you for the damages once replacement costs have been evaluated?'

227

'Yes, that's fine.'

'Good. And I hope your stay with us was worthwhile, sir.'

'Oh yes, very worthwhile.' Ty slid his arm around my back in a suggestive way and winked.

Ty! I wanted to get out of this place as soon as possible. How much more blushing could my cheeks handle this weekend before they spontaneously combusted?

The guy printed out a receipt and handed it to Ty, and we turned away from the desk.

'Oh, one more thing,' Ty said, turning back to Plastic Hair Guy and speaking loud enough for anyone nearby to hear. 'The springs in the bed were a bit... squeaky. Hope we didn't disturb the guests below. You might want to get that looked at. Cheerio!' He waved and we turned away again. I clenched my mouth tight and gave him a good, hard whack on the arm.

CHAPTER 22

After the elation of finding Nancy's ring, we were now hesitant about our next task: convincing Chris his wife was here in spirit, and that her death was an accident.

Despite our reluctance to repeat our disastrous attempt from yesterday, we both agreed it was worth a second shot now that we had the ring. Worst-case scenario — he throws us out again, but at least the ring would be returned to him, and I could still try the letter writing option and give him time to warm to the idea.

Ty made some joke about comparing our trek to that in *Lord of the Rings*, and we made our way out of the city and back towards the pretty country town of Wattle Falls.

Nancy sat quietly in the back seat, her eyes closed, humming a song I didn't recognise. She seemed caught in some sort of transitionary state between life and the afterlife. Maybe she was preparing herself, or distracting herself, from the likelihood of more disbelief from Chris.

Traffic was fairly heavy, but we made progress gradually.

My mind became restless. 'What's your favourite colour?' I asked Ty.

'Cobalt. Why?'

'Just making conversation to pass the time. Cobalt? Not blue, or green, or red, but cobalt?'

'Colours vary, it's good to be specific.'

'I guess. Then why aren't you wearing cobalt? And why is your car black?'

'I didn't say it was my favourite colour to wear or anything, it's just my favourite colour to look at, generally.'

'Fair enough. That makes sense.'

'What's yours? Wait... light purple?'

'Mauve. How did you know?'

'You were wearing it that night you got stuck in the toilet. Just a guess.'

And I thought the only thing he'd noticed was the fact that I'd *gotten* stuck in the toilet.

'Favourite TV show?' he asked.

I was having déjà vu. It reminded me of the twenty questions Nancy, or *Red* back then, had fired at me during dinner at the guest house when Ty was with us. As long as he didn't ask me my favourite sexual position like Nancy did, I'd be fine.

'*Doctor Who*, or *Midsomer Murders*.'

He smiled. Was he silently making fun of my entertainment choices?

'Oh, and *Friends*,' I added, to seem reasonably normal and hip, and to honour last Saturday night's laughter prescription. 'You?'

'*Friends*, too, of course, and *Seinfeld*. And *Game of Thrones*.'

'Oh, I don't think I could watch that. Looks too explicit and gory.'

'Exactly! I love it. Try it, I guarantee you'll be hooked.'

'Hmm.' I wasn't convinced.

'Okay, next question: If you could go back in time, when would you go?'

'The fifties. They seemed cute and fun. You?'

'Hmm, maybe the Palaeolithic period? You know, grow a beard and long hair, wear nothing but a loincloth, and hunt for food. Perfect.'

'Caveman, huh? Well, you've got the loincloth bit all sorted, in a modern sort of way.'

'True. Maybe I'll have to mix up my performances a little. Instead of Doctor Ty, I could be Caveman Ty.'

An image of him swinging shirtless from tree to tree flashed through my mind. 'Or Tarzan's naughty cousin.'

'Good idea. *Tyzan*, perhaps?'

I chuckled.

'How about we play I Spy next instead of Twenty Questions? It's a perfect game for road trips, Cody loves playing it.'

Being around Ty was never boring. And I appreciated the way he was taking my mind off the inevitable challenge of going back to Chris' house.

'I'll start,' he said. 'I spy with my little eye, something beginning with... I.'

'Umm... Incredibly infuriating guy indifferent to public displays of partial nudity?' I joked.

'Nope! And yes, sort of.'

'Impossibly irritating imbecilic Neanderthal?'

A laugh shot from his mouth. 'I didn't know you had such a witty way with words, Sexy Sally.'

'I'm full of surprises this long weekend.' I glanced towards the back seat and Nancy was still humming with her eyes closed, seemingly oblivious to our conversation. Or, perhaps, giving us a chance to get to know each other.

'So, any idea?' he asked.

'Of what?'

'Who's the imbecile now? Something starting with I of course!'

'Oops! Got distracted!' Caveman Ty. Loincloth. Pecs. *Goodness, Sally! Hold your hormones!* 'Okay, what about: incredibly irresistible intelligent nurse?' I fluttered my eyelashes. What was I doing?

'How'd you guess?' He took his eyes off the road and locked onto my gaze for a moment. 'Nice one. And true. But in this case, it was an ice skating rink. Didn't you see it way back there?'

'No, I didn't. Not fair!'

'You'll have to pay more attention from now on, nursey.'

'Your turn,' I said. 'I spy with my little eye, something beginning with D.'

Ty looked around, then said, 'Devastatingly handsome doctor-to-be?'

'Oh, you are just too self-confident, mister! Try again.'

'Dynamite dancer and driver of damsels in distress?'

I laughed. 'I am not a damsel and I'm not in distress.'

'Okay, I'll be serious. Dog?'

'There's no dog anywhere! Try again.'

'Duck?'

I shook my head.

'Deer? No wait, dolphin?'

'Stop it, you! We're not at a farm or an aquarium. Though I think you belong in one.'

He slapped my thigh gently. 'Hey, watch it, sunshine.'

I grinned. 'Give up yet?'

'Nope. I never give up on anything. Daisies? Doll's house? Donuts? Mmm, now I'm hungry.' He licked his lips.

'Drive-through restaurant!' I blurted.

'Hey, I was on a roll there!'

'Yeah, rolling in a completely different direction.'

'Okay, okay, I spy with my little eye, something beginning with C,' he said.

I glanced around and knew immediately what it was. 'Easy. Church.'

'Oh, c'mon! You're no fun, smartypants.'

'You picked an easy one.' I shrugged. Then I remembered the church I was supposed to get married in on the weekend. The tall pointed roof, the stained-glass windows, walking down the aisle...

'Sally? I said *your turn*,' he prompted.

'Oh. Sorry, I was just...' My voice turned quiet.

Ty glanced towards me twice, still making sure to keep focused on the road. 'Was it the church? Did it make you... think of stuff?'

I flicked my hand. 'It's nothing. Silly, really. So I was supposed to get married this Saturday, no big deal anymore. The guy's a cheat and it's lucky I found out before the wedding.'

Ty absorbed my words for a moment. 'But still. There's nothing wrong with being sad about it. Things are bound to pop up when you least expect it; memories, places, names... sometimes we don't know how we feel until something around us triggers something.'

'That is true.'

We were silent for a minute, until Ty said, 'Sally, the other night...'

'It's okay, we don't have to talk about that.'

'But I want to.' He brushed his hand against mine briefly, and returned it to the steering wheel. 'I know the timing was way off. I know the timing *now*, is still way off. And I understand you need to spend some time alone to sort through what's happened and move on.' He took a deep breath. 'So I won't call you, after this weekend. I want to, but I won't. I'll be here to help with Chris again if today doesn't work out, absolutely, but I don't want to get in the way of whatever you need to do to move on from your broken engagement. If you want to call me, or meet up again, or give things a go, I'll be ready. But only when you are.'

I nodded, taking in the meaning of his words. He liked me. He was interested. He wanted to see how things could work out between us. *When I was ready*. Part of me wanted to grab him and say 'I'm ready now', but I knew the truth. I wasn't ready. Not yet. No matter how attracted to him I was or how good I felt around him, it wasn't right just yet. I needed to re-establish my own life first, get over the crap that all this had become, and start fresh. 'Thanks. That sounds like the best way to go,' I said.

'Yep, probably for the best.'

'Yep.'

'I hope I didn't cause any confusion, or make things more complicated that night.'

'You didn't, not at all. If anything you made me see more clearly what a bastard Greg was.' A small smile crept up into one corner of my mouth. 'And also, what an incredibly inferior and so-so kisser he was.'

A smile grew on Ty's face. 'I'm flattered.'

And now I was embarrassed. This weekend had taught me to speak up, to get things out in the open, to not waste any minute of my life.

'And yes, it was rather... nice,' he added.

'Nice. Yes, it was.' I smiled. 'And a little bit exciting.'

'A lot exciting,' he replied. 'Quite intense, actually.'

'You're right. It was intense.'

'And mesmerising.'

'Electrifying.'

Our words were spiced with passionate memories of

Saturday night, and my tongue tingled. My chest rose and fell quickly, and I could faintly hear him breathing faster.

We slowed to a stop at a red light and Ty put the handbrake on and turned to face me. His eyes glowed with beauty, depth, and desire.

I opened my mouth and before I could stop myself I said, 'Maybe we could have just one last—'

'Hell yeah,' he cut me off, grabbing the sides of my face and pulling my lips to his.

Oh my sweet God in heaven... Warmth, softness, pressure; a symphony of sensations exhilarated my senses as our mouths became entwined. He ran his hands through my hair so urgently my ponytail came loose, and I moved my hands down the back of his neck, around the front of his shoulders, and over his chest.

Horns tooted and we broke away from each other, gasping for breath. At first I thought people were applauding our passionate kiss, but they were only informing us that the red light had turned green and could we please, according to one driver, 'get a move on, you bloody idiots'.

We laughed, our mouths still close, enjoying one last kiss before Ty released the handbrake and moved forward.

I redid my ponytail. 'I think I'll start the whole "giving myself time" thing tomorrow,' I said. Today was different. Today was for us. And for Nancy. Tomorrow my challenging reality would rise with me in the morning. I glanced back at Nancy in the seat, her eyes still closed, still humming. Just before I turned back to the front, she opened her eyes slightly and smiled, giving me a thumbs-up sign.

I tried to erase my big goofy smile, but it wouldn't budge. And anyway, why would I want it to?

As we drove through Barron Springs and neared Wattle

Falls, Nancy straightened up in the back seat, her eyes wide. She seemed to be looking out for something.

'What is it, Nancy?' I asked.

'I'm getting a strong feeling. Umm...' she turned this way and that, looking about in all directions. Then she closed her eyes and focused intently, before snapping them open. 'Quick, turn right up here!' She pointed to the street up ahead. 'It's Chris. He's not at home. He's at the cemetery. At my grave.'

CHAPTER 23

Ty chucked a right and followed Nancy's directions to the cemetery. He drove through the iron gates and down a driveway lined with small shrubs, which looked newly planted. We parked and got out of the car. The cemetery was deserted, apart from a tall figure in the distance. We walked to Nancy's grave, where Chris stood holding his young daughter. He turned at the sound of our footsteps.

He rolled his eyes and sighed. 'Oh, great. You two again.'

'Three, actually,' I said.

'Look, I'm having a private moment with my daughter at her mother's grave, so if you don't mind, I'd appreciate being left alone.'

I glanced at the headstone:

Nancy Silverton.

We'll never forget you.

We stayed put. Chris faced us again. 'Fair enough, then *we'll* go.' He turned away to walk off.

'Wait!' I called. 'I have your wife's wedding ring.' I quickly opened my bag and took out the ziplock plastic bag, then removed the ring. 'Here. Here it is!' I held it up to the low afternoon sun creeping through the surrounding trees.

He walked closer, brows furrowed. Curiosity enticed him forward. 'That could be any old ring. How do you know it's hers?'

'We got it from The Renshaw. Room 814. She showed us where she dropped it. It was still there, outside the balcony!'

'Give me a look at that.' He yanked it from my hand, turning the ring around and holding it up to read the inscription. 'Oh my God. It's hers. How did, where did...'

'I already told you.'

'But—'

'She's telling the truth, mate,' Ty said. 'We drove to the city today to get it and bring it back for you. Thought you might want it.'

Chris looked confused. 'So you found it, and I'm thankful, but do you really expect me to believe that my wife's spirit is here?'

'Expect, no. Hope, yes.' I offered a smile. 'She's still here. She can't go until you know and believe the truth.' I glanced at Nancy, whose face held grief and fatigue, but at the same time joy at being able to see her family.

'So you're telling me you're some kind of psychic medium, is that it?'

'No. I've never had anything like this happen to me before. Nancy showed up a week ago at my house, then followed me to Barron Springs where I was having a weekend away. She was able to show me things in my life I'd been blind to. Made me realise a mistake I was about to make. I owe her everything.'

'And you, what was your name again?' He looked at Ty.

'Tyler. Call me Ty.'

'Ty, you said you see her too?'

'Yes. And like you, I was disbelieving at first. But pretty soon

I realised the truth. She's here. She wants you to know what really happened to her.'

Ruby smiled and giggled in his arms, seemingly unaware of the drama unfolding.

'Look, thanks for finding the ring. But I think we'll head home now.' He turned away again.

Nancy raced after him. 'Chris! Remember how you used to kiss the heart-shaped birthmark on my lower back? I miss that! I miss you!'

'Her birthmark!' I exclaimed. 'Nancy had a birthmark on her lower back. In the shape of a heart.' Chris turned around, his mouth hanging open, though his eyes still held uncertainty. 'She loved how you used to kiss it. She misses that.'

He took a few steps forward, then stopped and shook his head. 'You were her nurse. Chances are you saw it or something. That doesn't prove anything.' He turned, and I urged Nancy to think of something else.

'She said that on your honeymoon you missed out on half the champagne in your hotel suite because you'd dropped the bottle before opening it. When you popped the cork it fizzed up and spilled all over the floor!' I repeated what she told me.

He turned around and tested me with his eyes. 'She could have told you that herself.'

'Well, she did, but only just now. She also used to joke that she only married you because you were tall and she thought it would be handy to have someone around to change light globes and turn off the smoke alarm when her disastrous attempts at cooking filled the kitchen with smoke.'

He stepped closer. 'Keep going.'

'When you found out you were having a baby girl and came up with the name Ruby, she asked what to do if there'd been a mistake and it was really a boy. You said you'd call him "Rudy",' I said, after Nancy relayed her memories to me. 'And she didn't like that name. You had her convinced you were serious, until you agreed that it wasn't your name of choice for a boy either.'

'Oh yeah, then what name did we agree upon if our baby was indeed a boy?'

I raised my eyebrows at Nancy.

'Benjamin Bradley Silverton,' I spoke with confidence. Ty had his hand on my back in a show of support.

Chris' mouth gaped and he shook his head, running his hand through his hair, the other cradling Ruby. 'No, it can't be possible. This still doesn't prove it. I can't, I just...'

'Chris, all you have to do is consider it's possible. You only have to open yourself up to the fact that it could be true. Start there.'

Nancy approached her husband, her eyes ranging all over him and absorbing every detail. Then she smiled lovingly at her daughter, who giggled. Ruby's eyes looked straight at Nancy, as though she could see her too. She reached out her hand towards Nancy's face. Nancy smiled and blew a kiss at Ruby, then turned to me. 'She can see me! Ruby can see me!'

Oh wow. It took all my effort not to break down in tears then and there. It was the most beautiful sight.

'Chris, Nancy is with you right now. She's standing there. Ruby can see her.'

He stiffened, unsure and uncomfortable, and watched his daughter giggling and pointing right in front of her.

'Mama.' The sweet, soft sound of a baby's voice floated from Ruby's mouth.

Nancy gasped and covered her mouth. 'Oh. Oh my God. Oh, Ruby! My baby, you said Mama!' She looked at me and Ty, then back again at her daughter. Chris' face was frozen in awe.

'She's never said that before. She can say Dada, but never Mama. How? What just happened?'

I came close to them. 'She saw her mother.' I smiled softly, reassuringly. 'Nancy's right here.' I draped my arm carefully around Nancy's figure, my arm tingling with her energy. 'Right here.' Nancy draped her arm around me too, and I closed my eyes for a moment and breathed in the pure love emanating from her in this moment.

A slight sheen covered Chris' eyes, his body started to tremble. Ty held out his arms to take Ruby off him and he allowed it. Chris brought his hands to his head, his eyes not knowing where to look. 'If this is true, then how come I can't see her?'

'Because you've been closed up. Not receptive. But if you concentrate, I'm sure you could feel her presence.'

Nancy placed her hand over her husband's cheek.

'Can you feel her?' I asked. His eyes searched for confirmation, and I said, 'Close your eyes. Feel her with you.'

He did, and after a few moments he lifted his hand to his cheek.

Nancy tipped her head back in delight. 'I'm here, baby, I'm here.'

He opened his eyes. 'Was I imagining that?'

I shook my head.

'And you say she didn't take her own life? Are you absolutely sure?'

'One hundred per cent.'

'She dropped the ring and tried to get it?'

'Yes. She wanted so much to come back to you, fresh and renewed, ready to get back to her usual self. She sneezed, and that's what caused her to drop the ring.'

'So she didn't think to ask for help? Wait. Don't answer that. She never was one to ask for help, she liked to think she could handle everything herself.'

'She was a strong woman,' I said, while Ty amused Ruby with funny faces.

'It still feels so strange, I don't know how to believe. It belies everything I've been taught.'

'I didn't believe in the afterlife either, before this,' I said.

'I need to be sure. I need to know… What was the last thing she said to me, before the taxi took her to the hotel on the day she died? I never told anyone.'

I looked at Nancy and my eyes asked her for the answer, hoping she could remember.

Nancy's eyes lit up, knowing she had the proof he so desperately needed. 'I said: "I don't know what will happen after this weekend, but I know that I'll never regret becoming your wife. You've been a wonderful husband to me and father to Ruby. I only wish I believed that I deserved you."' Nancy's eyes became shiny. 'I stepped off the front verandah and walked towards the taxi. He called out to me, as if he wanted to respond to what I'd said, but I just waved, got into the car, and that was the last time he saw me.'

I took a deep breath, then relayed her words.

Chris gasped, held his hand over his heart, and crumpled to his knees in tears. Nancy sat beside him, her hand on his back, telling him everything would be all right. I left them together like that, then placed a comforting hand on his shoulder, until he had the strength to stand. He took my hand as he got to his feet, and sandwiched it between both of his. 'Thank you,' he whispered. 'Thank you.'

In all my years as a nurse I had never been so overcome by pure, beautiful emotion. Had never felt such clear, wonderful, amazing purpose; that I was here to help people, in whatever way, shape, or form required. Ghost accomplices optional.

When Chris took Ruby from Ty's hands and embraced her with the strength and support that only a parent could provide, Nancy stood in front of me. 'I have to go now,' she said calmly. 'I feel it.' She looked beyond my shoulder and pointed. 'I see it too. That's where I have to be.'

I turned around, but all that greeted me was the emptiness of the graveyard; grey headstones sheltered by trees, mosaic-like patches of shade and sun, and flowers in various stages of bloom and degradation. Whatever she could see was beyond my perception, beyond my physical body. One day I'd find out, but first, I had a long, wonderful life to live.

Nancy turned to Chris. 'Goodbye, my love.'

I told him she was saying goodbye, and relayed her words of love and admiration for the gift he'd been in her life. I told him how Nancy knew things would get easier, and how Ruby would be the new light of his life, and she would watch over them.

He gratefully accepted each word, his eyes appearing so deep and open now to his new understanding of the world and of his wife, and he touched his face again when she placed her hand on his cheek.

Nancy caressed Ruby's hair and her daughter smiled and cooed, her eyes wandering over her mother's features. I stole a glance at Ty, who wiped at the inner corners of his eyes.

'Be good,' Nancy said to Ty after leaving her family's side. 'And sorry for freaking you out.'

'It's okay,' he chuckled. 'I'm glad you did. Take care, gorgeous.' He offered a small wave.

Then Nancy came back to me, her face soft and thankful, her curly red hair glowing under the afternoon sun like a rich sunset. 'Please forgive me for being so cheeky,' she said.

'I already have.'

She smiled. 'I had fun. Thank you for that. And words can never express how grateful I am for what you and Ty did for me.'

'It was an experience, that's for sure! And I had fun too, even though I probably didn't think so at the time!' We laughed, and I wished I could hug her. Properly.

'The look on your face when you got stuck in the loo. Priceless!' she said.

'Yeah, yeah, enough with the toilet jokes, girl.' I winked.

'And as for the Greg situation… You'll look back on it one day and feel only gratitude that his mistake led you to a much better life. Trust me.'

'I trust you.'

'And remember what I said about you-know-who,' she whispered. 'Don't let him get away. Take some time, sure, but when it feels right, follow your heart and grab every opportunity with both hands. Promise?'

'I promise.' I nodded, holding back tears.

'Good. Now go forth and live your life, girlfriend!' She gestured into the distance, and walked forwards, towards a new realm that awaited her.

'Bye, Red.' I waved.

She turned and fluffed her red curls with the palm of her hand and gave a cute pout. 'Oh, and Sally?'

'Yes?'

'Go out and buy yourself a goddamn dress!'

And in a swirl of sparkling colours, she was gone.

I exchanged phone numbers with Chris and promised to keep in touch, and he apologised for throwing us out of his house initially. I apologised myself, explaining that we hadn't been completely truthful with him, and that Nancy had wanted Ty and I to pretend we were engaged and that I'd nursed Nancy's broken arm. We decided we were even and wouldn't say anything further on the matter. I promised to visit Ruby for every one of her birthday parties, the first being in two months' time.

I walked back to the car with Ty, our arms around each other's waists. It was only for today, we knew, but it felt nice and natural and comfortable. As we walked, I sniffled, a few remaining tears escaping from my eyes. I would miss Nancy, but most importantly, I looked forward to living life with a renewed enthusiasm, in honour of her memory and to make the most of the gifts I'd been given.

At the sounds of my sniffles, Ty pulled me closer to his side, and when we reached the car, he leaned me against it and wrapped me tenderly in his arms.

Words weren't necessary. His touch said it all. We'd shared something amazing together this weekend, something beyond anything I ever thought possible. And I didn't just mean being around Nancy's spirit and solving the secret of her death. We had a connection. A *strong* connection. Things would not end here, today. Time would pass and I would focus on getting my new life on track, he would study and save money and prepare for his interview to get into medical school. We'd do our own thing for a while. But when the great healer called time had travelled enough cycles around the clock, I would take that next step. I would be ready.

Yes, I thought, as Ty kissed my cheek softly and caressed my hair, and I looked up into his beautiful, dark brown eyes. I would take Nancy's advice. I would not let this one get away.

CHAPTER 24

'It's okay, you'll be at peace now,' I said to the dead body lying on the hospital bed in front of me. George Wilkins. He'd suffered far too long, and although sad, I was relieved knowing it had come to an end after the last few months of being my patient. I adjusted the white sheet a little, wanting everything to be as perfect as possible for when his family arrived to say their goodbyes. I would comfort them and tell them that he was at peace, and this time I would mean it.

I stepped away from the bed and squirted anti-bacterial hand sanitiser onto my palms, rubbing it over my hands. As I went to walk out the door, a strange sensation that I wasn't alone turned my head back to the direction from which I came. A sharp gasp entered my lungs. George stood right there in front of me, looking down at his body. My heart pounded as he looked up and his eyes met mine.

'Thank you,' he whispered, his voice missing the usual rasp I'd become accustomed to. He held his hand over his heart and smiled, deep crinkles fanning out from the corners of his eyes. Then he gave a final wave, and disappeared in a swirl of light and colours.

My mouth hung open, then slowly turned upwards into a smile. I had not seen a spirit since my experience with Nancy eight months ago, and didn't know if I ever would. But this... this was amazing. A reminder that there was a whole other realm out there. My nursing had changed; I was more aware of people's feelings and better able to counsel them with their worries, fears and grief. I stood in awe for a moment, then turned and walked out of the room.

'Ouch!' Something ran over my foot. A crash cart. Wheeled by an attractive man with a stethoscope around his neck.

'Ty!' I said. 'I was wondering if I'd be seeing you soon in these halls.'

'Good to see you, Sexy Sally.' He winked. 'Though please forgive me for running over your foot, is it okay?'

'It's fine.'

'I wasn't trying to get you back for the supermarket situation or anything,' he added.

I nodded. 'Oh sure, whatever you say,' I laced my words with sarcasm. 'How have your first couple of weeks been?'

'Full on. But so great. I'm loving it.'

'And how's Cody?'

'He's doing well. He's learning to play a musical instrument now; the keyboard.'

'Good for him!' I smiled. 'And are you still stripping?'

'Nope. Thanks to all your referrals I had a ton of bookings, and saved up enough to quit. There's no time for that now, anyway. But I do get to play doctor here, which is fun. Except I have to keep my clothes on.'

I rose up and down on my toes. 'So, I was actually going to call you this weekend.' I hadn't seen him for six months, not since Ruby's first birthday party. I now lived in a small apartment about ten minutes from work, and forty minutes from Barron Springs. Lorena now had baby Callie keeping her busy and sleep deprived, and Mel and Michael were going strong. Georgie seemed happier too, had more of a glow about her these days, and she'd had her TV contract renewed.

'You were? Or are you only saying that to be nice?' He winked.

'I was, look.' I took my phone from my pocket and showed him the reminder I'd set in my phone calendar: *Saturday: Call Ty*.

He smiled. 'Looks like I saved you some time by bumping into you.'

'Yes, literally.' I grinned. 'Although I'm sure a phone chat is in order anyway. There's only so much that can be discussed in a hospital corridor.'

Ty tilted his head slightly. 'Why don't we make it a face-to-face chat? If you want to, that is.'

I raised my eyebrows. 'I think that sounds like a perfect idea.'

'How about The Valley Restaurant? I can book a table for, say, seven on Saturday night?'

'Deal.' I held out my hand and he shook it. Oh, how I'd missed the touch of his skin. 'I'll meet you there.'

'And will you be carrying a red rose or something, so I know how to recognise you in case you're all dressed up?'

I chuckled. 'No, but I *will* be wearing a dress.'

'Let me guess, a purple one? Mauve?'

I shook my head. 'Cobalt.'

A smile grew on his lips and he nodded his approval. 'I look forward to seeing you then.' He glanced down the corridor. 'I better get this cart back where it belongs; have to be a good student.'

I nodded. 'See you on Saturday.'

After he smiled and began walking off, he turned back

around. 'Oh, ah, will there be any other *guests* joining us for dinner?' He raised his eyebrows.

'No. Definitely not! It will just be you and me.' I smiled softly.

'Sounds good.'

We held each other's gaze for an extra moment. 'So, you've really given up stripping, hey?'

'Yes. Although... I *could* make an exception at some stage, if it was absolutely necessary.' He eyed me with that sexy, teasing look from his business card. *Ty Roxford ~ Quality adult entertainer and dancer* had now become: *Ty Roxford ~ Medical student and potential love of my life.*

'I'll hold you to that,' I said, with a teasing look of my own to rival his. And as I watched him walk away, I knew without a doubt that what happened in Barron Springs, certainly would *not* stay in Barron Springs.

THE END

Also by Juliet Madison

Acknowledgements

Thanks to my loyal readers for buying my books, telling your friends about them, and having fun with me online in between writing sessions. And thanks to those bloggers and book reviewers who've taken the time to read and thoughtfully review my work.

Special thanks to my writing buddies Alli Sinclair and Diane Curran for always being there to brainstorm with, laugh with, and talk writers' stuff! Also to my other friends in the writing community; it's great to interact with you and get feedback on names, titles, plot twists... etc. Thanks!

Huge thanks to Betsy Reavley and the Bloodhound Books team for believing in my writing and republishing this novel, and to my editor Belinda Holmes, thank you for making editing fun!

To my mum, thanks for always reading my first drafts and giving honest feedback, sometimes at short notice and with time limits! And to my son, Jayden, for all the years you put up with my often crazy writing schedule, late dinners, and noisy tapping at the keyboard when you were trying to sleep. Payback for those early years.

About the Author

Juliet Madison is a bestselling and award-nominated author of books with humour, heart, and serendipity. Writing both fiction and self-help, she is also an artist and colouring book illustrator, and an intuitive life coach who loves creating online courses for writers and those wanting to live an empowered life.

With her background as a naturopath and a dancer, Juliet is passionate about living a healthy and positive life. She likes to combine her love of words, art, and self-empowerment to create books that entertain and inspire readers to find the magic in everyday life.

Juliet lives on the picturesque south coast of NSW, Australia, where she spends as much time as possible dreaming up new stories, following her passions, being with her family, and as little time as possible doing housework.

You can find out more about Juliet, her books, and her courses at http://www.julietmadison.com and connect with her on social media at Facebook http://www.facebook.com/julietmadisonauthor and Instagram http://www.instagram.com/julietmadisonauthorartist

A NOTE FROM THE PUBLISHER

Thank you for reading this book. If you enjoyed it please do consider leaving a review on Amazon to help others find it too.

We hate typos. All of our books have been rigorously edited and proofread, but sometimes mistakes do slip through. If you have spotted a typo, please do let us know and we can get it amended within hours.

info@bloodhoundbooks.com